Reckless Abandon

A Cutters Notch Novel

By Michael DeCamp

Fiction and Literature: Inspirational
Thriller Suspense Mystery
Paranormal
Young Adult

Rated pg:13 because of mild horror, violence, and cursing

ISBN: 978-1-0880-5693-6

Dedication

To my best friend, my muse, and my wife. Nancy DeCamp, you are the light of my world and the one I love with reckless abandon.

Acknowledgements

Who could've imagined so many years ago that my first project, *Abandon Hope*, would lead to a trilogy and a companion book of short stories? Well, my wife could, my daughters could, and lots of friends and co-workers could. They've been there for me all along the way, encouraging me when I'd get down, keeping my ego in check when I'd be up too high, but always prodding me to keep creating. Writers gotta write.

Special thanks to my beta readers: Anni Carter, Amy Holland, Jeremy Garrison, and Kristina Seifert. Your feedback and help was so valuable to me during my early revisions. A massive thank you to my editor, Sherri Stewart for keeping me in an active voice and helping me fix so many details. A humble thank you to my agent, Sarah Joy Freese for continuing to believe in my work.

Lastly, I want to thank YOU. I appreciate so much the fact that you've picked up this book. *Reckless Abandon* was a labor of love and the culmination of an even larger labor of love. The Cutters Notch Trilogy along with the Cutters Notch Interludes represent the work from well over a decade of my creative life. I hope you enjoy the tale. I wish you good reading.

Mike

Prologue

Kay Sours, a grumpy and eccentric loner, lives by herself in a small bungalow at the end of a long, winding lane. Her house is hidden behind a finger of the Hoosier National Forest that shields her property from prying eyes. Her five acres are an island in the middle of a raging sea of leaves, ten miles from Cutters Notch, just across the Bowen County line. A locked gate blocks her driveway at the road. Packages from her mail orders are left in a large brown metal box that she positioned to the left of the gate. Her mailbox stands guard on the right with a plastic newspaper receptacle tacked on underneath. A *No Trespassing* sign dangles from the gate's crossbar. Kay only sees people when she wants to see them. She likes solitude.

Sitting on a simple wooden chair at her gray Formica-topped kitchen table, she's flipping through that morning's *Bloomington Herald*. The evening light filters through the cream-colored sheers covering the window above her dish-filled sink; the sun slowly sinks below the tree line as if pulled down with a string. An ornate teacup rests on the table with the tail of a teabag hanging out, steam still emanating from the hot liquid inside.

A deep breath. A sigh. Kay yawns as she sits there in her muddy jeans and soiled, long-sleeved flannel shirt—the red and blue checkerboard sleeves rolled up to her elbows. It has been a long day, dragging limbs she trimmed from the forest up beside her barn, then using her chainsaw to cut them into burnable sections. Some of the larger ones, she split down. Her legs, her arms, her back—they all ache. "I'll sleep well tonight," she mutters to herself. "If I can get comfortable," she adds as she ruffles the fur on Penny's head.

Penny rests at Kay's feet. The golden retriever peers up at her with loving eyes and whines. She trotted out of the woods a few months prior, at just the right time, with cockleburs tangled in her fur. Kay was feeling particularly down that day, stuck in a cycle of depression, but the dog lifted her spirits. A tag on Penny's collar supplied the dog's name but nothing more. For a while, Kay occasionally checked bulletin boards and posts for any notices of lost dogs, but in the end, she found a new friend. Now, they're inseparable. Wherever Kay goes, Penny is right there. She's Kay's companion, protector, and best friend.

Kay carefully refolds the newspaper, leaving it on the table as she begins her evening ritual of walking around the house, turning on various lights. She likes living alone, but she doesn't like darkness and her anxiety only worsens as the days grow shorter in the fall. All part of her evening pattern, she clicks on the bathroom vanity light. She flips the switch that lights her nightstand in the bedroom. Finally, she lights the decorative spotlights in her living room that illuminate her collection of swords.

On small tables to each side of the sword collection, decorative electric lamps with curving, floral ceramic shades rest on lacy doilies. She turns these on, as well. After fully brightening the space, she pauses to admire her collection.

Kay possesses five swords, each mounted on the wall. Real ones, not replicas. Two from the Civil War, two used by the U.S. Cavalry on the western frontier, and one broadsword from the Middle Ages—all shipped to her from various sources, left in the brown metal box near her gate, and then resharpened in her barn workshop. The broadsword is huge. She can't imagine the strength it must have taken to wield it. It was all she could do to hoist it up to the wall pegs from which it hangs.

After admiring the weapons, she turns and peruses her appearance in the large mirror mounted on the opposite wall. Kay grimaces as she fiddles with her stringy hair, counting the increasing number of wrinkles at the corners of her eyes. She checks her teeth as if someone were there to care if something were stuck in them. Finally, she smiles at herself, just to give herself a little cheer.

Convinced that she looks terrible, she smiles at herself one more time before returning to the kitchen to enjoy her tea and finish reading the paper. Penny follows, returning to her spot at Kay's feet. The dog circles once before lying down, resting her large jaw across Kay's toes. Kay reaches down, giving her friend a couple of strokes on her fluffy fur.

Outside, the night grows dark as she sits, sipping her hot tea. No moon yet. The darkness wraps around Kay's little house like a cold embrace. Night is where her fears live. They creep into her mind, stirring up swirls of dark thoughts. She hears things. She sees things. She feels things. She knows it's her imagination. Always has been. Since childhood. Rather than outgrowing them, the struggles only seem to expand as she ages. She sought counseling, but nothing seemed to work—until Penny. And the Remington 12-gauge shotgun she keeps within reach. Penny brings her some peace of mind; the shotgun brings her a sense of security. Kay reaches down and strokes Penny's soft fur again.

The paper isn't what it used to be. Mostly ads these days. "Pretty soon, there won't even be a paper," she says to the dog. "Then, I guess I'll finally have to use that internet thingy for the news."

Kay again refolds the paper, resting it on the table before taking another sip of her tea. Glancing down again at her companion, she allows the warmth of the dog's friendship to seep into her heart. Penny whines, looking up and cocking her head. "I guess I'd better get you your dinner," Kay says as she stands.

Stepping to the pantry near the back door, she scoops a pile of dry dogfood from a large plastic bin into a stainless-steel bowl. When she turns around, Penny is standing at attention, growling deep in her throat, staring toward the living room. Nose and tail in perfect alignment. Ears perked.

Ordinarily, Kay imagines all sorts of creatures invading her private space. Dracula in the closet. Rapists at the door. The boogeyman under her bed. Of late, she's read of the cannibalistic kidnappers in Cutters Notch and the human traffickers running the motel and limestone mine. It's all very disconcerting. Normally, all she needs to do is peer over to Penny's calm demeanor to know she's safe and sound. However, this time, it's Penny who's on edge.

"What is it, girl? You hear something?" Goosepimples rise on Kay's forearms. Carefully, she places the bowl on the mat near the backdoor. With a glance, Kay checks the lock before easing toward her shotgun. Penny's growl deepens. The dog cocks her head to one side with her hackles raised. Gripping the old double-barrel's stock, Kay lifts it, pulling the hammers back. Each give a small click as they lock into place.

Stepping lightly, she edges her way toward the living room. Listening. She hears metallic rattling. *The swords.* Penny barks before rushing into the other room. Kay follows with the gun barrels at shoulder level.

The scene that unfolds before Kay's eyes is like something out of a strange B-movie. Three odd little creatures wearing leather jackets and sporting orange, pukey-colored skin, pointy ears, and long noses are stealing her swords. As she steps through the threshold, one is climbing up toward the mirror with her Civil War swords. Another is right behind the first with her U.S. Cavalry swords. Yet a third is removing her broadsword from its spot on the wall.

Even as she watches, two more leather-clad arms extend out of the mirror, grabbing the first in line. The thief is yanked through the reflective glass, carrying the swords with it.

The second one moves to follow the first, but Penny charges over, grabbing hold of its leg with her formidable teeth. Kay is dumbfounded, frozen in place. As she watches, the second sword burglar kicks Penny off, sending her skidding across the hardwood floor. Penny yelps and crashes into a console table. One decorative ceramic lamp falls to the floor and shatters, scattering broken pieces in all directions.

Thief number two makes his escape even as Kay aims the shotgun at the third strange pilferer. *What am I looking at?* So strange. The small, leather-clad being turns to face her with the heavy broadsword in its left hand. As she pulls both triggers, the creature flings some sparkling dust in her direction. The lights blow out as the thief flies back against the far wall, dropping the broadsword clanging to the floor.

Then, Kay sleeps.

~

A couple of hours later, Kay wakes up disoriented as Penny repeatedly licks the side of her face. *Crazy dream. Where am I?* It takes a while for her to come fully awake. She's weirdly groggy. Sitting up, she finds herself on the hard floor of her living room with the shotgun nearby. The smell from the fired shots still hangs in the air of the closed-up house. Kay springs to her feet, locates the wall switch, and turns on the ceiling light.

Her end table lamp is obliterated. Her Civil War and Cavalry swords are gone, the broadsword rests in the middle of the floor. To top it all, across the room, against a blood-spattered wall, rests the strangest—*person?*—sight of all. It has yellow-orange skin, pointed ears, and a long nose. Each hand has six fingers. It appears to be dead, a large wound in the center of its chest.

Kay calls her county sheriff. After arriving on scene, the sheriff calls a friend he has in the State House in Indianapolis. That guy calls a contact in Washington, D.C. Four hours later, the Feds arrive.

One
Saturday, October 30

Hope Spencer sat on one of the benches ringing a round, wooden picnic table. Across from her sat her new friend, Teresa Terrell. Nearby, a huge boulder was the centerpiece within the cement-floored pavilion in the Terrell backyard. The roof of the open-sided structure blocked the welcome rays of the late morning sun leaving Hope feeling a bit of a chill despite her hoodie.

It was late in October and the whole forest had turned shades of yellow, orange, and red. The fall color was at its height, and the air was cool. There was no wind. That helped. Tim, Teresa's dad, had raked up a huge pile of leaves nearby. Hope briefly allowed the beauty of the forest to capture her eyes. *I love watching the leaves fall.*

Each girl sat with a dinner plate and a bowl in front of them. Red Solo cups completed the lunch arrangement. Teresa's mother, Traci, provided bologna sandwiches, some homemade potato salad, and bowls of chicken noodle soup. Steam rose from the bowls in the cool air. Hope lifted a spoonful of the soup, blew lightly on the hot liquid, then carefully tasted it. "Mm, that's good."

Teresa was older, a senior at the Cutters Notch High School, so Hope was startled when the girl approached her after school and invited her over for lunch. She might have declined, thinking it was a senior prank, but Teresa had explained her interest.

"Tomo thought we should get acquainted," Teresa had said.

The reference to her new Native American friend who lived in the Arboreal Realm did the trick. Now, here she was, having lunch with the senior class president and one of the most popular girls in school. With all that had happened in recent weeks, Hope was reticent, but only a little. She couldn't help but be excited on the inside.

The Terrell family didn't live far from Basketball Court, only a couple more miles south on Robbins Creek Road. Hope surveyed the area. The house was old and had a back porch that stretched the width of the structure. Near the corner on one side stood a tall sycamore. To the right of the house, a long, gravel driveway snaked uphill toward the road. A medium-sized barn, dark gray from weathering, sat off toward the forest on the left.

The pavilion they sat under looked new. The timbers bore little weathering and were stained with a clear-coat finish. A wooden railing encircled the large rock. Concrete had been poured where the slab met the stone, forming a berm around the base of the boulder.

"What's with the giant rock?" Hope inquired.

"Have a look at it. It's got Native American markings on the top. We found it after we moved in. We were gonna move it to put in a pool, but my folks… well… they changed their minds."

Taking a quick bite of her sandwich, Hope stepped over to take a closer look as she chewed, examining the markings on the top. She made out a large spider-like creature surrounded by human forms with various weapons in hand, some fallen, some still battling the monster. She ran her fingers over the surface. The edges were smooth and weathered.

"Isn't it weird to think there used to be a whole different civilization living right here where we're standing?" Hope was peering off into her mind's eye, into what she imagined it must have been like.

"You and I both know there still is another civilization living right where we're standing." Teresa joined Hope at the rock, giving her a warm smile. "It's nice there's someone else around that I can talk to about them." The girl pulled her long, dark braid over her right shoulder and played with it as she spoke.

Returning to her spot at the table, Hope asked, "And how do you know Tomo? Did he drop by for some of your mom's soup?" Grinning, she lifted another spoonful of the tasty liquid, carefully enjoying the savory goodness.

Teresa returned a brief smile but lingered by the rock, resting her hand on its surface. "He, umm…" She turned back around to face Hope, her voice breaking. "He visited us shortly after we moved in here. Like I said, my dad was determined to move this rock to put in that pool I told you about. Tomo tried to stop us, but my dad was stubborn. He moved it anyway." Clearly shaking, the girl rejoined Hope at the table. "Terrible things happened. Things I wish I could forget."

"Wait," Hope interrupted. "Is this the gate? The Gate to Abandon?"

Teresa nodded. "I still relive that day in my memories." Tears welled in her eyes.

"What happened?"

The older girl looked down, then turned to stare at the trees. "There's a deep tunnel—so deep you can't see the bottom—and a thing lives down there."

Before Teresa could continue, the forest on the far side of the yard began to rustle. Then all along the same tree line, the brush shook violently, branches flew, dead and dying leaves burst forth, and streaks formed like pathways in the lawn. From the opposite side, the process started anew. Rustling. Brush flying. The grass being tromped down in lines that progressed toward the pavilion.

Hope didn't know what to make of it. Both girls stood, turning in a circle to take it in. "What's happening?" she asked.

"I don't know," Teresa replied, grabbing Hope's hand.

Apparently, they were surrounded, but by what? Hope had no idea.

~

Rick reached over, taking Maggie's hand into his own, interlacing his large fingers with her small, delicate ones. His heart began to pound in his chest. He felt it up into his throat. Her palm was soft and warm as it rested against his own. She squeezed. He squeezed back. Looking down at their simple hand embrace, he felt an excited sense of new beginnings, of renewal, swirling in his mind. His life had come full circle.

Rick Anders and Maggie Spencer were finally on a date. Perhaps it was only a picnic lunch at the Cutters Notch town park— Maggie had prepared some ham-salad sandwiches along with some mixed fruit on the side—but Rick could think of nothing he wanted to do more than sit with her under the trees. He studied the delicate shape of Maggie's jaw and the way her curly black hair fell across her flannel-covered shoulders. Rick enjoyed how her angular eyes led into the curve of her nose. She smiled. That simple up-curl of her lips spoke volumes to him. Sure, it was only a simple picnic date, but it was also hope and joy—two concepts absent to him for the last couple of years.

It was Saturday, the day before Halloween. Large puffs of clouds floating above the trees speckled the wide expanse of blue. The air was cool, but the lack of a breeze kept the chill at bay. Leaves fell here and there, joining their counterparts on the ground.

Rick took easy breaths as he relaxed in his jeans and State Police sweatshirt. The previous six weeks had been beyond crazy with multiple kidnappings, a shoot-out, a daring escape from a locked silo, and a battle with a dark entity that Rick hoped he'd never meet in person. He'd grown up in church, but the concept of evil spirits never seemed real to him. That had changed.

Rick leaned back, gazing up into the tangled branches within the canopy of towering oaks, maples, and sycamores that filled the park grounds. "Did Hope have a good week at school? She must have some real catching up to do."

Maggie released her grip on Rick's hand and took a sip of her drink. "It went pretty well," she replied as she joined him in leaning back, her left elbow sinking into the blanket they'd spread under the nearby giant oak. "But you're right. She's buried in homework. Hope's got plenty of time on her hands, though, with Josh and Danny still healing up. All she can do is go visit some, maybe watch a movie. They can't really go anywhere or do anything."

Rick let his view expand to take in the park and the surrounding houses that wrapped the park on all four sides. The structures looked like Legos set up around the old-growth timber that populated the Cutters Notch Park. Movement caught his eye across Rock Street. He spied Calvin, his deputy, trotting over to visit Linda, his long-lost love returned. Rick waved; Cal waved back.

"How are the boys?" A sudden gust of wind carried fallen leaves across their blanket. Throughout the park, the unexpected breeze pushed leaves in a line from west to east, picking up more as the wind traversed the grounds.

"Danny's coming along well," Maggie replied as she brushed the leaves away. "His ribs are still wrapped, and he's supposed to be carrying his arm in a sling, but I see him slipping it off a lot. He's still has a lot of scabbed-over scrapes."

"And Josh?"

"He's gonna be laid up for a while yet. Luckily, his head injury doesn't seem to have caused any lasting issues, but that busted-up leg…" She paused. "Did you know his cast extends from his foot all the way to his thigh? I don't know if he's sleeping well or not, either. He's had problems with that in the past."

"Trouble sleeping is understandable." Rick sipped his Sprite. "Is Hope with him today?" He reclined fully onto his back and peered into the upper branches. A squirrel skittered about, jumping from limb to limb. The rodent's large nest sat on one of the uppermost limbs. Here and there were some small birds, sparrows mostly. For the last two weeks, Rick constantly scanned the skies for one particularly large black bird, but none grabbed his attention.

"Actually, no. Hope has a new friend from school. She went over to the girl's house for lunch today."

"That's good. Anything lately from Kenny?"

"What is this? Twenty questions?" Maggie laughed. "He's doing good, I guess. When Hope's not doing homework, she pops through that portal thing every evening to visit with him. She says he's adapting and he's still his old self. Apparently, he's happy over there. I'm glad he's better, but after all that's happened, he makes me nervous. I worry he'll revert. He was like a real live nightmare, and I'm afraid he'll turn again."

Rick sat up. A few silent seconds passed. He nervously smoothed the blanket around him. "Maggie…I…" He started, but the words wouldn't come out.

Maggie smiled. "Rick," she replied, continuing to smile.

"Well…" The words caught in his throat again.

"Come on, now, big boy. Spit it out."

The blood surged into his cheeks. He couldn't speak. The words wouldn't flow. Maggie lifted their intertwined hands, pulling him toward her. She surprised him as she leaned in. He gazed deep into her eyes, then closed his own as their lips met. The kiss was sweet like honey butter on a homemade biscuit. It lingered. Rick's heart raced. His arms shook. The world around him disappeared, leaving only Maggie's soft hand and warm lips. And her presence in his life. All his longing from the previous two months found fulfilment in this one long-anticipated moment.

"Hey! That's a public park, ya know." Calvin's voice carried from Linda's front porch, breaking through Rick's romantic bubble.

"Nobody wants to watch you smooching in the grass."

Rick waved him off with his free hand, then used it to pull Maggie in closer. He'd been waiting for this moment for weeks. And right now, he didn't care who saw or what they thought.

Slowly, Maggie pulled away. She smiled, her eyes glimmering. "That was so nice."

Rick found that he still had no words. She'd taken his breath away. He smiled back as he studied the curve of her cheekbones, the sharp lines of her eyebrows, and the slope of her slender neck as it dropped toward her flannel shirt. Maggie leaned back in. He met her halfway, and her soft lips rejoined with his.

This is where I want to be. I never want to be anywhere else.

Without warning, a strong, steady wind began to blow in from the west, and a falling limb broke their embrace. Four inches in diameter and ten feet long, it landed just behind Maggie. Looking up, Rick saw that the massive oak was flexing and vibrating. Beyond the oak and across the park, branches were whipping in the breeze, dead ones snapping free and falling to the ground. It was as if a herd of giant, invisible squirrels were all leaping from limb to limb, moving as a unit from one end of the park to the other—from the west to the east.

"What's going on?" Maggie bolted up. "Is there a storm coming in?"

"Not sure. The last forecast I saw said the day would be clear and maybe a little chilly, but there's obviously a pretty strong wind hitting the trees up high."

~

Deputy Gator Randal reclined in the rickety office chair behind his metal desk in the sheriff's main office. Lifting both arms in the air, he stretched and yawned, his open mouth resembled a coffee-stained entrance to a deep, dark cavern.

"Cut that out," Judy Steinkamp ordered from across the office. Then, she yawned in response. "See what you've done? I'll be yawning all afternoon, thanks to you."

"Sorry," he muttered as he leaned back toward the computer screen. He was there to catch up on some paperwork—on his own time. "I stayed up too late last night watching the news."

"You're off today. Why didn't you just sleep in?"

"Can't. My body clock doesn't work like that. Six a.m. comes and *bing*, I'm awake."

"What was so engrossing about the news that kept you up?" Judy walked over to the coffeepot and poured herself a fresh cup, adding some sugar and powdered creamer. "Something big happen in Indy?"

"Naw. It's the usual in Indy. Two or three shootings. Political wrangling. Stuff like that. What got me hooked was a story about weird break-ins in rural areas. Homes invaded and weapons stolen, but no actual evidence of a break-in. No busted locks. No broken windows."

"Why's that so weird? Homes get burgled out in the country all the time." Judy sat back down at her desk, her laptop open in front of her and the radio base station on a credenza behind her. Three stacks of papers sat piled in front of her. One stack of papers for Rick to sign. One stack of papers to be filed. And finally, one stack of correspondence to which she needed to write an official response. The third stack had grown exponentially taller after all the events of the last few weeks.

"It's the lack of evidence left behind, lack of any sign of a break-in, and the type of weapons stolen. Seems these thieves are specifically looking for blades. Old swords and machetes, stuff like that. One man's knives were stolen from a case that also held several guns. Plus, the break-ins are random—happening all around us."

The bell hanging over the door at the front of the office jingled. Gator glanced up to see two men and a woman step inside. The men wore dark suits with red ties, their hair trimmed sharply around their clean-shaven faces. The woman was older with gray hair styled into tight curls above her shoulders and over her ears. She wore a dark brown pantsuit with a blue scarf looping around her neck. She carried a large, leather notebook.

Rising from his desk, Gator stepped up to meet them at the reception counter. "Can I help you folks?"

One of the men handed him a card. "We'd like to speak with Sheriff Anders. Official business."

"Official, huh?" Gator took the card and examined it, scratching his chin.

James L. Franklin
National Security Agency

"Are you all with the NSA?" Gator asked.

The second man handed Gator his card—Anthony Sheldon, also with the NSA—then stood toward the back, hands crossed at the waist, remaining silent. The woman shook her head. "I'm Cynthia Sweet. I'm with SETI." She handed her card over, as well. "Are you the sheriff?"

"SETI? You mean those folks looking for space aliens and UFOs?"

"SETI stands for Search for Extraterrestrial Intelligence. We're a scientific organization." The woman looked perturbed. "We need to speak with your sheriff. Is he here?"

Gator was intrigued. "Why in the world is the NSA and SETI in tiny, little Cutters Notch?"

Impatience crept up Franklin's otherwise stolid face. "Deputy…" He paused, looking around for some identifier, but Gator was off duty and out of uniform. "Look, we really need to speak with Sheriff Anders. Can you get him for us or not?"

Judy Steinkamp ambled over, shoving Gator aside. Smiling sweetly, she looked the visitors over. "Sheriff Anders is off duty today. Deputy Randal here is also off duty. He's only here to be a pest and do paperwork. Can I find another deputy to assist you?"

"I'm afraid not," Franklin said. "We need to speak with the sheriff himself."

"He's off work until Monday," Judy explained. "He comes in around 7 a.m., so you can meet him here at that time."

"Would you call him for us? Please." Cynthia Sweet from SETI smiled back at Judy as she leaned on the counter. "We need to speak with him today."

Judy was having none of it. "Look, things around here have been extremely stressful in the last couple of months. Sheriff Anders has been in the middle of every situation. I'm not calling him in unless you give me a really good reason why I should interrupt one of the few opportunities he's had to rest and relax."

Franklin raised his rectangular black briefcase to the counter, opened it, pulled out a file folder, and then slid a photograph across so Judy could see it. Gator leaned across her shoulder so he could see, too. "This photo of a dead alien was taken in a home just over the county line, a little northeast of here."

"Wow." Gator reached for the picture. "Let me see that."

Judy smacked his hand away. "Back off, Gator."

"Now, will you please call the sheriff for us?" Franklin asked again.

Without another word, Judy returned to her desk, lifted her phone handset, and dialed Rick Anders' number.

~

Josh sat in a chair at his kitchen table. His leg, covered in a cast to his upper thigh, was elevated on a neighboring chair, resting on a pillow. The boy wore a pair of sweats. It was the only thing he had that would stretch over his cast. He sported a Colts hoodie on the top half of his body. His buddy, Danny, sipped a glass of milk at the table across from him. The boy still had visible scabs on his face, neck, and hands, acquired during his courageous jump from the silo two weeks earlier. Danny wore jeans, a t-shirt, and a blue windbreaker.

"Where's your sling?" Josh asked, whispering so as not to draw his mother's attention.

"Mom said I didn't need to wear it anymore." Danny obviously fibbed. He'd just slipped out without putting it on.

Josh's mother, Cindy Gillis, her blond hair pulled back in a ponytail, placed a paper plate in front of each boy. Bologna sandwiches with American cheese and mustard on white bread. Rippled potato chips garnished the sides. Pulling a carton of French-onion dip from the refrigerator, she popped it open before positioning it on the table between the boys. Immediately, Danny lifted the top slice of bread and began piling his potato chips into his sandwich. Transfer complete, he returned the bread and smashed the concoction, crumbling the chips inside.

"Why do you do that?" Josh asked.

"I dunno. It tastes good. My Aunt Rose does it, too. She showed me and I like it that way." Danny took a bite, the chips crunching as he chewed.

"Oh, what the heck?" Josh flipped his bread, added the chips, and then smashed the sandwich, just like his friend. He took a bite. "Mm. This is pretty good."

Sheba rose from her place next to Josh's chair and trotted over to lap up water from her bowl. The dog had not left Josh's side since his return from the hospital. A few moments later, she returned, lying down between the boy and the sliding door to the backyard, placing her head on her paws. Josh reached down and scratched her behind one floppy ear. Casually, he dropped a potato chip nearby for the dog to snatch up.

After nearly dying following his fall inside the silo, Josh had experienced about a week of rest and recovery, aided by pain meds. The specter left him alone, so he'd slept well. With each passing day, the pain in various spots on his body dissipated. He was on the mend. Hope came to see him every evening. His mother doted on him. His dad made all sorts of promises about things they were going to do together. All at once, life was lining up in front of him like an easy layup. Until a couple of days ago.

"Danny, it's back," he said under his breath. He didn't want to tell his folks.

"What?"

"It left me alone for a week. Ever since I saw it on the beach in my mind. But a few days ago, it came at me again. It taunts and threatens and laughs at me." His hand quivered as he lifted his sandwich for another bite. Glancing at his mom, he lowered his hand to the table.

"Have you told Hope?"

"No. Not yet. I haven't seen her much. Short visits or maybe a movie. You're the only one that knows."

Whining, Sheba rose and trotted to the sliding door. Her ears were perked, and her head was cocked to one side.

"Mom," Josh called out. "Sheba needs to go outside."

"We need to let Hope know," Danny whispered.

His mother opened the patio door, but Sheba stood and peered toward the trees, continuing to whine. "Well, go on," she said. "Go do your business."

Suddenly, Sheba began to bark. She raised her haunches, bared her teeth, and added a deep growl. Then she backed off a couple of paces.

Cindy stuck her head through the open door, looking for the cause of Sheba's reaction. Josh and Danny angled for a view beyond the woman. As they peered toward the forest, trails suddenly formed in the dried weeds and grass along the berm between their yard and the woods. Then, the brush undergrowth began to slam about as if an invisible army were pushing through. Sheba's aging body stood in an aggressive mode, accompanied by a flurry of snarls, growls, and barks. Yet, she made no move to go outside.

15

Cindy turned to face her injured son. "Something's going on, but I can't see what it is."

The boys looked at one another. Josh's arms were shaking.

"Mrs. Gillis," Danny said, "can I use your phone? I need to call Hope."

~

It was a lovely morning in the Arboreal Realm with the pulsating blue of the forest just visible despite the sunshine overhead. Most of the twinkling leaves had given up their grip and fallen to the earth, losing their colorful aura. Only the oak leaves, now pulsating a deep red, resisted the annual urge to descend to the ground below. Shafts of sunlight sliced through the sparse canopy, brightening the normally shaded, yet colorful woods.

Alone, Kenny Burton ambled along a trail winding through the hills behind the Adena village. He'd only lived here for two weeks, but already it felt more like home than anywhere he'd ever lived. His mind was clear; he could breathe. The only dark clouds were the guilt he carried and the concern that he could lose himself again. With the specter no longer cluttering his mind, he could remember in vivid detail all the horrible things he'd done to his family, his wife and daughter. He ached deep in his heart.

In his arms, he carried firewood. When he first joined the Adena, he'd been relegated to learning about the people, their history, and their way of life. Tomo devoted hours to his instruction. Now, he was taking on tasks in support of the community, like gathering firewood, cleaning up after meals, and carrying water. Kenny didn't mind; everyone else had tasks, as well. He appreciated having a useful role to play.

His modest lodging was in a tree. He was surprised when Tomo had shown him to his spot, but soon he'd felt like a boy again, climbing to his treehouse. "We live in the trees so that we leave little trace on the ground that could draw attention from your realm," Tomo explained. "In this ancient forest, it is easy and comfortable. Yet, we are always watching for the encroachment of men, removing the old trees. We place our homes far from any man-made trail."

Kenny's assigned task was to gather wood in preparation for the coming winter. They needed to stockpile. Unlike the elves, who had metabolisms that could carry them through the cold months, the

Adena required warm clothes and fire to survive.

The trail he traversed was remote, most likely a deer trail formed in the Human Realm. It meandered through the underbrush, crossing steep hills before descending into deep gullies. Because his new people had lived there many years, he needed to search long distances from their village to find sufficient wood that would already be seasoned enough to burn well.

Walking on a cliff high above a lake, Kenny paused to rest on a large rock. The sunlight was reflecting off the rippled surface of the reservoir below. A couple of colorful fairies skimmed along just above the surface of the water. He took a deep breath. The sun soothed his face, and the fresh air worked to cleanse his cigarette-stained lungs.

Megan was on his mind. *It's Maggie now*, he reminded himself. *How can I ever make up for what I've done to her?* Even before the specter, their marriage had not been perfect. They married too young. Argued too much. But they'd also loved one another. He knew it to be true. With a clarity he hadn't experienced in close to three years, he also knew he was to blame for both his own troubles and the destruction of his family. Tears leaked from the inside corners of his eyes, dribbling along both sides of his nose.

"Maybe I'll write her a letter," he mumbled. Leaning back, he took in the scene. It was beautiful with the fall leaves floating on the water and the low, pulsating blue of the forest aura. *Where would I start?*

Movement caught his eye from across the lake. An elf stepped free of the trees and peered at the lake. Then, another. And another. Soon, there was a large group gathered on the far shore. They lacked the greenish aura of the elves he knew. These were all an ugly orange color like those two fallen elves he'd met on his first day in this realm. Kenny spotted a sword reflecting the sun. Then he saw more weapons. Knives. Machetes. Spears. Pitchforks.

Having not been noticed yet, he slipped back under the cover of the trees, continuing to spy on the group. Kenny counted twenty-eight, but he couldn't see far into the trees. There could be many more under cover. Leaving his pile of firewood where he'd laid it near the rock, he sprinted away. He had to find Tomo. Kenny hadn't been in this realm long, but he knew trouble when he saw it.

~

In the two weeks that followed Nozomi's battle with the dark specter, Queen Hesed had lingered, staying with her sons, Gavin, Gronek, and Smakal, in their forest abode. She'd missed her sons. It surprised her how much, but now that they were reunited, she was hesitant to part again. The queen procrastinated her departure, using the excuse that she needed to stay until the Gate to Abandon was secured. That would only happen after Dargo and his security forces arrived. In her heart, she knew the feeling for what it was—separation anxiety. Still, she wished to make the most of her time with her children.

Her children's home was a comfortable nook within a cave set between some large boulders. The cave descended slightly, curling below a ridge of limestone in a portion of the forest uninhabited in the Human Realm. On the human side, one of the only mountain lions in the area lived in that very same cave.

She sat in a swivel rocker with a padded seat and threadbare armrests. It leaned a little to the right, but she was quite comfortable. The cream-colored stuffing poked through a broken seam in the fabric. There was a faint odor of smoke.

"How did you move this chair through a shimmer and up into this cave?" she asked Gavin.

Her oldest son stood in his makeshift kitchen, making tea. He smiled, pausing for a moment, apparently recalling the effort it took to acquire and transport the chair to the cave. "It was a bit of an effort," he admitted. "The chair was left behind in that large burned-out house in the human village. The one where Hope's…I mean Nozomi's father had taken her. We passed it through a large shimmer that appeared up high in the night sky. When we investigated, we found that the light of a full moon shining through a hole in the roof had activated a portal through a very large mirror. I think it was the same mirror that Nozomi drove her father through. We climbed a tree, tied off a rope—"

"Okay," she interrupted, "I do not want to hear details about how you risked your life to secure a chair." With her slender green fingers, she smoothed wrinkles from the fluffy blue bathrobe draped around her shoulders.

Gavin smiled again. "It was a bit of an adventure. Do you want some more tea?" He carried a kettle with steam slipping out of the small, curved nozzle.

The two of them were alone in the cozy, subterranean abode. Gronek, Smakal, and Sacqueal were out and about. Sacqueal had gone in search of more walnuts to add to his already bulging collection. He gathered during the day and munched on them in the evenings. The shells were piling up in a corner. Gronek and Smakal were on a mission to check in on Tomo's people and see how Kenny Burton was coming along.

Hesed gazed around the chamber, enjoying the twinkling lights emitted by the moss and algae growing on the moist walls. "I am beginning to worry about Dargo," she stated. Hesed raised her teacup, accepting more of the delicious, hot liquid. "He and his team should have arrived by now; I have received no messages."

"He will be here. I have no doubt. Something unforeseen must have delayed him."

Hesed's cup shook slightly as she lifted it to her lips. "Yes, yes. He is very good at what he does, but these days are suddenly fraught with dangers he has never known. Bayal is cunning and more than willing to do unspeakable acts. He may also know that I am here."

"How?" Gavin asked. "How could he possibly know?" The elf poured himself some tea and sat next to his mother. He pulled back the hoodie of his child-size Indiana Hoosiers sweatshirt, then fingered the single tuft of hair on his head.

"Any number of ways. Perhaps one of those fallen ones that I pardoned. Or the specter that Nozomi defeated. Ambassador Karma reported that Bayal is using specters to carry out some of his wishes."

"Gavin? Mother?" Smakal rushed in. "Come quick! There are armies of fallen ones approaching the Gate from two directions."

~

Al Havener never returned home after his cousin inadvertently released him from the caged compound at the limestone mine, allowing him to escape justice for kidnapping Josh and Danny. The authorities would be looking for him, so instead, he'd picked up a burner phone at a convenience store in Evansville, called ahead to his family, and arranged for short-term lodging at a rundown safe house in East St. Louis. His family may have started out as farmers in rural Indiana, and he may utilize a cover as a pharmaceutical rep, but he and his kin ran a substantial crime syndicate headquartered in Missouri. Their fingers of nefarious activities extended as far west as Kansas City and as far east as Evansville.

He spent the ensuing two weeks in the dilapidated apartment studying maps, regrouping, and making new plans to complete his original mission. It was the day after his escape when he learned the boys had somehow survived the silo. As he watched the TV news reports of how the chubby one had jumped from the top, Al almost gained a new-found respect for the kid. Almost. They still had to pay, though. The family demanded it. Giving up wasn't an option available to him. He had to go back and finish the job.

This time, he hoped to slip in and out on the same day. The silo was no longer an option, as much as he loved the irony and simplicity of the original plan. Instead, Al managed to communicate with his Uncle Earl, as the old man sat in jail awaiting trial. His uncle gave him the lowdown on how things had transpired at the abandoned quarry when Earl and Faye had been captured. This time, he hoped to grab all three of the punks at the same time, take them back to the original scene, and finish locking them up inside the stone tomb behind the old shack. The new plan carried even more irony.

Al smiled as he crossed back into Indiana. It was a beautiful October Saturday morning. He couldn't ask for better weather. Perfect for the work he had planned. Glancing in his rearview mirror, he caught sight of a line of dark clouds following him on the western horizon. He hoped that wasn't a bad omen.

Two

Dargo walked among the ruins of the queen's compound. Smoke wafted skyward from charred trees. Here and there, fellow elves were bandaging one another. Anger welled up and threatened to overwhelm his senses. *I should have left a stronger force behind.*

As he stood there, holding his dagger, and glaring about, Dorcas hobbled up, carrying her own sword. A cloth circled her left thigh, and a large bruise colored her forehead. She wore a blanket over her shoulders to cover the rips in her royal garments.

"There was no way for you to anticipate the attack," she stated, as if reading the self-doubt in Dargo's mind. "There was no warning. The queen requested your presence, and you had to go to her."

"Yes," he answered, his eyes dropping to stare at the bare earth at his feet. "But did I need to take so many? I should have left a larger force in defense of the queen's home. If that fairy had not reached us when it did—"

"Stop." Dorcas placed her six-fingered hands on Dargo's shoulders. "It serves no purpose for you to second-guess yourself. In your three hundred years of life, there has never been an attack. You had no way to know one was imminent."

"Still," he began as he turned away. "It is my job to know, to anticipate. I am the queen's minister of security."

Dorcas pulled him back to face her. "I said for you to stop, and I mean it. We are alive. Sure, we have some injuries, but no one among our people died. Perhaps there will be time for self-pity later, but right now you need to attend to Queen Hesed. She still awaits you in the northern forest."

"Yes." Dargo resigned himself to the task at hand. "You are correct, of course. I will depart again this afternoon, but this time I will leave more of our forces here. Just in case they decide to try again."

Dorcas smiled at her friend, her green eyes twinkling as she and Dargo stood beneath the shade of a large pine. "Now, there you go. That is the Dargo I know." As she spoke, she wiped the curved blade of her sword on the light blue blanket draping her shoulder. "And that will give me time to pack."

"What do you mean?" Dargo returned his dagger to its sheath. "You mean to join us in the journey? Are you not needed here?"

"I am not. Maxon and Maxle have the situation well in hand. You are leaving other security forces behind to ensure their safety, are you not? I believe I am more needed by the queen's side."

"You want to see Gavin." A smile formed on Dargo's lips. He reached up and cleared a smudge of dirt from Dorcas's chin.

"That is a pleasant side benefit." Dorcas smiled back, her cheeks flushed, adding a red tint to her glowing, greenish aura. "I will not deny it."

Giving Dorcas a sideways glance, Dargo turned away. "Very well. I will enjoy your presence during my travels. Be ready to depart after the noon meal. As for me, I mean to interrogate our captives." Dorcas had a way of soothing his emotions, but anger returned as he marched into the trees. His forces had captured and bound four fallen ones left behind by their hateful companions. Dargo carried a pouch. The Leaf of Necessity. He would have his answers.

~

Hope stood back-to-back with Teresa in the shade of the pavilion near the Ancient Gate to Abandon. Together, they watched as the yard's scattered, fallen leaves formed into lines as if by shuffling feet. All lines ended an equal distance from the stone, about fifteen feet out on each side.

Teresa's mom, Traci, stepped out the backdoor onto the porch, dishrag in hand. "Is something wrong? You both look a little scared. I was watching through the kitchen window when you jumped up."

"Something's going on, Mom," Teresa said. "The brush began to rustle all around, and then lines formed in the yard. See?" She pointed.

Traci joined the girls on the pavilion. "That is weird. Maybe we should go inside?"

"You should all leave the area," Tomo stated as he stepped around from behind the large sycamore that grew near the corner of the old house. His eyes were wide, and his dark hair flowed out behind him as he strode toward them. He wore a leather tunic adorned with colorful beads. His deerskin shirt sported a metal plate affixed across his chest with leather straps. A large knife in hand, he fingered a stone hammer hung in a sling from his waist. "Enemies approach from two directions. We have formed a defensive perimeter." The man ducked his head to join the trio of women beneath the roof of the picnic shelter. "If we lose the battle, our enemies may open the gate."

Hope's companions gasped. Neither spoke, but Traci grabbed Hope by the elbow and pulled her toward their family car. "Come on, girls. Let's get going."

"Wait!" Hope's eyes were wide. "What about my dad? Is he okay?" Jerking free of Traci's grasp, she turned back to Tomo. "Can you protect him?"

"Your father stands with us, not ten feet from where you are. He carries a spear and a small sword and will fight alongside his new people."

"Tomo, no!" Hope shouted. "Send him home. Send him through a shimmer or bring him to me, however you do it."

"I cannot do that." Tomo's face held a grim countenance. "The shimmers are not active during the day, and there is no time for me to retrieve him. Besides, he wishes to stand with us." Turning to Traci, he motioned toward the car. "You must go. You must go now. Are your husband and son in the house?"

"No," Traci answered. "They've gone to Indy for the day."

"Good. Take Hope and your daughter and leave the area. Get far away. I do not know how this will turn out."

Traci again tugged at Hope's arm. Teresa took the other. Together, they pulled the resistant girl toward the vehicle.

As they shoved her inside, Hope's cell phone rang. She pulled it from her jacket pocket as Traci hopped behind the wheel and fired the engine. Staring back at the pavilion even as the phone continued to ring in her hand, Hope saw Tomo disappear behind the large sycamore tree.

It was Josh's home number on the screen of Hope's phone. The Gillis's had not yet given up their land line. "Hello," she said, desperation in her voice. "Is something wrong? Is Josh okay?" She hit the speaker button.

"Hope." It was Danny. "Something weird is going on outside."

"I know. Weird stuff here, too, and my dad's in danger."

"Josh says the specter is back," Danny added. "He's started in on him again."

Her two weeks of relative peace were over. She felt her heart racing in her chest. Hope shivered, and the phone shook in her hand. Out the window and through the trees, a line of black clouds formed in the western sky. Darkness was again descending on Cutters Notch. Evil was back for a third round.

~

"What do ya suppose made all those limbs start falling?" Calvin asked Rick from the swing on Linda's front porch. His girlfriend sat beside him, leaning her head on his shoulder, letting her blonde hair fall across his chest. Rick stood at the rear of his cruiser with the trunk lid open, loading in the lunch materials while Maggie folded the blanket nearby.

"I don't know. Some upper-level wind, maybe. It was weird, that's for sure. But I guess it's like Gator says, 'weird stuff seems to happen in Cutters Notch all the time.'"

"I've lived here all my life, 'cept for my time in the military," Calvin said, "and I can officially confirm that statement. This place can really give you the wiggleworms sometimes."

"The what?" Maggie asked.

"Wiggleworms. You know. It's like little worms under your skin, making you wiggle." Calvin stood and leaned against the brick pillar supporting the right side of the porch.

Linda stepped beside Calvin, sliding her hand around his waist. Her bright red lipstick stood out against her blonde hair and light complexion. "You two looked sweet out there under the trees." She winked.

"You saw that, did you?" Maggie said as she carefully laid the blanket in the trunk. "It was a long time coming." She smiled and winked back.

Rick blushed. It seemed like a long time to him, also. Just last month, they'd been thrown together by circumstance, but he'd been attracted to her for well over a year, ever since Maggie and Hope had moved in. He'd always felt he had too much baggage to pursue her. Then, the Hicks snatched Hope, throwing Maggie into his life. *Out of a burnt forest springs fresh growth.* Rick found himself feeling a touch embarrassed by this one turn of good events in his life.

"Well, razzlesnatz. Look, Linda, he's blushing."

Rick's phone started ringing from inside his jacket pocket. "Saved by the bell," he quipped as he retrieved the device and stepped away. Maggie finished loading the trunk. Still chatting with Calvin and Linda, she stepped around to the passenger door.

"Hey Judy," Rick spoke into the phone. "What's up?"

"Sheriff, you've got visitors down here at the office. They're demanding to see you right away."

"Demanding?"

"Yes, demanding. Two men from the NSA and one woman from SETI. I think you should come see them."

"Roger that. I'll be right there. Maybe ten minutes." Rick tapped off the call and stuck the device back in his pocket. "I've got to stop by the office for a few minutes," he said to Maggie. "Do you have time to hang with me, or do I need to run you home?"

"I'm good," she replied.

They waved at Calvin and Linda before sliding in the car and pulling out. Leaves were blowing across Park Street carried on a brisk breeze. As they cruised toward the main road, a seriously heavy line of clouds approached from the west.

"What's going on, Rick? You've got a crinkle in your forehead."

"Do I?" He smiled and tried to rub it out. "I guess I do. Judy told me there are two men from the NSA and one woman from SETI waiting to see me at the office."

"The NSA and SETI? Really? What in the world do they want?"

Rick rubbed his face again. A glance in the rearview mirror showed the crinkle on his forehead still firmly in place. "I don't know for sure, but I've got a guess or two." He glanced at his date. "I'm betting you do too."

Maggie turned in her seat to look at him. Rick read the concern in her eyes.

"How would they know?" Maggie paused; she turned and

stared at the passing foliage. "You can't tell them anything, you know. Hope would be devastated. Who knows what they'd do?"

"I know, I know. Why do you think my forehead is crinkled?" He forced a smile. "It's probably not that, anyway. I mean, how *would* they know anything about it?" Rick rubbed his face again. "I'll just see what they want and go from there, but our secret is safe. Okay?"

"Okay," Maggie muttered before leaning back on the headrest. Rick could see a crinkle on her beautiful forehead, too.

The car fell silent as they continued west on 257, passing the General. They crossed Robbins Creek Road, heading toward the sheriff's office, located behind the post office. Maggie had her arms crossed as she stared out the passenger window toward the dilapidated bank building and the boarded-up school.

"I won't say anything," Rick promised.

"I know," Maggie replied, but Rick could sense the worry, nonetheless.

~

The Bowen County Justice Center, the fancy name for the sheriff's office, was a low-set, limestone building with two wings— one for cells, the other for offices. Rick parked around back and walked in the rear entrance. Normally, he would throw his hat on a row of pegs along the left side of the hallway, stop in the break area for a cup of Judy's strong coffee, and head straight for his office in the front west corner of the building. Today, though, he had no hat, and it was afternoon, past his coffee time. Unlike Calvin, whose body ran on coffee, he'd never sleep if he drank the caffeinated fluid after noon. Instead, he strode directly to the main reception area, spotted his waiting visitors in chairs on the other side of the counter, and stopped in front of Judy's desk. Gator, sitting at another desk and pecking away at a computer, glanced up and waved.

"Judy, did they say what they wanted?" Rick asked in a low voice. "Any idea why they're here?" He glanced at Maggie. She stood where the back hallway spilled into the office, her anxiety evident from the set of her jaw.

"Apparently, a woman just over the county line killed an alien," Judy replied. No smile. No smirk. She kept a completely straight face. "They have pictures. Seems it's close enough to our little village they want to know if you've heard anything about strange goings-on."

"Pictures? You've seen 'em?"

"Yep. Little guy with sort of orange-tinted skin, long nose, pointy ears, six fingers on each hand. He was wearing a leather jacket of all things." She shook her head. "I always thought aliens were little green men, not little orange men." Acting as if she were disinterested, Judy shuffled papers around on her desk. Rick noticed an uncharacteristic shake in her fingers as she lifted then replaced several folders into the same spots.

Rick approached the reception area. "I'm Sheriff Anders. Welcome to Bowen County. How can I help you?" His waiting guests stood as one.

Moments later, Rick, James L. Franklin and Anthony Sheldon from the NSA, along with Cynthia Sweet from SETI sat around the table in the conference room, while Maggie waited in Rick's personal office.

Rick decided a little caffeine might be a good idea after all, so each person at the table had a Styrofoam cup of coffee sitting on a white napkin. Franklin's briefcase was open in front of him. Sweet sat next to him poised with a notepad and pen. Sheldon looked on with his hands crossed on the table.

Rick sipped his brew. "I'll pay for this later," he murmured.

"What was that?" Franklin asked.

"Oh, nothing," Rick replied. "I'll probably have trouble sleeping tonight." He raised his Styrofoam cup like it was show-and-tell time.

Franklin slid the folder with the pictures across the table. "These were taken a few hours ago at the home of Kay Sours. She lives just across the county line. Cutters Notch is the closest town to her home."

"I know Kay," Rick said. "She comes into town for supplies. I just met her about a week ago. Is she okay?"

"She's fine," Sweet stated, "maybe a bit shaken up. Take a look at what she shot in her house."

Rick pulled the folder across, opening it to find four 8x10 glossy photos. He spread them out, side by side. "Are you sure you didn't pull these from one of those tabloid papers?" He chuckled and rubbed the crinkle on his forehead.

"I took those photos myself," Agent Sheldon answered.

"They're legitimate."

Franklin explained the circumstances, the chain of communication, and the timeline.

The crime-scene photos documented a dead creature from different angles. The body was what Rick knew to be an elf—a dead elf. It wore a leather jacket with the front shredded by a shotgun blast. "What exactly am I looking at?" He asked anyway, doing his best to manifest a curious demeanor. "And what does it have to do with Bowen County or Cutters Notch?"

"You're looking at a deceased alien," Sweet stated, as she sat up straight and tapped her notepad. Rick noted the sparkle in her eyes and the giddiness in her voice.

"We're here," Franklin added, "because Cutters Notch has a reputation that has reached our offices. What can you tell us about this thing?"

Rick laughed nervously. His hand quivered slightly as he loaded the snapshots back inside the folder. "Cutters Notch has a 'reputation' that's reached the NSA? Really? That's nuts. And I'm afraid I don't have any information on aliens that would be of any help to you. I've never seen anything that looked like that creature around here." It wasn't exactly a lie. The one he'd seen was green and wearing a stocking hat. Still, he felt a little guilty for fibbing to the NSA.

"Fair enough," Franklin said. "Still, we'll be around town today. We wanna chat with folks Ask some questions. You know."

"Help yourself."

With nothing more to be said, the meeting ended, and Rick escorted his guests out the front door of the Bowen County Justice Center. His gaze followed them as they drove off, turning right on 257.

"This place just keeps getting more interesting," he muttered, stepping back inside and waving at Judy and Gator.

"Oh, it most definitely does," Gator quipped. "So, what's the scoop?"

"You know as much as I do," Rick replied.

After retrieving Maggie from his office, he led her through the back door, and they slid into his cruiser. Before starting the engine, he turned to her. "They've got the body of a dead elf. Someone shot one in the next county."

Maggie's mouth dropped open; she covered it with her hand. "Oh, no. No, no, no. You don't think it's one of Hope's friends, do you?"

"I don't think so. It wasn't green. It was orange. But I can't know for sure. Seems a group of them were caught by a homeowner while they were stealing some swords the woman had on display in her house. She shot one and the others escaped."

Maggie's phone rang. Hope's face appeared on the device's screen. "Hey, honey." Rick could tell Maggie was trying to force the nervous energy from her voice. "What? Where are you?"

Rick watched the crinkle re-form on Maggie's forehead as she spoke into the phone. The tone of her voice told him something was wrong. He started the cruiser, pulling toward the road as she spoke to Hope. He paused at the highway until she explained the situation.

"Take me home," she blurted as she tapped off the call. "Tomo appeared at Hope's new friend's house. He interrupted their lunch and told them to evacuate right away. There's some sort of big fight about to happen on the other side. Hope's friend and her mother are at my house right now, waiting for us."

~

Clarence glanced in the rearview mirror of the 1989 two-tone, black-over-white GMC pickup as he slowed to turn into Basketball Court, catching the wrinkles around his eyes and the tight gray curls above the caramel-shaded skin of his forehead. "Man, I'm lookin' old," he muttered with a chuckle. The hands on the wheel were bony and dark brown with flecks of white—dead skin in the crevices around the knuckles. "I must be a pretty picture."

A Dodge Caravan rushed toward him, so he waited for it to pass. Instead of speeding by, it slowed only enough to turn into the cul-de-sac, tires squealing. "Some folks are in too much of a hurry." Clarence pressed on the gas. The engine popped, and a puff of blue smoke trailed in his wake as he followed the much newer vehicle into the neighborhood. His engine rumbled as he rolled past the ball court and into the ring of pavement surrounded by the little ranch-style homes. The residual leaves on the surrounding trees fluttered violently in the wind.

The Caravan pulled into the first driveway on the left. Clarence drove straight across, pulling beyond the for-sale sign and into the driveway that used to belong to Earl and Faye Hicks. Moving the stick shift on the steering column to park, he turned the ignition off and listened to the engine continue to rumble for another thirty seconds. As the big V-8 coughed and spit, Clarence gathered his belongings—his duffle bag, a Mark Twain novel, his walking cane, and the keys to his new house.

Clarence D'Angelo had hobbled into the realtor's office just seconds after the house hit the market and laid down cash for the property, the exact amount of the asking price. The flabbergasted agent, knowing the family wanted a quick sale, recovered quickly, and expedited the closing, giving Clarence immediate possession of the keys. Now, the feeble-looking old man stood on the slight slope of the driveway and surveyed his new neighborhood.

To his right sat the sheriff's house. The shrubs were trimmed, and the grass was mowed—a smart, simple landscape except for the smashed bed of mums that bordered his own yard. No flowerpots. No seating arrangement on the front porch. To his left stood two houses with lots of yard accoutrements—neat shrubs, potted plants, landscaped flowerbeds, baseball bats, a bike, a basketball, and a large pile of fallen leaves. The list went on.

Clarence ignored much of that. Instead, he watched the women pile out of the Dodge Caravan on the other side of the sheriff's house. He recognized Hope Spencer and Teresa Terrell. Limping toward the rear of the truck bed, he slid his left hand along the side to steady himself, then he saw Hope stop and stare at him. He gave her a little wave and smiled.

He hadn't expected to see the two girls so soon after arriving, but he was glad to catch a glimpse of them. After all, they were the reason for his presence.

~

As the Terrell van pulled into her driveway, Hope stuffed her phone back in her jacket pocket. "Let's get inside," she said. "My mom's on her way." Pulling the lever, she slid the side door back and jumped out. Grabbing her bag, she turned to peer around the cul-de-sac.

Hope spotted the stranger right away—an old man who had parked his ancient pickup truck in the Hicks' driveway. As she watched, he exited his vehicle, then pulled a satchel and a few other items with him. The man leaned on a cane and moved slowly, as if he might fall at any moment. Teresa and Traci chattered behind her, gathering their own things before moving toward her porch.

"I think it's gonna rain," Traci said.

Hope didn't take her eyes off the man standing across the way. The old guy didn't appear dangerous, but she'd recently learned that appearances can be deceiving. She'd developed a new sense of extra caution around people she didn't know. Still, the man caused her no alarm. He was simply unexpected.

As she stared at the old man, he hobbled to the rear of his truck, peering around. He looked her way and they locked eyes. He smiled and waved. Hope smiled and waved back. *I wonder who he is?*

"Hey, Hope," Teresa called from the porch. "Do you have a key? Or do we need to wait out here on the stoop?"

"I've got a key," she replied, continuing to watch the old dude as he turned and ambled up the driveway. He hobbled all the way to the front door of the "House of Horrors." Danny had given it the nickname. She and Josh liked it. Between the Hicks and their nephew, Al Havener, the place would always be a terrifying, haunting presence to them. The police had even found pieces of missing people in that house.

"Let's go inside," Traci said. "We don't know what's going to happen. We need to get out of sight."

Hope broke from her thoughts. Turning, she hurried to the front door, key in hand. "Sorry. I wasn't expecting anyone over at that house."

"Is that the Hicks' house?" Teresa asked, glancing over just in time to see the old man step out of view.

"Yeah," Hope muttered. She unlocked the door and shoved it open. "Come on in."

~

When Kenny reached the Adena village, he discovered that his new neighbors were already aware of the approaching danger. Men, and even some of the women, were gathering weapons. Someone tossed a spear in his direction. He caught it in his right hand. Someone else handed him a large knife, which he slid into his belt.

Tomo approached. "Quick, we must guard the Gate," he said. "Now that you are one of us, it is your duty as well. Come with us."

Most of the women and all the children were hidden away, while the balance of the Adena village rushed to the large stone. Kenny didn't understand the significance of the big rock except that it was supposed to be some sort of gate that held back an ancient evil. His new-found Native American family seemed terrified yet determined that the so-called gate would not be compromised. It felt surreal. It was like he was caught up in some dream world. He rushed along with the others as the pulsating blue of the forest blurred past him on each side.

Suddenly, they stopped in a clearing, forming a semi-circle. They faced outward with a large boulder to their backs. The ground was bare around it in a rectangular shape.

Tomo stood before them, raising his arms to catch their attention. He wore a leather tunic with a plate of armor across his chest. Tassels hung from his sleeves. With his long black hair blowing in the wind, he brandished his weapons and bared his teeth as he spoke.

"My people," he said, "for many centuries, our ancestors have guarded this portal to the dark realm. Ever since our people were rescued from the jaws of the spider shaman, we have been tasked with keeping him locked inside. Most of those many years have been safe and quiet, but now our purpose in this place is being challenged. Now, we must stand firm, and for the sake of our people and our cousins in the Human Realm, we must prevent Bayal from removing the stone and opening the gate. They will be here soon. I will go and warn our fellow guardians on the other side. Keep watch. Stand firm. I will return quickly."

Without another word, he muttered some phrase that Kenny didn't understand and ran headlong into the side of a nearby sycamore. Just as he reached the trunk, a portal opened. The large man slipped through the shimmering window.

Kenny stood there, shoulder to shoulder with his new family. He rested a hand on the hilt of the knife tucked behind his belt.

Quickly, he had come to love the Adena people. They were warm, loving, and they'd embraced his presence despite the terrible things he'd done. For the first time in a long time, a sense of hope crept into his soul. Maybe, just maybe, he could find redemption. He peered around at the Adena warriors, then set his focus on the forest, watching for movement.

The sun was high in the sky; a bank of clouds was rolling in from the west, and the rumble of thunder rode the breeze. The wind swirled fallen leaves at his feet. He was afraid but alive at the same time. Every muscle in his large frame groaned as he stretched, tensed, and flexed in preparation for whatever came next. Gavin the elf slipped into the line next to him. The elf queen stood at the top of the nearby ridge with her sasquatch guard.

"Greetings, Kenny Burton," Gavin said. The elf carried a sword, but it shook rapidly in his small hand. His normally bright green aura carried a tinge of yellow, the universal color of fear.

"Are you okay?"

Gavin looked up at him. "I am well, but I have never fought a real battle. I do not wish to kill my fallen brother elves."

Kenny thought about that. He didn't wish to kill them either. Still, he had a responsibility to his new community. If they believed in the need to defend the stone and whatever was locked below it, then he would stand with them.

Suddenly, *it* was there, floating directly in front of his face. The black billowing darkness with the red pinpoint eyes. Kenny could see no mouth, but he could feel it smiling at him, probing, poking dark fingers into his mind. The specter had left him for the first week, then it returned, trying to move back into his soul. It poked and prodded and muttered to him. Kenny kept pushing it away, but it wouldn't relent.

"*Let me in, Kenny Burton. Open the door to your mind. With me driving you, we will reap delicious destruction on these puny creatures.*"

"No," Kenny bellowed. "Get away from me."

In this realm, the specter was visible to all. The eyes of his new family turned in his direction. His knees wobbled, so he stiffened his stance, steeling his will.

"Is it speaking to you?" Gavin asked.

"Yes. It wants me to let it back in. It says it'll make sure we wipe out the enemy."

"It lies," Gavin replied. "Remember that. It thinks only of the taste of hatred, pain, and bitterness. Keep your mind locked against it." Then, the elf turned its attention to the specter itself. "Be gone, you evil phantom. Or do you wish me to retrieve the young one that you battled before?"

At the mention of Kenny's daughter, the specter turned its attention on Gavin. It hovered silently in front of the elf for a few seconds. Kenny could no longer feel the smile emanating from the floating entity. Now, he could feel the specter's fear. Without pressing Kenny's mind again, the entity dashed away, retreating to a position floating above the forest canopy. With or without Kenny, it was there for the battle and the misery that would come with it.

The underbrush shook violently around them as the fallen elves emerged, leering and grinning at the defenders. The Adena warriors raised their weapons as their enemies paused a few feet away.

"Bayal has shown himself." Gavin pointed to the left, toward the top of the ridge across from where Queen Hesed was standing. "Look!"

Kenny saw the notoriously evil elf standing just outside the tree line, silhouetted against the now gray sky. The wind picked up. Thunder cracked loudly. The assembled defenders jumped at the sound.

~

Queen Hesed peered down upon the Ancient Gate to Abandon from a ridge a couple of hundred yards away. Sacqueal stood to her right, his swords held at the ready in both his hairy hands. A low growl emanated from his throat. Hesed sent Gavin to join Tomo and his people in defense of the gate, while Gronek and Smakal scouted the forest on each side, watching for the enemy's final approach. The sun turned gray as dark clouds rolled in from the west. A brisk breeze fluttered the golden magnolia leaves on her royal tunic.

The queen dreaded what was about to happen. There had been no violent bloodshed in her realm in centuries. "Oh, Mighty One," she whispered. "Please rescue us from Bayal's evil intentions."

As she watched, two specters arrived, floating above the trees on opposite sides of the clearing below her. Their billowing dark forms chilled her soul as they circled above the impending fray, waiting for the violence. They'd come for the feast of anger and pain. No doubt, the force of fallen elves was nearby.

"Sacqueal, you will stay with me unless I give you leave to go. Do you understand?"

The large guardian grunted in reply, but Hesed could tell he was eager for the fight. His blades chopped at the wind blowing his fur back from his face, even as he leaned toward the likely battle.

"Do not worry, my friend. If the Adena need you, I will release you. Until then, we cannot give Bayal an opportunity to use me as a hostage. You must guard me. Eventually, Dargo will arrive, and I do not want him to be in conflict because I am being threatened."

One of the dark phantoms fluttered downward. It floated directly in front of Nozomi's father. *Is it the same one that Nozomi fought off?* It lingered, billowing in front of the large human briefly before darting away.

Gronek returned, taking a position near Hesed, as the forest underbrush began to rustle all around the defensive line below. Shapes moved through the trees. From her vantage point, she saw Tomo rejoin his people, standing next to Nozomi's father. Gavin stood, armed on the other side of Kenny Burton. They all raised their weapons.

"Where is Smakal?" Gronek asked. "Has he not returned?"

"Not yet."

There was silence as the fallen armies emerged from the trees all around the human defensive line. The ragtag fallen elves wore tattered clothing of all types with some being too large and others too small. The weapons they carried were as varied as their clothes. Pitchforks to swords, machetes to sledgehammers. Luckily, they did not outnumber the Adena forces.

Gronek drew his sword. "Should I join them?"

"No. We are behind the enemy's line. Stay here unless I release Sacqueal."

The battle did not immediately engage. Instead, the force of fallen elves stood patiently around the Adena forces as if waiting for some signal to proceed. Hesed's sharp eyes caught Gavin speaking to Kenny Burton and pointing off to her right. Following his point, she turned to see Bayal. He had emerged from the trees on the same ridge on which she stood. Bayal emitted no aura; instead, his skin was charred, streaks of red glowed in fissures across his face. Ignoring the impending battle below, Bayal stood facing Hesed. He held a hostage, a gleaming knife blade at his captive's throat. Smakal hung there, his aura pulsating a greenish-yellow glow against Bayal's burnt face.

~

Havener cruised into Cutters Notch in a late-model dark-gray Ford F150 Crew Cab pickup. Two-weeks' worth of growth covered his face. An Indianapolis Colts hat sat on his balding head, and he wore a checked, flannel, long-sleeved shirt. His goal was to blend into the scenery. He wanted to look like any other random person that might pass through the area.

He was entering from the west on Highway 257. The sheriff's cruiser pulled out from behind the post office and turned east in front of him—Rick Anders with Hope Spencer's mother in the seat next to him. Al smiled. *Maybe I can fit in a little adult revenge, too.*

The sheriff turned south on Robbins Creek Road. Havener continued east. He needed to find the road that led back into the forest toward the old, abandoned quarry. Al would get the lay of the land there, make his final plans, then return and make his move.

As he crossed the intersection, he peered through the plate-glass windows of the General and recognized the redhead behind the counter. He'd seen her on his last trip. She appeared to be alone; there were no cars in the store's lot. Driven by impulse and with tires squealing, he swerved into the convenience store's parking area. *Might as well test the disguise.*

Al rolled beyond the gas pumps and parked at the curb, positioned so he could see the woman between advertisements plastered on the windows. He liked the looks of her with her red hair, healthy skin tone, and shapely body. Al had always had a little thing for redheads. She wasn't fat, but she wasn't skinny either. Her red curls hung to her shoulders, pulled back from her face so he could see the curve of her neck. A leather cord held a crystal to her throat. Its twinkle caught his eye.

Popping the truck door open, he pulled his booted feet out, stepping to the pavement. The wind caught his hat, nearly blowing it from his head. He grabbed it and shoved it back in place. Hiking up his jeans and sucking in his gut, Al ambled into the General and peered around. Rows of goods sat on display inside the rectangular room. Motor oil to potato chips, candy bars to individually wrapped rolls of toilet paper. Giant refrigerators lined two walls in an L-shape, and glass display cases sporting various fried foods sat beside the cash counter.

"Good afternoon," the redhead said in greeting. "Welcome to the General."

"Afternoon," Al mumbled, glancing at his watch. Not wanting to be too obvious, he wandered around the store. He grabbed a Coke from one cooler and a pre-made egg salad sandwich from another before stepping up to the counter. On impulse, he added some Lifesaver peppermints to his snacks.

"Need anything else?" the attractive young woman said. Her nametag identified her as Rose. Her green eyes sparkled in the fluorescent light. Al Havener was smitten but not in a good way.

"That'll do it for now, Rose," Al replied, leering at her neckline.

Rose smiled at the use of her name. "Have we met before?"

"Don't think so. I'm just driving through town. Needed a little something to keep me going." The sparkle of the crystal at Rose's throat again caught his eye and wouldn't let go. It almost seemed to glow as it shifted colors, blue to green to purple to red. Al stared at it as Rose rang up his order. "That's an intriguing stone on your neck. I've never seen one like it."

"You like it? I've had it practically forever." She smiled again as she reached up, fingering the crystalline shape. "This is the first time I've worn it in months. I'd put it away, but I recently moved and … well, I found it again in the process." Her eyes grew distant like she was thinking back on old memories.

"How much do I owe you?" Al pulled her back to the present.

"Oh, sorry. That'll be $5.37 total."

Thunder boomed nearby. Pieces of loose paper blew across the parking lot.

Havener pulled six dollars from his wallet, placing it on the stainless countertop. After grabbing his snacks, he paused. "You know, I'll be coming back through town later. Maybe I'll stop and see you." He winked.

Rose blushed. "You do that." Again, she reached up and fingered the intriguing necklace at her throat. With a flirty grin, she winked back.

Al crawled back in his pickup before continuing toward the east side of town. As he passed the now-defunct motel, he slowed and studied the unlit neon sign and the empty parking lot. The gate across the entrance was closed; a large padlock dangled from the latch. It was still unreal to him just how close he'd come to ending his life as a captive working in a slave camp. He was lucky that kid had escaped when he did, or he'd be down working in that pit right now. Anger toward Mabel Robbins welled up inside him. She was still out there, he knew. "I'd give up chasing these kids if I could tighten my hands around that old woman's neck," he mumbled.

~

Rose watched as Al Havener crawled back in his pickup and

drove away. She'd recognized him right away, and it was all she could do to contain herself. In many ways, she was the eyes and ears of Cutters Notch, working behind the counter every day at the General. Besides, he'd tried to kill her nephew by locking him in an abandoned silo. She'd studied pictures of the man, memorizing every feature on his ugly face. Rose had been on the lookout for two weeks, and her vigilance had just paid off.

The store was empty, so she picked up the phone and pushed the buttons. She should call the sheriff's office, but that wasn't who she called. Someone else was also looking for Havener.

"*Hello?*" Kevin Flannery said.

"He's back in town," Rose stated.

"*Who is?*"

"Havener. He just bought a sandwich and a drink in my store. He's disguised, but I recognized him."

"*Did you call Rick yet?*"

"Nope. You're my first call."

"*Good. Don't call him right now. I'll come see you. I want that man to myself before the authorities catch up to him.*"

The call clicked off. Rose placed the receiver back on the phone's base and stared off toward where her nephew's kidnapper had driven. Again, she fingered the necklace. She'd seen how it had done its work, capturing Havener's mind. "Maybe you'll get your chance," she whispered to the jewelry.

She'd only just put the unique piece of jewelry back on that morning. It tingled against her skin. Such serendipity. For months, it had been buried in her backyard, but she dug it up when she moved and carried it back home. *Its* home. For two decades the huge old house sat empty after Minerva Woodstock disappeared. When it finally went to a county auction, Rose had been the only bidder. The place was hers now.

Rose's mind drifted to the memories she carried from that old house. A few terrifying ones were her own, but many more belonged to others—Minerva, who had lived there for over one hundred years, and her victims, who had generally only visited once.

Rose picked up a cloth, sprayed some cleaner on the countertop, and began to clean as she waited for her brother to arrive. Kevin wanted to give Havener a beating, but Rose had other ideas. Her brother didn't know about the power she possessed. She'd never used it, but this seemed like a good time to start.

~

"Hope's home," Danny yelled from his position at the front window. "She just pulled in."

"Awesome," Josh replied from his spot at the kitchen table. "Help me into the chair, then wheel me over there." He motioned for Danny to hurry up. "Mom, we're going over to Hope's house," he shouted toward his mother in the other room.

Danny grabbed the wheelchair from the corner and positioned it next to his friend. Then, he grabbed Josh from behind, under his armpits, lifting him into the seat. It pained his still-bruised ribs a little and his shoulder hurt, but he bore the ache without complaint. After setting Josh's feet on the metal pads, Danny maneuvered him toward the door.

"Don't stay too long," Cindy Gillis said as she stepped from the hallway. "You still need extra rest."

Josh glared at his mom. She gave it right back at him. "And don't give me that stink eye either," she added.

"Don't worry," Danny replied. "I'll make sure he doesn't overdo it."

Cindy's countenance was doubtful as she held the door. Danny pushed the chair through, being careful not to tip it over. After they were off the stoop onto the sidewalk, Cindy closed the door from inside and the boys headed toward the cul-de-sac.

"There's a new dude at the House of Horrors," Danny said.

"Really? Another relative of the Hicks?"

"Don't think so. He's a really old guy."

"Cool," Josh stated. "Do you think he bought it?" The boys had been in Danny's front yard when the realtor installed the sign just the day before.

"I dunno. That'd be awful fast."

"It'd be nice to have somebody new in there."

"For sure."

Both boys studied the old man's truck as they hurried toward Hope's house. Before rolling up the driveway, they paused, gazing over at the neighborhood's newly appointed 'haunted house.' They spotted the old man as he stepped to the window, looking out at them. Danny thought he had a friendly sort of smile.

"He seems nice," Danny said.

"Really? I figured he would give you the creeps."

"Why?"

"Everything gives you the creeps."

Three

The two government agents and the one scientist left the sheriff's office, turned right on Highway 257, and headed west away from town. The sun had edged into the western sky, and a heavy bank of clouds approached. Litter rustled toward them, carried along by the stiff breeze ahead of what looked like a serious incoming storm. A clear plastic lid from a fountain drink rolled like a tire down the middle of the road in their direction.

"Let's grab some lunch," Franklin said as he accelerated, "and let that storm pass. There's a diner down this way. They're probably open for lunch."

"It's *probably* the only restaurant in town," Sheldon quipped.

Cynthia was riding shotgun with Sheldon in the backseat behind her. She shifted slightly in her seat so she could see both agents. Both men had removed their suit jackets, having hung them on hangers behind the driver's seat.

"Well, that meeting wasn't particularly useful," she said. "The sheriff didn't give us anything." Cynthia picked up her purse from the floorboard, rustling around inside it.

"He knows more than he shared," Sheldon said. "The man was fidgeting."

"I saw that too," Franklin added, glancing in his mirrors as if looking for a tail.

"Why would he hold back on us?" Cynthia asked. She pulled a compact mirror from her purse and checked her eyes and lips. "I mean, he didn't grow up in this little town. And he's only been sheriff for what—three weeks?"

Franklin glanced over at his passenger. "Great question, Cindy. We'll keep digging and see what we uncover." He began to slow. "Here we are."

The black Suburban with the government plates swerved into the paved lot of the 50s-era diner with the shiny, aluminum siding. The daytime running lights reflected off the metal like a mirror. The sign on the top read: *The Quarry Pit*. Printed underneath the restaurant name was a smaller catchphrase: *Dig the food*!

"Well, isn't this quaint?" Cynthia snarked.

"I bet the food is awesome," Sheldon replied. "These little places know how to do it right."

"Come on," Franklin said. "They're only open 'til two. We can question anyone who happens to be hanging around."

~

Gator left the sheriff's office a few minutes after the visitors, leaving Judy Steinkamp to enjoy some peace and quiet. Jumping in his county-provided Ford Explorer, he realized he'd missed lunch. Plus, he'd seen the Feds turn toward the diner and figured he could kill a couple of squirrels with the same shot. Off duty, he hooked his phone into CarPlay mode and cranked up some music. Hoping for some Bob Seger, he switched to a classic-rock station, but he had to settle for Creedence Clearwater Revival instead. *That's all right. I won't be in the car long.*

Gunning the engine as he pulled onto the highway, he spotted the impending weather. He picked up his radio mic, turning down his jams. "Judy, looks like a pretty good storm rolling in from the west. You heard anything?"

"Let me check the radar."

Judy reported back as he parked his vehicle in a roadside spot in the diner's lot. His headlamps reflected off the shiny siding. *"Yep, Gator, looks like a line of storms moving through. I'd guess it'll all break loose in about ten minutes. Lots of red and purple on the screen."*

"Roger that." He grabbed his rain jacket and carried it inside the restaurant. After looking around, he took a stool at one end of the counter. He positioned himself so he could see the whole dining area, especially the booth where the Feds were seated. The woman, Cynthia Sweet, sat opposite the guy Gator assumed to be the senior NSA dude, James L. Franklin. He was the one who did all the talking, anyway. The other NSA agent was seated next to the SETI lady. Rhonda Lake, one of Gator's old high school classmates, was busy taking their order. He'd always had a thing for Rhonda, and she still looked pretty good to him.

A couple minutes later, Rhonda stood on the other side of the counter in front of him, platinum blonde hair in a ponytail and pad in hand. "What can I get you, Sandy?"

"Come on, Rhonda. Just call me Gator. You know I don't like to be called Sandy." His mother had meant well. She liked the name—Sandy Randal. But she hadn't considered what other kids would do to it. *Sandal Randal. Sandy Randy. Sandy Pandy Randy.* On it went.

"It's your name and I like it." She smiled. Rhonda liked to tease him, and the truth was, Gator liked it, too. He grinned, despite himself.

Gator blushed and quickly looked down at the laminated menu. He already knew what he wanted, but he couldn't keep looking at her—not with her amazing blue eyes looking back at him. "I'll take a Mountain Dew, a Pit Burger platter. Double fries." He smiled and chanced a glimpse at the woman. She still made his heart race.

"That's my boy," she blurted. Then she turned and called the order out to Roger Gillis in the kitchen.

As Rhonda turned in Gator's order, NSA Agent Franklin stood and walked toward Gator, heading to the restroom. Their eyes met. "Officer," the man said as he passed by.

"Hey, Gator," Roger called through the little serving window opposite the griddle. "What kind of cheese do you want on that burger? Regular American, cheddar, or maybe some pepper jack?"

"Let's do cheddar today, Rog," he replied. Gator was glad when Roger bought the diner last year. The place truly was a pit at the time, and the man had completely remodeled it, giving it a whole new life. Even the food was stepped up about three levels. "And can you give the fries an extra thirty seconds in the frier? You know I like 'em extra crispy."

"You got it."

Gator sensed him before he heard him. Agent Franklin sat on the stool across the corner from him.

"Officer Randal, right?"

"Deputy Randal. But yeah, that's me."

"You've lived here your whole life. Right?"

"Yep. Pretty much. I did a couple of seasons in minor-league baseball but came home after I tore a ligament in my shoulder. I was a pitcher. That injury pretty much ended my major-league dreams."

"Ah, that's tough."

"What can I do for you, NSA Agent Franklin?" Gator shoved him to the point. He knew the guy didn't just stop by to make a new friend. The Feds may have been squirrel number two, the second reason he was about to have lunch in the Quarry Pit—hunger being number one—but he now found himself more interested in squirrel number three—Rhonda. He looked past the middle-aged dude in the slick suit and let his eyes rest on the attractive blonde wrapping silverware at the other end of the lunch counter.

"Okay. I'll get to the point, Deputy Randal. I'm a man who does his research."

"That's nice. An educated Fed."

"For a tiny little town, this place has sure seen its share of strange criminal activity the last few weeks. Cannibalistic kidnappers. Motel owners running a human trafficking operation in a stone quarry. Another kidnapper locking teenagers in a silo."

"It has been a wild ride."

"But the fact is, tiny little Cutters Notch, Indiana, has a huge file of weirdness going back decades. Did you know that?"

"Is that so?"

"It is most definitely so. What else can you tell me about this little town? What stories can you add to the pile?"

Outside, lightning flashed, and thunder boomed. Rain began to ping off the metal roof. The sun disappeared as the storm rolled in.

Gator didn't immediately respond. Instead, he watched Rhonda deliver sandwiches to his pest's companions. He didn't like the guy, and he didn't like his questions. The man had a smug look and a condescending tone. There was something else intangible that he found annoying. Maybe it was his air of authority. Maybe his haircut. "I've got nothing for ya," Gator finally said. "And your food's getting cold." He pointed at Franklin's table. "Your friends are starting without you."

"Come on, Officer…"

"Deputy. I'm a deputy. Got it?" Gator's tone was low, deep in his throat. "And I'm done talking. Go on back to your table and leave me to enjoy my lunch in peace."

The man shrugged before ambling back to his booth. Gator watched him go with a level of anger boiling just under the surface.

He had lived in Cutters Notch his whole life. He loved it. Sure, he'd seen some weird stuff, but that wasn't Franklin's business. It wasn't anyone's business from outside their county's borders.

"Rhonda? Can I have some more Mountain Dew?" He rattled the ice and smiled at her pretty face floating above her classic pink, form-fitting uniform.

~

Dargo rushed into the clearing. "Where is Dorcas? We need to leave. We need to leave now!" He was shaking, clutching the hilt of the blade at his waist. Motioning for one of his lieutenants, he stopped and spun in a circle. "Gather all the forces," he ordered. "We leave in ten minutes."

Dorcas ambled out of the mouth of the royal cave carrying her duffle. "What is wrong, Dargo? What has happened?"

"I forced one of our captives to drink the Leaf of Necessity," he answered. "This attack was a ruse. A distraction to hold me here. The main force of Bayal's fallen army is gathering around our queen even as we stand here and converse."

"Oh, Mighty One, help us," Dorcas mumbled.

"Follow me. My carriage waits. You will ride with me."

Dargo stormed off. Dorcas followed, running to keep apace. When they both were loaded up, the reindeer charged forward, lifting into the air as they gained speed. Dargo looked around him as his elven forces lined up. It was a formidable battalion but one that was largely untested. The elves were good-natured, friendly, peaceful creatures. Whether they would be able to act as they should in battle was a huge question looming in their leader's mind. *We likely will soon find out.*

~

Traci Terrell held Hope's front door open while Danny wheeled Josh through. Hope greeted her boyfriend with a kiss on his cheek. "Hey, where's mine?" Danny demanded with a smirk. "Am I the odd man out now?" It didn't earn him a kiss, but Hope did give him a hug.

Hope knelt in front of Josh, resting her hands on his knees. Her left hand sat on the bulky cast protecting his right leg. "Danny told me the specter is back. What happened?"

"I don't wanna talk about it," Josh replied. "Not in front of everyone."

"Come on," Danny interjected. "Tell her."

"What's a specter?" Teresa asked.

Hope glanced up at her new friend. "It's a black billowing evil spirit-sorta thing. We learned about it from the elves—"

"Elves?" Traci said as she closed the door.

"Oh, we have a lot more to fill you in on than I thought," Hope said. "I figured if you knew about Tomo, then you knew about the rest of it, too. Let's go sit down so we can talk."

Traci put her arm around her daughter, pulling Teresa toward the sofa. Hope wheeled Josh in front of the television, then pulled up a kitchen chair. Danny sat in a side chair.

Hope peered at the two new women in their circle. "Tell us your story. Then, we'll fill in the gaps."

A car pulled up outside. Two car doors slammed. Danny stood, glancing through the sheers at the front window. "It's your mom and Rick."

"Okay," Hope said. "Let's wait until they're in here, then we can trade stories."

Lightning flashed and thunder rumbled a couple seconds later. The storm would hit any second.

~

"There's a truck sitting in the Hicks' driveway," Maggie pointed out as they wheeled into the cul-de-sac.

"I see it," Rick replied. "Probably someone doing work on the place. I'll check it out." He tried to see the license plate, but he couldn't make it out. It was a beat-up old GMC; he could see that much. Rick parked in his own driveway, backing in as usual.

Maggie jumped out, sprinting for her front door.

As Rick exited, he watched an old man amble over to the "For Sale" sign, kicking through fallen leaves as he went. He struggled to pull the sign from the front lawn.

Rick joined the aging gentleman on the grass. "What are you doing with the sign?"

The man chuckled. "I'm gonna lean it up against the house over there." He pointed to a spot between the garage and the front door. "—so, the agent can pick it up whenever he gets around to it."

"Why would he want to pick it up? The place just went up for sale."

As he shuffled toward the house with the sign under his left arm, his cane tapping along in his right hand, the old man laughed again. "I suppose suspicion is a side-effect of your job, Sheriff." After he leaned it against the brick wall, he turned back to Rick. "Let me introduce myself. I'm Clarence D'Angelo, your new neighbor. I bought the house yesterday, right after it went up for sale."

"You got possession already?"

"Cash makes the wheels turn," he said through a grin. "Nice to meet you, Sheriff Anders." Switching his cane to his left palm, he stuck out his right hand.

"Nice to meet you too." Hesitantly, Rick shook his hand in response. "You know who I am?"

"I did my homework. A fella wants to know who he's gonna be living next to."

Rick opened his mouth to speak, but for a moment nothing came out. One month ago, the Hicks were living there. Two weeks ago, their nephew showed up and kidnapped the boys. The sign had only been put in the yard yesterday. He'd never known a real-estate deal to happen so fast, but money did seem to grease the gears sometimes. That was true enough. He pushed his suspicious thoughts aside and forced a smile onto his face. "Well, that's true enough. It's nice to meet you too, Mr. D'Angelo. Welcome to the neighborhood. Forgive us all if we're a little slow to embrace you. Things have been scary around here lately. If folks…um, well, if I'm a little suspicious, it's nothing personal."

"Oh, I fully understand. Like I said, I've done my homework. I'll keep my distance and simply be a good neighbor until y'all feel safe enough to make my acquaintance." He smiled warmly.

Rick studied the old man's eyes. His irises were a beautiful golden color. He saw no deception there. The smile seemed genuine. He'd still check out Clarence's story, but otherwise, the fellow seemed okay. "Look," Rick said. "I have a situation I need to attend to, but do you need any help moving in? Anything I can do?"

"I've got it covered. Thanks. I do appreciate the offer, though. From the way our neighbor ran into her house, I'm guessing you probably need to go anyway."

Rick peered over his shoulder toward Maggie's place. "I do." He turned to face Clarence again. "Can I come visit you later?"

"Sure. Come anytime, Rick." The warmth of the man's smile lowered Rick's defenses. "My door will always be open to you."

Rick backed slowly off his new neighbor's leaf-strewn lawn. Somehow, he already completely trusted the old man. It felt confusing, like his sharp suspicious nature had dulled. He waved, then trotted to Maggie's door. He was still feeling the tickle of what seemed like butterfly wings in his gut as he stepped into the crowded living room. As he closed the door behind him, thunder cracked again, lightning flashed, and rain burst forth in a torrent.

~

Bayal sneered at Queen Hesed as he held the blade tightly against Smakal's throat. "Imagine my surprise, Agahpey, when I crawled out of the pit only to learn that you were a queen." He laughed. "You were only a tiny one when I was forced to flee. You had only recently tied on your apron. And here you are, a mighty royal, in charge of a vast queendom."

"Release my son!" Hesed coolly ordered. Sacqueal clearly wanted to attack. "Hold," the queen whispered harshly. The large hairy bodyguard held, struggling against his impulses.

"Perhaps I will release him." The ancient evil elf grinned. "Perhaps not. Grant me the stone and I will consider your demand. I may even let those humans below live to breathe again tomorrow."

Pulsating red cracks were glowing even in the skin on Bayal's hands. He looked like a molten piece of lava with arms and legs. Hesed could see that he wore armor—where he could have gotten it, she had no clue. Metal plates covered his shoulders. Chainmail draped his arms with small gaps where it attached to the plates. Leather chaps hugged his thighs. The blade he held was large with a serrated edge.

"You cannot win this fight," Hesed stated. "You do not have the numbers. Our forces are better armed, and they have been training for an event like this for centuries. Your forces are all fallen, weak, and unprepared."

"Oh, do you think the small force you see is all I have at my disposal?" The dark elf laughed again. "Even as we speak, I have a larger force preparing to ravage the human village nearby—the one on the other side." He chuckled. "They await the storm." Bayal motioned toward the western sky. "See how it is rolling in? The darkness it brings will open the portals as their artificial lights kick on."

Acid rose in Hesed's throat. Would he really send a large force into the Human Realm, risking their entire culture? "You would do that, Bayal? You would risk us all for the evil held under the rock?"

"Agahpey, my dear, you do not know the power it holds. Yes, I would trade everything in this realm for that one gift. Then, I will rule the human world, taking all their wealth and power and adoration. Give me the stone, and I will spare most of what you hold dear, starting with your son. I might even spare that human girl you are so fond of, the one you call Nozomi."

The queen's heart sank. *How can he know so much?* Then, she saw the soiled trousers her son wore as he hung from Bayal's grasp, and she understood. *He has used the Leaf of Necessity.*

"I am sorry, Mother," Smakal groaned. "I could not resist."

Bayal motioned with his free hand. Below, another ring of fallen elves emerged from the trees, essentially doubling the size of the forces squaring off against the Adena warriors.

Sacqueal growled deep in his throat.

"What do we do, Mother?" Gronek asked from her side.

Queen Hesed, frozen in her indecision, peered down on the pending battle, then quickly returned her focus to Bayal. The sight of her son being held under Bayal's blade terrified her, but the thought of the evil elf gaining control of the Human Realm was unbearable. It would bring disaster upon the entire Arboreal Realm even if he kept his word about sparing what she held dear. The decision was an impossible one. Besides, she did not believe for one moment that Bayal would be true to his word.

Further complicating matters, Hesed's dominion over the Adena people was mostly ceremonial. Voluntary. Their priority was the protection of the Gate of Abandon. There was no guarantee they would comply even if she ordered their withdrawal. Gavin would be the only defender fully obligated to stand down, but he was within the circle of fallen ones and would need to defend himself anyway.

"Come now, Agahpey," Bayal said. "Surely, you do not want your son to die. I see another of your sons among the forces below. You may lose two in one day. The choice is yours. You can save both with one decision. Let me have the stone peacefully, and you may take your children and go."

"What of the Adena people?"

"They are mere mosquitos. Most will flutter away, others will be smashed, but you and your sons will live to see another day."

As the dark elf spoke, the storm clouds rolled overhead carrying with them more gusts of wind blowing the fallen leaves like small missiles through the arrayed potential combatants. The sky grew very dark as vaporous curtains completely enveloped the sun.

Hesed knew she was trapped. Regardless of her decision, disaster awaited. Bayal was a liar. Even if she complied, Smakal was lost to her, and likely Gavin, as well. Further, the charred elf that stood so smugly on the ridge, spouting his falsehoods, would use whatever power was hidden below the boulder to dominate the Human Realm, leading to destruction across the world—in both physical realms. Both choices would lead to the same result, so she chose a third path—silence.

Seconds passed into minutes. Thunder rumbled. Flashes illuminated the swirling clouds. The specters were floating in lazy circles above the ring of defenders below, oblivious to the wind. Still, the queen stood silently resigned to the imminent defeat and the end of her long, peaceful reign.

"If you will not speak and you will not choose, then you leave me to make the decision for you." Bayal, still holding Smakal around the neck, raised his knife hand, swinging the blade in a circle. Below, the double loop of fallen elves began to approach the Adena defensive ring. They were chanting something unintelligible as they moved in for the battle. Then, Bayal turned the blade, preparing to bring it down in an arching blow to Smakal's gut.

CRACK! Boom! Boom! Boom!

Before Bayal's blade could reach Smakal's stomach, a lightning bolt hit the tree behind him, knocking them both to the ground. Smakal broke free, scampering toward his mother.

"Get him!" Hesed screamed at Sacqueal. The massive guardian sprang forward, reaching the young elf before Bayal could recover.

Just after the first lightning bolt hit the tree on the ridge, two more struck trees on either side of the Ancient Gate to Abandon, scattering defenders and attackers alike. Elves and humans regardless of their status, fled to find cover.

It seems that another power altogether has made my choice for me. Hesed nearly collapsed as the pressure to decide was taken from her shoulders. *There will be no battle—at least not now and not under these circumstances.*

Sacqueal, swords replaced in the scabbards on his back,

grabbed Smakal in one arm and Hesed in the other. Together with Gronek, they also fled into the trees, retreating to the safety of the cave the brothers had made their home.

~

Al Havener found the nearly overgrown gravel road before the rain began to pour. He'd passed it twice, doubling back each time. This time, he'd slowed to 20 mph on the county road, looking for the abandoned entrance that had to be close. When he finally spotted it, he wondered how he could have missed it. The brush that encroached the old driveway was broken and shredded from the dozens of investigative vehicles that had passed through only about a month before.

He wheeled in. The trees hung over the sides, and weeds spread across the tire ruts, effectively camouflaging the roadway. Rolling slowly, Al maneuvered about a hundred yards along the path before he came to a closed steel gate, blocking his progress. It consisted of a single horizontal steel pole mounted to a concrete post on one end and locked to another concrete post on the other. A Do Not Enter/No Trespassing sign dangled from rusty wire in the middle.

He cursed.

Crawling out of the cab, he approached the padlock, glancing here and there, checking for anyone who may be looking. No one was around. Thunder rumbled overhead. With the sun blocked by the impending storm, it had become very dark under the cover of the trees. The lock was a typical keyed version. Al grabbed it out of frustration, and it fell open in his hand. Cut. Someone had left it hanging there for show. He smiled as he tossed the worthless piece of metal into the forest, swinging the gate wide.

The trees around him swirled in the wind as he drove deeper into the forest. Rain found its way through the tree canopy, splattering on his windshield. The assault on the Ford's glass intensified as he left the cover of the trees, emerging along the edge of a lake. His wipers flew across the windshield, throwing waves of water in every direction. Still, the rain obscured his vision.

The road swung to the right, running parallel to the cliff that dropped about twenty feet to the surface of the lake below. Rolling his window down, rain drenched the bill of his Colts hat as he peered across the water to the collection of outbuildings on the other side. Here and there were large stone slabs stacked on top of one another.

Old conveyors with rubber strips flapping in the wind. Rusty barrels and large machines had sunk into the soil.

Havener smiled again as he spotted the small block building where his aunt and uncle had done their wet work, disgusting as it was. Towering above it was the largest oak he'd ever seen. Behind the building and in the shade of that huge tree was the "tomb" his uncle had described. Al needed to see it for himself.

Raising the window and pressing the accelerator, he swung right and then left to avoid broken-down equipment and leftover piles of stone, then bounced over the muddy ruts. The lake below him was full of breakers created by the surging wind. An island sat toward his end. The wipers in front of him continued to fling torrents of water with each swipe.

Steering around the low building that used to be a maintenance office before it was a party house and later a slaughterhouse, he spotted the piled slabs his uncle had described. These particular rectangular stones stood out because one was precariously tipped up on end, balanced just so it would fall over, creating the tomb his uncle had described. *That'll do it.*

Al backed up and turned around. He should investigate the old office and look in the outbuildings, but the rain was coming down like he was driving inside a waterfall. It was obvious the place was deserted. No sign of anyone around. He'd seen what he'd come to see. *Time to go. Maybe I'll stop and see that redhead again.* He couldn't shake Rose from his mind.

Havener was smiling with anticipation as he pulled out of the closed industrial compound into the cover of the forest canopy. *This is going to be a very fun day.*

~

"Ma, someone's coming," Robert hollered. He'd been standing at the door, looking at the lake. His cousins, Parker and Boyd, were playing a game of rummy across the old oak desk in the center of the room. Oil lamps lit the space, the flames flickering on the block walls.

"Quick! Douse the lanterns," Mabel Robbins hissed. "Close that door, Robert." The old woman picked up the AR-15 she'd propped against the wall and joined her son near the window as the room fell into darkness. "Make sure that door's locked. It's probably just another gawker, but let's be ready just in case."

"We need to pull outta here," Boyd stated. "We can't stay out here in these woods all winter. Eventually, someone's gonna spot us."

"You doin' the thinkin' for us now?" Mabel snapped. "Got that big brain of yours cranked up, do ya?"

"Come on now, Mabel," Parker said. "You know he's right."

"Yeah, yeah. I know. I'm workin' out a plan. We just need to make sure all the searching has died down a little before we make our move."

Outside, the vehicle sloshed past the front of the building and curled around the side—a dark-colored Ford F-150 with a crew cab. "That's a nice truck," Robert observed. "Doesn't look like a typical scrapper."

"I told you, it's probably a gawker. But he won't likely get out and look around in this rain."

Robert retrieved his own AR-15. Mother and son watched from the shadows behind the dusty glass at the front of the old maintenance building as the stranger in the Ford turned around and headed back the way he'd come. Mabel got a good look at him as he rolled past.

"Ha!" she cackled. "I'll be a cooked turnip if that ain't Al Havener."

Parker and Boyd joined them at the window. Together, they watched their former captive maneuver his way out of the industrial lot and back into the trees. Mabel scratched her chin. She knew they were searching just as hard for Havener as they were for her and her crew. Maybe harder. *What's he up to?*

She replaced the AR-15 against the wall and watched Havener's rain-obscured taillights disappear into the forest beyond the lake. Something told her his visit was a bad omen.

~

The air inside the Quarry Pit smelled delicious. The aroma of grilled cheese, hamburgers, onions, and frying potatoes all mixing in the air with the freshly brewing coffee. Outside, rain continued to pound in hard waves, splattering off the cars, running off the roadway, and pooling into massive puddles. The bright lights mounted on the poles around the restaurant lot kicked on automatically. The water seemed to magnify their reflection as they illuminated every surface like massive, wet mirrors.

Gator, knowing he would be there longer than originally planned due to the downpour, moved to a booth near the front windows. He picked one in the corner so he could see outside and keep an eye on the Feds inside. But mostly, he trained his eyes on Rhonda. She was much more interesting with her long, wavy blonde hair and tight uniform.

The shapely server peered over at him and smiled as she poured a fresh cup of coffee for someone. He smiled back. Then, he blushed.

Scanning around, Gator's gaze met Cynthia Sweet's. The scientist from SETI averted her eyes immediately. Franklin's back was to him, but he noticed Sweet and the other Fed, Sheldon, the quieter one, periodically glancing over the man's shoulders at him. Curiosity gripped Gator as to what "file" they had on Cutters Notch, but his gut told him to keep his distance.

Gator had lived in Cutters Notch for nearly forty years. Sure, it had its share of crazies and weird happenings, but he doubted it was any stranger than any other small town in America. *Weird stuff happens everywhere. Right*?

He drained his second glass of Mountain Dew until the straw gurgled. "Rhonda?" She looked over. "Can I get one more?" he said as he again rattled the ice and grinned.

"You got it, sweetie," she replied.

A warm feeling again spread from Gator's gut to his face. *Sweetie*? Sure, it was probably a term of endearment she used with lots of customers, but she'd just used it on him, and he liked it. He liked it a whole lot.

A large semi roared past on 257. Large waves of water spewed up from its tires, splashing all the cars, his Explorer included. Lightning flashed, then it flashed again. The thunder followed almost immediately. All that water outside made him realize that his morning coffee and afternoon Dews needed to be relieved. Gator slid out of his seat, strode beyond the end of the counter, through the overflow seating area in the rear, and entered the men's room.

"Nothin' feels better than a flatter bladder," he mumbled as he exited a couple of minutes later. "And I'm feeling a lot better now." He grinned. Then he froze in his steps.

The room was silent except for Rhonda's whimpers. She was being pulled up and backward onto the lunch counter. Everyone else had their backs shoved hard against the outside walls. A tiny, orange-skinned man (*creature?*) wearing a leather jacket stood on the counter above her. He gripped her blonde hair in his left hand. In his right, he held a massive blade. The thing smiled at Gator, the fluorescent lights reflecting off his yellow teeth.

"Hello, human," the thing said. "Come back out here and return to your seat." It giggled with delight. "My friends and I wish to see what treasures you may be carrying. Do you have a gold coin? Golden chains? A silver timepiece?"

Gator's eyes landed on two more of the creatures, one in each corner of the diner. The one closest to him brandished a sword. On the opposite end, the third held a butcher's chopping knife at the throat of James Franklin. The federal agent had been pulled to the floor. All three beings grinned from pointy ear to pointy ear.

Slowly, Gator inched to his booth. As he slid in, he glanced outside. There were dozens more of the things moving across the lot toward town. It looked like they were coming right out of the side walls of the diner itself. *Okay, this place is weirder than any other small town.*

Rhonda screamed. Gator whipped around to see the weird monster on the counter rip an earring from her pierced ear. Blood trickled down her neck, staining her blonde hair and her light pink blouse. As he moved to help her, a sword tip met his Adam's apple.

"Halt, human," the creature ordered. "Do not move again."

At the opposite corner of the diner, NSA Agent Anthony Sheldon also jumped up in response to Rhonda's scream. He was not as fortunate as Gator. A knife blade entered the side of his neck and exited the other side. That was when Cynthia Sweet began to scream.

Four

Rose was alone inside the General when the storm rolled in, eagerly awaiting Kevin's arrival. They needed to make plans regarding Al Havener. A slight twinge of guilt told her she should call the sheriff's office to report the criminal's presence, but they wanted their pound of flesh out the man first. She stared out the window as rivers of water poured from the sky, a real gully-washer.

As she peered through the glass, she considered her options. They could take Havener to her house across the road, the secluded, old Woodstock mansion. She'd finally acquired it after all those years since she'd first encountered the old Woodstock woman. Minerva, long gone now, was the one responsible for the necklace dangling from her throat. She'd transferred ownership unwillingly.

Another option was to cart Havener down Robbins Creek Road and chunk him into the same silo where he'd locked up Danny and Josh. They could leave him in there a couple of days. *That would serve him right.* She kind of liked that idea—poetic justice of sorts. They might receive a slap on the wrist when they finally turned him in, but no one would convict them of anything more serious after what he'd done to her nephew. She was pretty sure, anyway.

The phone rang. Her brother's number.

"Hullo?"

"*Rose, I'm gonna be stuck at the hardware store until this storm passes over. I've got a leak in the warehouse roof and I've gotta make sure the whole place doesn't flood.*"

"What about Havener?"

"*I dunno. I guess maybe we better just report him. I wanna kick the crap outta him, but I also don't want him to get away.*"

Rose's heart sank, but she also felt a touch of relief. Despite what happened with Minerva Woodstock so many years ago, she wasn't in the habit of hurting people. Still, the man had nearly killed her nephew. He needed to pay. The muscles in her shoulders tightened. She took a deep breath to loosen them up. "All right," she said, aimlessly wandering the store as she spoke. "I guess you're probably right. Give me a call when the water thing is under control, and I'll let you know what's happened."

They said their goodbyes and hung up. Rose returned to her spot behind the register and placed her phone on the counter before lifting her gaze to the window again. Al Havener's Ford F-150 sat at the curb just outside the door. Rain fell through his headlight beams and pelted the sidewalk, bouncing off like little water pellets. The criminal peered back at her, grinning. It was a chilling gaze. Lifting her hand, Rose fingered the stone at her neck. It again tingled at her touch.

~

Hope, along with Rick, Maggie, and the boys spent about thirty minutes exchanging stories with Teresa and her mother, Traci, as the storm raged outside. Teresa and Traci learned about the elves and the specter while Hope and her crew learned about the ancient gate and what it contained. Or rather, what it held back. Hope was shocked to learn just how close her new friend had come to total disaster. From the look on her face, Teresa was equally shocked by the battle Hope had fought to free her dad.

"What do you suppose today's fight is all about?" Rick asked the room.

Everyone was silent at first. They exchanged glances to see who might have some clue. Finally, it was Teresa who spoke up. "Tomo and his people guard the gate. He said the fight was about protecting it."

"It's happening in the Elves' realm," Hope added.

"Could some of those fallen elves Gavin told us about be trying to open the gate for some reason?" Josh asked.

Hope scratched her chin as she watched Josh engage in the discussion. She was so happy to have him back. Hope still couldn't believe how close she'd come to losing him. "I suppose it could be. My dad told me the Adena people are worried about some elf named Bayal."

"Bayal?" Teresa grabbed her bag, pulling out a small Bible. "My youth group just read a story about an ancient false god named

Baal. That's too close to be a coincidence." She started flipping pages.

Lightning struck nearby. The house shook. The power surged. Something beeped in the kitchen. The sky was very dark from the heavy clouds, so the flash illuminated every corner and down the hallway. Hope glanced toward her bedroom door and caught sight of a small creature with pointed ears staring back at her. Gavin. He motioned for her to join him. Hope slipped down the hall and into her room.

"Gavin!" Hope whispered with hushed excitement, slipping into her bedroom, and closing the door behind her. She embraced the small green elf. "I'm so glad to see you. Is everything okay? Is my dad okay?"

Gavin returned the hug, patting her back with both of his six-fingered hands. He wore a child-size bicycle helmet on his head, causing his pointy ears to jut out to the sides. Pulling away, he held her by the shoulders. A small lamp in one corner lit the room, but the lightning kept throwing shadows across the space. "Your father is safe. There was no battle. The storm drove everyone off."

"Oh, thank God," Hope remarked.

"Yes, thank the Mighty One. Smakal was taken captive, but he escaped."

Hope sat on the side of the bed and glanced briefly at her reflection in her bedroom mirror. She was quiet. Thinking.

"Our reprieve from battle is only a delay. Bayal will reassemble for another attempt. He has a large force, which is why I am here." Hope returned her gaze to the elf, so Gavin stared directly into her eyes. "You need to cover your mirrors, and I need you to tell everyone you know to cover their mirrors. You must close all the portals. Bayal intends to invade your world, seeking to cause enough destruction and mayhem to force my mother to give way to him. With this storm, his invasion may have already begun." The tiny elf removed his helmet, cupping it under one arm. "He is evil enough to do it."

~

Maggie noticed Hope slip away. She leaned back to peer down the hallway as lightning continued to flash outside, causing the space to alternate between bright light and deep shadows. Danny was sharing about the large bird that somehow urged him to make the precarious climb and subsequent leap from the silo. Maggie stood and followed Hope, curious why she would leave mid-story.

Stopping at her daughter's door, Maggie leaned her ear to listen through the surface. Voices. She carefully turned the doorknob, cracking the door open to peek inside. Hope was sitting on the bed with a child standing in front of her—a child holding a bike helmet. But it wasn't a child.

"…his invasion may have already begun," the small being said. "He is evil enough to do it. Furthermore, he is aware of you, my dear Hope. Bayal knows what you mean to us and to our mother, the queen."

Maggie stepped inside. Her daughter's eyes flashed upward, and the elf jumped back. All three stood speechless as several moments passed, then Maggie quietly closed the door.

"Mom, this is Gavin." Hope broke the shocked silence. "Gavin, this is my mom, Maggie Spencer."

For his part, the elf recovered quickly. "I am well pleased to finally meet you," he said, sticking out his right hand. "As you know, I am very fond of your daughter."

Maggie's hand shook as she hesitantly reached out to accept the elf's gesture. Was this even real? Despite all the stories she'd been told, despite all the events of the past month, she'd still maintained a fragile grip on the idea that the stories of the other realm were all a delusion. That grip was now lost.

"What did you mean just now?" Maggie's words burst forth like the torrential rain outside. "Who is aware of Hope? Is she in danger? Can you protect her?"

The elf peered at her intently before responding. His face was solemn. "There is one of our kind nearby, an evil elf named Bayal. He has a large force of other fallen elves with him. Bayal is intent on breaching the Ancient Gate to Abandon. That is his objective, but we stand in his way. He announced to us a few moments ago that he knows of Hope. It was a clear threat, and we believe he wants to use her as a tool to force our retreat. I came here as quickly as I could, despite the storm, to warn you."

Maggie stumbled, feeling faint. She dropped to the bed next to her daughter.

"You must lock all your doors and windows," Gavin continued, "and you must cover all your mirrors. The portals must be closed after I return to my realm. All of them. He cannot hurt Hope if he cannot reach her."

"Can't you stay?" Hope asked. Her eyes darted toward the mirror, then back to Gavin again.

"No, Hope. I cannot. I must go now. My mother needs me, and I must stand with the others." Gavin gave Hope another hug, then hopped on the dresser and waved before ducking through the surface. Maggie watched it ripple from the center to the edge and back again. She stared after the elf, her mouth agape. "He...he's real. He's really real."

Hope gazed at Maggie's reflection in the mirror. Maggie stood and pulled her daughter tightly against her side. "We need to warn the others," she said.

"Yes, we do," Hope replied. "Let's go." She softly pushed Maggie to lead the way.

Maggie turned toward the hallway, but something wasn't right. Hope had dropped behind her. Her daughter was always one to charge ahead. Maggie turned back to encourage her only to see Hope standing on the dresser. Without looking back, Hope leapt through the portal, leaving only ripples in her wake. "Hope, no!" Maggie rushed after her, but the mirror was again just a mirror.

~

Rick was engrossed in the story of the spider shaman when Maggie screamed. He rushed down the hall with Danny on his heels. Josh couldn't maneuver his wheelchair around quickly enough and ended up at the back of the line behind Teresa and Traci. "What's going on?" he yelled.

Rick reached the door to find Maggie bent over Hope's dresser, her right hand resting on the mirrored glass, sobbing. "She's gone again, Rick. Hope knew the danger, but she went anyway."

"What're you talking about?" he asked. "What kind of danger?" He gently pulled her toward him with Danny standing aside. "Maggie, please tell me, what's going on?"

The sudden disappearance of Hope was a shock, and to Rick, one more problem on top of a new pile of mounting problems. One moment, they were gathered in the living room exchanging stories; the next minute, Hope was gone and Maggie was hysterical. "Come, sit down and tell us what happened," Rick urged.

Rick guided Maggie to Hope's bed. He sat beside her while the others looked on. Josh jammed his chair into the doorway, straining to see into the crowded room. Danny paced at the foot of the bed. It took a moment, but Maggie gathered herself.

"I saw Hope slip down the hallway," Maggie explained. "It seemed odd that she'd just go off in the middle of the story, so I followed her. When I reached the door, I heard voices and peeked in. It was one of those little people, one of the elves. I saw one, Rick. I actually saw one. It spoke to me." Maggie looked up suddenly, her eyes as big as walnuts.

Traci's hand covered her mouth. Teresa sat down on Maggie's other side.

"Do you know which one it was?" Danny asked. "Wha'd he want?"

Rick's eyes shot spears at Danny, demanding silence. The boy closed his mouth and stepped back against the far wall.

"Okay, Maggie," Rick said. "Take a deep breath. What happened next? Did this elf take her with him?"

"No," she answered. "He came to warn us. Hope introduced us. His name is Gavin. He said we needed to cover all our mirrors, to close the portals because the evil elves are looking for Hope. Then, he left." Maggie was shivering. "We were heading back to fill you in, but I felt her pause behind me. I turned around just in time to see Hope jump through the mirror." Maggie looked directly into Rick's eyes. "I saw her do it this time. The glass rippled like a pond, and…she was gone."

Rick stared over at the mirror. His curiosity about the other side of that portal was gaining a huge foothold on his mind. *Cover the mirrors to close the portals? Evil elves searching for Hope?* He'd heard all the stories from the kids. He'd heard about the colorful auras, the flying reindeer, the sasquatch guard. It was all so crazy. Rick thought it was a delusion, too, but then he'd seen one for himself, hanging through the mirror in Maggie's living room. *I want to see the other side for myself.* Rick pushed the idea away. "Okay, let's get you back to the living room," he said. "We need to get a handle on all this and figure out what we can do."

"Should I cover this mirror?" Danny asked.

"No!" Josh exclaimed. "How would Hope come home?"

"Leave it," Rick replied. He motioned for Danny to clear the room, then helped Maggie to her feet. "Let's leave the light on in here, too."

~

The store was empty, as were the streets outside. It seemed the storm drove everyone inside their homes, so when Al snatched Rose from the General, there wasn't a soul around to notice. He watched her on the phone behind the counter and saw her eyes widen when she looked up to see him outside. It was then clear to him that his disguise hadn't really fooled her. Al didn't know who she'd called, but on the outside chance it wasn't the sheriff—he didn't think it was or they'd already be everywhere looking for him—he decided she was a loose end that needed to be tied off. Besides, she was cute—like a redheaded puppy.

He marched inside as Rose snatched up the phone again, beginning to dial. He knocked it out of her hand as he jumped the counter, slamming her against the wall of tobacco products. She screamed but there was no one there to hear. After shoving her face-first to the floor, he dragged her around the counter and zip-tied her wrists and ankles. Then he flipped her over, placing a strip of tape over her mouth. Rose glared up at him as the strange necklace twinkled under the fluorescent lights.

He enjoyed her angry eyes. They gave him a sense of excitement he hadn't felt for several years. He paused, soaking up the fear she exuded, then he dragged her out the door and into the rain before flinging her into the bed of his truck like a rolled-up rug.

Al stood in the downpour, watching her struggling. Again, he was briefly mesmerized by the twinkle of the stone at her throat as it rested against her wet, lightly freckled neck. It was dark under the bedcover, but somehow the jewel still sparkled. *My daughter might like that trinket*. He slammed the tailgate closed as rain drained across the bill of his hat, soaking the sleeves of his jacket. Al's eyes locked with Rose's green eyes as they again glared up at him, this time matching the color of the stone, glowing in the darkness. As he closed and locked the cover, a tiny warning bell sounded in his brain. He ignored it.

Those eyes bored a hole in his psyche. He tried to drive them from his mind as he pulled out of the General's lot, heading south on Robbins Creek Road. Al had three teenagers to add to his new collection, and the rain would give him just the cover he needed to pull off the job. *I hope I can get them all in one swoop*.

Glancing in his rearview, he spotted five small figures splash across the road. They looked to be carrying clubs or knives. One even looked like it had a sword. He did a doubletake, but they'd apparently scurried behind the General Store. *Probably just kids up to no good.* He chalked it up to Halloween and forgot about Rose's unsettling eyes.

~

At the Quarry Pit, Gator heard Cynthia scream until the monster with the knife pointed his weapon at her nose with Sheldon's blood still dripping from the edge. The woman swallowed hard, averted her eyes, and slid back in her booth—cowering and whimpering in the corner. The fallen elf allowed Agent Franklin to slide into the booth opposite her. The agent positioned himself with his back to the window, feet up on the seat, and his hands on his ankles.

Gator backed away from the sword tip at his own throat, dropping into his own booth on the opposing end of the restaurant. Like Franklin, he put his back to the window and pulled his knees up toward his chest. His hands felt the lump near his right ankle. As he looked around, everyone in every booth was backed as far from the monsters as they could get.

Rhonda knelt on top of the lunch counter in the lead monster's grip, blood from her wounded ear trickling down her neck. Her eyes darted from creature to creature. Her hands kneaded the apron at her waist.

The pukey-colored creature holding Rhonda stood beside her on the counter, grinning with jagged teeth. It was at least a foot shorter than the woman, even as she knelt. Gator studied it. In fact, all three of the monsters were short. They all carried that ugly yellow-orange tint to their skin. Their ears and noses were pointy. They looked like how he'd always imagined the trolls under the bridge in that old fairy tale, except the Brothers Grimm didn't dress their trolls in ill-fitting leather and denim.

None of their clothes fit right. Baggy pants, rolled up at the feet. Boots that looked too big. Leather jackets with the ends of the sleeves cut off. They wore a hodgepodge of mis-fitted and roughly modified apparel. The one standing on the counter wore a black bowler hat. Its ears poked up beyond the brim on either side.

Gator's mind flew back to those pictures the NSA agent carried in his folder. Same weird-looking face. Same hodgepodge of clothing. *Aliens?*

Wrapping his hands around his ankles, Gator felt for his snub-nose revolver. He always kept his backup weapon strapped inside his pantleg. Glancing toward the remaining NSA agent, he saw James Franklin peering back at him. Then, the man looked away toward the creature closest to him before he peered back at Gator. Franklin's hand was resting on the seatback. His thumb and forefinger loosely forming the shape of a pistol. The message was sent and received. Gator gave Franklin an almost imperceptible nod.

No doubt, the federal agent was armed, and he surmised the agent assumed he was also. The saying "Don't bring a knife to a gunfight" sprang into his mind. His teeth clenched.

"Hey, Officer," Agent Franklin called out from his corner, "do you know the first three numbers?"

The three small, dangerous creatures turned in unison, glaring at the NSA guy. Their facial expressions revealed a lack of understanding. "Shut up!" the one on the counter ordered.

"I do," Gator answered. "Let's say them together."

The creatures peered back at the deputy, all three creepy faces turning in unison. "Shut up," the one holding Rhonda repeated.

"One," said Franklin.

"Two," Gator replied.

"Three," they said together.

At the same time, Gator and the NSA agent pulled their respective weapons, took aim, and fired. The monsters directly before them fell, their blades clattering to the floor. Elfin blood pooled around each body. The remaining creature took cover behind Rhonda, swinging her back and forth, glaring with fear in its eyes.

Both Gator and Franklin stood. "I don't know what you are," Gator stated, "but if you want to live, you'd best take your hands off that woman." The deputy spat the words through still-clenched teeth. "You let her go and put that weapon down, or this will be your last day on this planet."

The troll-looking alien thing bared its teeth as it peered out from behind Rhonda's torso. It didn't reply but seemed to be considering options as it glanced at its fallen comrades and the armed human men. Finally, its eyes fell on the restaurant's exit. The door was at the halfway point between Gator and Agent Franklin.

It happened in a flash. The creature lifted Rhonda in the air and leapt from the counter, landing near the exit between the men. Turning its back to the door, it kept Rhonda as a shield until it backed against the metal frame. Lightning flashed and thunder boomed. The troll shoved Rhonda against the lunch counter as it pushed its way out the door, fleeing into the raging storm.

Gator dropped to his knees to see to the injured waitress while Franklin followed the creature into the rain. Several diners took the opportunity to escape, fleeing to their vehicles outside. Yanking his phone from his pocket, Gator hit speed dial for Rick Anders. His boss answered on the second ring.

"Hey Gator. What's up?"

"Those things from the pictures..." He took a deep breath. "They're in town. They just attacked the Quarry Pit. One of the NSA agents is dead. His partner and I, we killed two of the little monsters."

"I'll be right there." The phone went silent.

Gator applied a napkin to Rhonda's wounded ear as she sat on the floor, her back against the counter and her legs splayed out before her. Franklin stepped back inside, dripping water from his drenched body. He replaced his weapon in its holster as he stood next to Gator.

"Well done, deputy," he said.

"Did you get it?" Gator asked.

"It was too fast. I took aim but it disappeared into the blowing melee out there. Headed toward town." Then Franklin's eyes went to his fallen partner. "Ah, Tony," he cried, moving to kneel beside his comrade's body.

Gator may not like the man, but in that moment, he gained some respect for Franklin, his new impromptu partner. Another bolt of lightning struck a utility pole at the edge of the parking lot, killing the power inside the diner. Everything in the restaurant went silent. The only sounds were anxious breathing and his own heart as it pounded in his chest.

~

Rick clicked off Gator's call and peered around Maggie's living room at anxious eyes all staring back. Lightning struck nearby. Everyone jumped.

"What's going on?" Traci asked, holding Teresa's hand. Her daughter was silent, leaning against her side.

"The evil elves attacked the diner. Gator said one man is down, but they killed two of the little monsters. I've gotta get over there." He paused a moment, considering the situation. Feeling torn as usual. "Danny, wheel Josh home. If you can, cover the mirrors in your house. Maggie, it's not safe for you here. You need to go with them."

"No," she blurted. "I'm not leaving."

"I don't have time to argue, Maggie. You need—"

"What if Hope comes home? What if she needs help?"

"We'll stay with her," Traci said. "She won't be alone. If I were her, I wouldn't leave either." She glanced at Teresa as she spoke, pulling her daughter closer.

Rick paused again. "Okay. Cover all the other mirrors then. Leave only one portal open for Hope. Can you handle a weapon?"

Traci looked a tad sheepish. "Actually, I have a pistol in my purse. I have a permit."

Rick wasn't fazed. Neither was he surprised. He lived in southern Indiana, after all. "Good, good." He paced in front of the door. "Traci, with your gun, you take the lead, but be careful. Maggie, you and the girl should find some sort of weapons, too. Knives, maybe. Watch that bedroom door."

"We'll be fine," Maggie said, determination replacing her earlier hysteria. "Those creatures will be sorry if they come crawling in here." She kissed him on the cheek. "Now, go."

Rick rushed out, shielding his head from the showers without success, and jumped in his cruiser, soaking wet. As he started his engine and lit his lightbar, he saw Danny carefully maneuvering Josh's wheelchair through Maggie's front door. *Good boy.*

Once in the cul-de-sac, he turned the wheel and gunned the engine. The tires slipped a little on the wet pavement but caught and drove him fast toward Robbins Creek Road.

Rick couldn't imagine the horror of what must have just occurred at the diner. The friendly, green-skinned face he'd seen in Maggie's mirror a couple of weeks back was weird enough. Those folks who faced evil versions of the beings at the Quarry Pit were probably in shock.

He accelerated the Ford Crown Vic toward town, the steel grating surface of the bridge rumbling as he passed over. His wipers were swishing at top speed and water was flying in every direction.

Heck of a storm. A pickup passed him going the other way. His mind registered it. *Ford F150 Crew Cab, Gray.* Typical vehicle in the area. It meant nothing to him.

~

When Hope leapt through the portal during the storm, she'd given no thought to returning home. She didn't consider the closing of the shimmer when the storm passed. All she cared about was finding her father. She had to make sure he was safe.

Now that she had him back in her life, she was determined never to lose him again. All the hope and love and affection she'd felt for him had been lost when he was under the specter's control. Now, it had all returned and then doubled, maybe tripled. Those who hadn't seen the evil phantom didn't understand her quick embrace of him, her forgiveness of his actions. Hope *had* seen it, though, and that made all the difference. She meant to make up for those lost years, and she'd given her heart over to him completely. Hope loved her mom and she loved Josh, but her dad had become her mission.

She landed in ankle-deep water in what was her own backyard—on the other side. Storms, it seemed, did not respect dimensional boundaries. They raged just the same. The sky was dark. Lightning flashed. Thunder boomed. The myriad blue hues of the forest aura dimmed in the haze of the falling rain, rising mist, and blowing water. Even without leaves, the trees bent under the force of the wind.

Hope hadn't brought a jacket. She stood there a moment with water soaking into her hoodie and drenching every square inch of her body—cold water dripping from her nose and ears. Peering around, she had a decision to make. Run to the elves' cave? Rush to the Adena village? She hadn't jumped into the storm with a plan. Hope wasn't there to see Gavin, Gronek, Smakal, or even Queen Hesed; she needed to see her dad. Two paths angled away from her window toward the forest. She took the one on the right, the one her heart dictated. The one leading to her dad's tiny cabin in the trees.

~

Two of Bayal's soldiers watched from within the forest underbrush as the human girl emerged from the shimmer. Looking at one another, they each smiled. They had heard the captive prince talk. They knew only one human had the power to traverse the portals. The fallen elves were amazed that she was making it so easy for them.

As the wind wailed through the leafless trees, blowing the slender ones from side to side, the pair of troll-like elves followed the human girl as she ran into the forest. She was loud and reckless, paying no mind to stealth.

"She is running to join the native humans," one said as he led the chase. "Her aura is so bright it hurts my eyes."

"We will cut her off," his companion replied.

"Yes, and Bayal will reward us handsomely."

~

A third pair of eyes, red like pinpoints, watched both the girl and the two fallen elves as they raced through the forest. Unseen by both the girl and her pursuers, the specter followed them all, undaunted by the blowing rain and the violent wind. Slipping between the trees and gliding smoothly through the brush, it kept pace, watching, waiting, biding its time.

~

Kenny Burton sat on a cushioned bench inside Tomo's warm hut nestled against a rock ridge deep in the forest. It was one of only a handful of Adena homes set up at ground level, positioned beneath a stone outcropping where foliage would be sparse. A fire was burning brightly in the center firepit. Tomo's children were absent, tucked safely away in another location far from the potential conflict that still loomed over them like the wood smoke in the air. Mala, Tomo's wife, handed Kenny a steaming mug of tea. Like the rest of the defensive force, Kenny was soaked to the bone from the unusually strong, late-season storm.

Outside, the storm continued to rage, but the ridge protected the small hut from the wind. Even so, shutters hung across the windows with strips of leather rattled as they kept out the swirling rain. Inside, the air was warm. The fire, illuminating their faces as they each sipped their drinks, cast fluttering shadows on the outer walls.

"Tomo, why does this Bayal want that stone?" Kenny asked. "What does some rock sitting in the middle of nowhere have to offer him? I don't get it. He's going to a lot of trouble just to fight over a boulder." He took another sip of his tea, both his large hands wrapped around the warm mug.

Mala sat next to her husband. She removed the stone-armor plate she wore as one of the defenders of the gate. Glancing at Tomo, she gave her husband what Kenny took to be a sad smile.

Tomo rubbed his face and took a deep breath before beginning the story. "Many, many years ago, our ancestors lived in your realm. They were scattered across the land in various villages. We had a thriving, interconnected community of farmers, hunters, and traders. However, one foolish shaman, dabbling in magic, nearly wiped us from existence. He became a monster, killing first his own family, then his village, then other villages.

"Those of us who were left gathered here, calling out to the Mighty One to rescue us. The shaman found us, and we battled. All was nearly lost, but the Mighty One sent a bright warrior to rescue us. A gate in the earth was formed, the Ancient Gate to Abandon, and the shaman was banished to await his judgment. The stone we defend was placed over the gate, and we became its guardians; we must never let the evil shaman escape."

"The shaman isn't dead? After all these years?"

"No," Mala stated.

"But what does Bayal want?" Kenny pressed. "What could he gain by opening the gate besides his own destruction?"

Tomo shook his head and lowered his eyes. Mala placed a caring hand on her husband's shoulder. "That I do not know," he replied. "The spider shaman is a danger to all other creatures. Fallen elves will not be a match for his magic or his voracious appetite. It would be suicide for Bayal to open that gate."

A commotion arose outside with much splashing and shouting. Tomo rushed to the door with Kenny and Mala at his heels. Warriors were rushing toward the trail. Another man dressed in stone armor approached Tomo. He was young with long dark hair and muscular arms. Rain pelted his face as he stopped in front of his leader.

"There has been a struggle in the forest not far away," the man said. "A girl screamed for help. It must involve the fallen elves. We are rushing to investigate."

"Was the girl one of our people?" Tomo asked.

"We do not know. All our warriors are accounted for. It could be a messenger from the children's camp." The man's eyes darted back toward the path. Water dripped from his nose. "We do not yet know who else was involved. Perhaps it was Gavin or one of his brothers. Maybe the sasquatch guardian."

Grabbing a cloak from a hook next to the door, Tomo pulled it around himself and followed the man into the rain. Mala also pulled on a covering, splashing off on the muddy path. Kenny had no cloak, but he trailed the others.

When they reached the spot, Kenny muscled to the front next to his friend. There was no sign of the combatants. Only mashed brush and stirred-up mud leading into a new trail in the woods. And one shoe. Kenny's heart sank. He recognized it. It belonged to Hope.

~

The eyes in the trees watched the rushed approach of the native men and women. They also watched as Kenny Burton joined the others and reacted to the shoe left behind in the muck. The pain in the man's eyes was tasty. Silently smiling, the phantom turned away from the scene into the forest canopy in pursuit of the two fallen elves and their newly captive young woman. Its time was nearly at hand.

Five

Rose was uncomfortable inside the covered bed of the pickup truck. She was cold and wet, and the surface was hard and uneven. It smelled of oil. After Havener dropped the cover down, she heard the lock engage as the darkness enveloped her. She hadn't felt this much terror since the day she'd acquired the stone on her neck, the day that Minerva had locked her in the room with the wooden box. Her body began to shiver uncontrollably through her wet clothes. Her feet were bound, but she kicked at the cover as much as she could though there wasn't space to get any leverage.

I should've called the sheriff. She kicked her own conscience in the head. Rose knew better. Despite what they showed in the movies, vengeance never worked out. It's more like a canker sore that keeps growing until it covers your whole face.

The truck was moving. Rose rolled to the side as the Ford turned, then rolled back as it evened out. Pooled water in the truck's bed sloshed around, splashing her in the face. She wasn't sure which way she was traveling until the tires rumbled over the steel grating on the Robbins Creek bridge. A few moments later, it slowed. She felt a turn to the left. *We're going into Kevin's and Anni's neighborhood.* Water was rushing through the wheel wells as the F150 circled into the court and came to a stop. Hard rain pelted the bedcover. Wind whistled through the cracks along the edges.

Muffled voices. A door slammed. Something banged into the side of the truck. Then a key turned in the bedcover lock.

~

Danny watched Rick speed away in his county cruiser, water fanning out from the wheels. He maneuvered Josh's wheelchair onto Hope's porch, ready to push it as fast as possible across the cul-de-sac toward his friend's front door. They'd get soaked, no way around it. The rain looked like a waterfall from the sky. Lightning flashed and thunder boomed as the trees bent under the force of the storm.

"Danny," Maggie said from behind him, "you may as well make a run for it. It ain't slowing down anytime soon." She handed an umbrella to Josh. "Hold this over your cast."

"I guess you're right," Danny said, "but I doubt that umbrella will hold up in this wind." As he eased the chair down the two steps to the walk, the door slammed behind him.

"Hurry up, dude!" Josh blurted. "My cast is gonna be soaked. They said not to get it wet. I should've asked Hope's mom for a garbage bag to cover it."

"I didn't think of that. Maybe hold that umbrella out like a shield."

As fast as he could make his legs move, Danny rolled Josh out into the rain, down the walk, across the driveway, and onto the cul-de-sac pavement. Almost immediately, the breeze grabbed the nylon umbrella, jerked it from Josh's hands, and sent it sailing into the trees beyond Rick's house.

The downpour hit Danny's face so hard that he could barely see a few feet ahead. Pools of water filled low spots in the roadway. Headlights came from his right. A pickup he didn't recognize cut off his path. The window came down. A semiautomatic pistol emerged, pointed directly at him.

"Stop where you're at, boys."

Danny knew the voice immediately. Apparently, so did Josh. "It's Havener," Josh yelled above the roar of the storm. "Get us outta here!"

Danny froze. He was staring at the black hole on the business end of the pistol. He'd outgrown a lot of fear in the last six weeks, but he still knew enough to be afraid of a bullet. With his friend squirming in the chair in front of him, and rain soaking every square inch of his husky body, he slowly began to back away.

"I said to stop," Havener repeated, pulling the hammer back on the pistol. Danny complied.

"Where's the girl?" Havener asked. Not waiting for an answer, the criminal opened the driver's side door of the Ford and stepped out in the rain, slapping his hand on the side of the truck. "Quick now, wheel him back here." He motioned toward the tailgate, keeping his gun pointed squarely at Danny's forehead.

Danny's mind raced. He could run, maybe get away. A huge maybe. But he couldn't abandon Josh. He could ram the man with the wheelchair, maybe make him drop the gun, but he'd be using Josh as a weapon. His buddy was depending on him. What choice did he have? Havener inserted a key in the lock of the bedcover, raised it open, and lowered the gate, keeping the gun trained on Danny's face.

Peering toward his house, Danny hoped with all his might that his mom was peeking out the front windows. She did that a lot but not this time. He glanced at Josh's house. Same result. Danny even chanced a look at the Hicks' former house where the old man had just taken possession. No luck anywhere. They were alone with a madman. Again.

At the sight of the now-open bed of the truck, his heart sank some more. There was his Aunt Rose, bound and gagged, struggling inside the gaping darkness of the pickup's storage bed. A tiny twinkle of light reflected from the necklace she wore.

"Get the cripple inside," Havener ordered with a smirk, waving the gun in the rain. "Then crawl in after him. Do it now."

Danny peered down at Josh who had gone silent. He was helpless, and his friend knew it.

"Come on, Danny," Josh said. "Get me in there outta the rain."

Lightning struck behind Josh's house. Everyone jumped. Danny bent down, looping Josh's arms over his neck, lifting him free of the chair. Pivoting, he placed him on the tailgate. Josh dragged himself inside. Danny followed, squeezing between his buddy and his aunt.

"Roll over," Havener ordered. He zip-tied their hands and feet. "Where's the girl?" Al asked again. "She at home in her warm bed?" Danny saw the criminal glance at Hope's house.

"She's gone," Josh snapped. "You leave her alone, or—"

"Or what?" Havener asked with a grin. "You ain't gonna do anything. You won't be around to do anything."

Danny twisted and glared at the grinning face of Al Havener, willing his anger to hit the man in the face. Instead, the gate came up and snapped into place. The top was lowered and latched. Cold, wet darkness descended on the trio. Josh sobbed. Danny, however, didn't cry, nor did he despair. The two of them had been in this situation before. Ever since he leapt from the top of that silo, a sense of hope had become a resilient resident in his heart, replacing the demon of fear that used to reside there. They'd get out of this mess. He'd find a way.

~

Rick Anders burst into the diner, water dripping down his face and off his jacket. He stopped in his tracks, surveying the scene, taking it all in.

"Did you see any of 'em?" Agent Franklin yelled. The man was at the front window with his eyes darting to the right and the left. He turned to Rick and pointed to the creature he'd shot, lifeless on the floor. "There were a lot more of those things. They seem to come out right from under this diner."

Rick didn't respond. He stood there for a moment, scanning the scene. The SETI woman, Cynthia Sweet, was curled up in a ball in one of the corner booths. His neighbor, the owner of the diner, Roger Gillis, plus one of his kitchen helpers stood behind the counter with large cleavers in hand. They both looked like something out of a B-movie with white hats and stained t-shirts. Gator sat on the floor holding the blonde waitress, Rhonda, blood splattered on her blouse. One dead elf corpse lay at each end of the room, weird-looking blood pooled around them.

As Rick stooped in front of the injured waitress, Franklin repeated his question. "Sheriff, did you see them? There's got to be dozens of 'em running loose in your town."

Rick again ignored the question. He wanted the details from someone he knew and trusted. "Gator, fill me in. What exactly happened?"

"Rick, it's like Franklin said. A bunch of those…those things emerged right out of the side of the diner. It was weird. I saw two of 'em emerge myself after the ones in here forced me into my seat." He paused a second and took a breath. "I'd gone to the bathroom. When I came out, there were three of the little monsters inside. The two dead ones you see on the floor and a third one standing on the counter holding Rhonda hostage. After we shot two, the third one escaped out the door into the storm."

Rick's cell phone buzzed. Peering at the screen, he saw it was Judy Steinkamp. "Anders," he said as he clicked on the call. "What's going on, Judy?"

"*Sheriff, I'm getting calls from all over town. It's weird.*

Burglaries, vandalism, reports of strange creatures. The town's gone nuts. To top it off, the General's unlocked and empty. Rose is missing."

"Call in everyone," Rick said. "Get 'em responding and patrolling. Look for anything strange." After a pause, he added, "Judy, lock the office doors and cover any large shiny surfaces, even the mirrors in the bathrooms. Do that first, right away." After clicking off the call, the sheriff addressed Roger. "When I leave, lock the door. Then cover anything that resembles a mirror." He saw the question arise in the man's eyes. "Don't ask me why. Just trust me and do it."

"Got it," Roger replied.

"Gator, I'm going to leave you here to control this scene and protect the rest of the civilians." Finally, he turned his attention to the NSA agent. "Franklin, you're with me. Let's go."

~

"The boys left the wheelchair in the middle of the cul-de-sac. Why would they leave it in the middle of the street with it pouring down rain?" Teresa turned away from the living room window. The storm had not let up. Thunder was still booming all around. The trees were thrashing about. Water was everywhere.

"Are you serious?" Traci asked as she approached the window, peering over her daughter's shoulder. "Maggie, are those boys that careless?"

"No," Maggie replied, joining them and peering out for herself. "No, they're not. They may be reckless, but they wouldn't do that. It makes no sense." She pulled her cellphone from her back pocket and called Cindy Gillis.

"Hello?"

"Cindy, are the boys over there?"

"No."

Maggie shook her head to the others. "Danny was supposed to bring Josh right home, but Josh's wheelchair is sitting empty in the middle of the cul-de-sac."

"Maybe they went to Danny's house. Maybe it just rolled down their driveway. If that's what happened, I'm gonna ground that kid for a freaking month."

"Call Anni and check, then call me back, okay?" Maggie hung up. She stared out into the storm at the empty chair sitting in the road. Even in the blowing rain, she could tell that the brake was engaged. It wasn't rolling around at all. It couldn't have rolled down the driveway with the brake engaged. *It's all happening again.* Maggie's heart raced as she clutched the phone to her chest. Teresa and Traci flanked her, holding her.

The phone buzzed. "Hello?" she said, her voice frantic.

"They're not over there either. Anni and I are coming to you. Be right there." The call ended.

Maggie stepped over to the door. As she opened it, she saw Anni running to meet Cindy at the end of her driveway. They bolted across the court in the rain. Cindy grabbed the chair as she rushed through the blowing storm.

The boys' mothers paused on the porch, staring at Maggie on the other side of the storm-door glass. It was Cindy that spoke first. "It's happening again, isn't it?"

Maggie nodded as she opened the door. She hugged her neighbors as they dripped water all over the entryway floor. Maggie pulled away, hit a button, and spoke into her phone. "Call Rick Anders," she told the device.

~

Rick and Agent Franklin sped to the General in Rick's cruiser. The sheriff pulled a clear, plastic rain poncho from his backseat, handing it to Franklin. "You may be needing this." The agent took it, silently.

Lights were on inside the store and the fluorescents were bright underneath the gas-station canopy. The water in the air seemed to give each bulb a glowing halo. Flashing blue lights enhanced the effect. Waves of water spewed from the cruiser's wheels and wipers as they rushed toward the store.

Rick's cell phone rang. He looked at the screen. "Maggie, I can't talk right now. I've got two major scenes going at once."

"You now have three. Someone's grabbed the boys again."

"How? When? I just left there."

"We don't know much. Danny was wheeling Josh home through the storm. A few minutes later, Hope's new friend, looked out the window and saw Josh's empty wheelchair in the middle of the cul-de-sac. I called Cindy, and she checked with Anni. The boys are gone. Anni and Cindy are at my house."

"I'll send a deputy. I'll be there myself as soon as I can." After hanging up, he glanced over at Franklin. "It's raining and pouring in more ways than one around here. My neighbor kids have apparently been snatched again. I need to send someone, ASAP."

"Roger that."

Franklin pulled the poncho over his shoulders and the two men stepped out in the rain in front of the big plate-glass windows of the General. Inside, Jerry Steinkamp in uniform and Calvin Churchill in civilian clothes were examining the area behind the counter.

"Sheriff," they said in stereo as their boss entered the store.

"Fellas, before you give me a report, I need one of you to hightail it over to Maggie's house. It seems that Josh and Danny have been kidnapped again." Rick paused to catch his breath—and his emotions. "Cal, you're off duty. You're now officially back on duty. Head over there and start investigating."

"You got it, Sheriff," Calvin replied. "On my way." He hurried around the counter, side-stepped Agent Franklin, and burst through the doors. Moments later, his vehicle sloshed through the parking area, then turned onto Robbins Creek Road.

"Jerry, you can get me up to speed here, right?"

"Yessir."

As was the case just two weeks prior, Rick was conflicted, pulled in multiple directions at the same time. Again, he had to trust his team. Gator was solid and would handle the weird scene at the diner. Calvin was a long-term veteran deputy; he would get things rolling in the search for the boys. And, Jerry Steinkamp, though the youngest of his deputies, was sharp and well-trained. He knew his stuff.

"Walk me through it, Jerry," Rick instructed. Agent Franklin was a silent shadow, taking it all in.

"Well, looks like Rose was behind the counter. Whoever did this trapped her back here. There was a struggle." Packs of cigarettes from the wall display littered the floor, interspersed with sticks of beef jerky and tiny red bottles of an energy drink. "From the way the products on the floor are scattered, I'd say she was dragged to the far end of the counter and out into the display area. She was fighting the whole way. See how things are knocked off the lower shelves?"

Rick glanced around. Up in the corner, he spotted a camera. Turning around, he saw two more. He pointed. "Let's find out if those work. Maybe we'll catch a break."

Two minutes later, the three men gathered around a screen in the tiny office behind the wall of tobacco. Steinkamp was manipulating the video feed with Rick watching over his shoulder. There were three views inside the store and one from the outside showing the parking and fueling areas—all in high definition. "Okay, Sheriff, I think I've found the right spot. Here we go." He hit play.

The camera angle showed a man jump up on the counter, then attack Rose. He acted quickly, knocking her to floor, dragging her to the shopping area, and using zip ties to restrain her. Another angle showed him drag her out the door. He wore a cap, and nondescript clothes. They couldn't see his face, but the impression he gave was of a middle-aged man.

"Let's look at the outside footage," Franklin said.

Jerry cued it up. The video picked up as the two exited the store. The man dragged Rose across the sidewalk, dropping her roughly onto the puddled pavement as he continued to the rear of a gray, Ford F-150.

"I saw that truck," Rick mumbled. "It passed me on Robbins Creek Road as I headed toward the Quarry Pit."

The man picked up Rose before depositing her under the bedcover in the rear of the truck. As he closed her inside, he glanced upward. "Freeze," Rick ordered. "Back up so we can see his face."

"Is that who I think it is?" Steinkamp asked.

"Yep."

"Who is it?" Franklin asked.

"Al Havener. He's come to finish the job," Rick answered. "We're looking for one kidnapper. He's got Rose and the boys, too."

~

After capturing Hope in the forest, the two fallen elves bound her hands behind her back and laughed at her screams for help as they dragged her through the trees. They didn't bother gagging her in the blowing storm. Before long, Hope stood before a fire under a rock ledge staring at what almost seemed like a living, breathing black hole with red crevices in its skin and bloodshot eyes. Bayal, she presumed. A few dozen minions surrounded him, all huddled out of the storm.

Water poured off the overhanging rock and flowed away in mini rivulets toward the forest. The crevice they stood in protected them from the nasty weather. Hope's cold face absorbed the warmth of the fire. Beyond Bayal and his audience, the forest swayed under the force of the wind.

Staring at the evil elf's face, she noticed his lack of aura and the fact that the fire didn't reflect from his skin. It was as if the pigment absorbed the flickering light.

"I have heard stories of you, young one," Bayal said. "They are carried on the whispers of the specters. You seem to have become one of Queen Hesed's pets." He approached. Hope was taller, forcing him to peer upward, letting his eyes land only briefly on hers and pointing his charred nose toward her chin.

Hope stayed silent. She had nothing to say to this creature. Instead, she glared down at him, trying to drill holes in his face with her mind.

"Come now, child," Bayal prodded. "No pleading? Why, you do not even appear to be frightened. For a human, you are most amazing with your brilliant aura and your intense determination. We will see how long you can maintain this attitude."

Hope was indeed scared, terrified even, but she refused to display it. She'd even stopped struggling against her bindings. Instead, she straightened herself and stared even more intently at Bayal, willing her already bright aura to new levels of intensity. Hope's fear was more for the safety of her father than for herself. After she was kidnapped by her neighbors, having met everything from fairies to an overgrown sasquatch and battling an evil specter, Bayal didn't seem that intimidating in the overall scheme of things.

Bayal appeared to resist looking at her directly. "Fine," he said as he turned away. "I have no real need for your words. You are nothing more than bait." He gave his attention to his followers. "This child will force Hesed's contrition. The queen will not allow an innocent to be harmed simply to keep us away from the stone. We will have our objective, and this human child will assure our success."

Bayal paused before a leather-sleeved elf—one that seemed to be his lieutenant. He motioned toward Hope. "Bind her feet. Position her near the fire so that her clothes dry. Then assign two of the soldiers to keep an eye on her. She is our decoy. Word will reach the queen and she will seek us out, likely dragging the Adena in her wake." He slowly glanced around before adding, "The girl must not be harmed. Do you understand? She shall not be harmed in any way. I must learn more of her apparent power."

Bayal rushed into the darkness of the storm, leaving Hope standing before the staring, bloodshot eyes of a few dozen fallen elves. Their clothes were shabby and worn. They held various weapons, swords to pitchforks. "The rest of you," Bayal called from the forest edge, "follow me." All but her chosen guards complied, splashing away in the muck.

The remaining two, wearing black leather jackets with roughly trimmed sleeves, stepped forward. One jerked her toward the fire, then shoved her to the ground. The second quickly wrapped twine around her ankles and knees. They glared at her briefly before wandering off to sit around another fire. Hope was left alone, leaning against the cold stone wall at the back of the overhang, but with a warm fire to heat her face and dry out her soaked clothing.

~

Agahpey Hesed, Queen of the Elves, rested safe and cozy in her sons' cave, a cup of peppermint tea with mist rising from its surface sat on a table nearby. Her son, Smakal, having cleaned up, sat with his back against her knees, his head drooping. Firelight flickered against the stone walls, enhancing the glowing aura of the moss and reflecting in her large elfin eyes. Agahpey bent forward and stroked Smakal's ears. "My son, it is not your fault. Put your heart at ease. No one can resist the Leaf of Necessity."

Gavin was not so forgiving. He stood at a serving table, pouring his own steaming cup. "Is it not his fault, Mother?" Turning his attention to his dejected brother, he added, "Could you not hold out for even a little while? You have put our friend at risk."

"Gavin," Hesed snapped, anger in her eyes. "Have you ever been subjected to the Leaf of Necessity? Have you ever felt its chemical fingers worm their way into your brain even as others coil around your intestines?"

"Well, no," Gavin replied. "But I—"

"Then you had better show more mercy to your brother. Until you have experienced it, you cannot understand. There is no resistance. This I know as fact."

Gavin lowered his gaze. His mother was right. Peering at Smakal, his heart began to ache. "I am sorry, my brother. I am anxious for Hope, and it has spilled over onto you."

Smakal glanced up and nodded. Gavin tried to offer his cup to him, but the younger elf refused.

Lightning struck nearby. They jumped at the simultaneous flash and boom. "This storm is a bad one," Gavin remarked. "Very unusual for this time of year."

"I am thankful for it, though." Hesed peered toward the cave mouth. The forest swayed furiously in the wind. Her bodyguard stood at the entrance, just out of the rain. Sacqueal seemed to enjoy the violent weather. He casually munched on walnuts as he gazed into the maelstrom. "If it were not for the storm, many may have died in the battle. Perhaps the Mighty One sent the storm to prevent the bloodshed."

"What of Bayal, though?" Smakal asked as he leaned into his mother's touch. "Will he not simply regroup and attack again?"

Hesed didn't immediately reply. Instead, she continued to gaze toward the blowing forest. After a long pause, she turned her attention back to her sons. "Yes, Bayal will make another attempt on the gate, and I am worried because the Adena guardians were driven from their defensive positions. My hope is that Dargo will arrive in time to turn the ancient evil one away."

Gronek burst into the cave, rushing before his family, breathing heavily. Water dripped from his nose, his ears, and his fingertips, forming pools around his nervous feet. The old fedora sagged around his head. "Bayal has her. Hope has been taken!"

Queen Hesed sank back in her chair with a groan. The air left her lungs; she couldn't breathe.

"How do you know?" Gavin asked.

"There is an Adena messenger outside," Gronek explained. "It seems she was on her way to check on her father and was taken in the forest. They found her shoe. Her father identified it."

"I should have known she would not listen. That she would go to her father," Gavin cried. "She kept looking at the mirror as I warned her of Bayal." He began to pace the room, waving his arms. "Hope is so strong-willed and refuses to think of her own safety. She only thinks of others, especially her father. I should have known."

Agahpey rose from her chair, pulling Smakal to his feet with her. "We cannot sit safely in this warm cave while Nozomi is in the hands of that evil fallen one. He has a heart as dark as his burnt skin.

There is no telling how he will use her. No telling what he might do. We must go to the Adena village."

~

Dargo and Dorcas rode in the lead transport carriage pulled by a team of ten reindeer, flying in unison. There were twelve armed elves riding in the cargo hold. As they crossed the great river, passing over the wasteland of Louisville, huge storm clouds loomed ahead.

"That looks ominous," Dorcas stated.

"Yes," Dargo replied, "and we cannot fly into it. It is yet another delay." He paused to consider his options. "It appears too large to go around. We could lose a full day. We must go higher and attempt to pass above the storm." Dargo looked up. "Very high, indeed."

"How will we find them if we cannot see the landmarks?"

"That is an excellent question." Dargo tried to prevent the worry from appearing in his countenance. He could feel Dorcas's eyes on him as he scanned the horizon. As he did not have the electronic instrumentation that the humans possessed, Dargo would be forced to make the balance of the journey based on a keen sense of direction and an estimate of the speed of his team against the remaining distance. In other words, he would be guessing.

Six

A l Havener hurried back into Cutters Notch after grabbing up the boys and adding them to his growing collection of captives. Here and there, out of the corner of his eye, he caught movement. More of those weird kids out playing in the storm. *What's wrong with their parents?* They'd dart from bush to bush, house to house. One set of two rushed across the street about a football-field's length ahead of him. Something gleamed in one of the pair's hands; it looked like a large knife. *This really is a strange town.*

As he drove, he began to have second thoughts about taking Rose and the boys to the old quarry. Now that he'd added Rose to the mix, he preferred somewhere warmer and nicer. Someplace he could gaze at her freckled, slightly plump cheeks. Besides, he still needed to find that girl, Hope Spencer.

The necklace Rose wore leapt into his mind. A moment later, his eyes landed on Rose's purse in the passenger seat. She'd grabbed for it as he dragged her from behind the counter, so he did her a favor and carried it out for her. *Hmm.*

Al steered the Ford off the road toward one of the dilapidated cubicles at a deserted carwash. "Floyd's Carwash" was spelled out in faded letters on a metal sign hanging from a pole and swinging in the wind. Paint hung in flakes off the cinderblock walls. Old rubber hoses dangled loosely from the ceilings of a couple of the wash slots. He circled around, sloshing through large pools of rainwater, and came in from the rear, wanting a view of the road.

After shifting to park, he yanked the handbag into his lap and rustled through it. A makeup pouch. A loose mascara. Lipstick. Tweezers. A key ring with about a hundred keys. Hairbrush. Comb. Envelopes, both opened and unopened. A paperclip. "Geesh, she has everything in here," he mumbled. Finally, in the bottom, he found her wallet.

Flipping open the red zippered, leather case, he saw that it held countless plastic cards—credit cards, membership cards, expired medical coverage cards. He doubted she'd ever need any of them again. Opening the money slot, he found forty dollars—a twenty and two tens. He removed the bills, sliding them into his front pants pocket. "She won't need these either."

Rose's driver's license was tucked behind a plastic window. Al pulled it out and checked the address. Lifting his phone, he plugged the location into his GPS app. *She lives in one of those old, giant houses.* He grinned. *Perfect.* He suddenly knew exactly where the house stood—he could almost picture it, although he'd never been there.

Carefully, he replaced the ID card behind the transparent plastic and zipped the wallet closed. Then, he rolled down the driver's side window and tossed the wallet and her bag, minus her keys, into the puddled water gathered underneath a coiled hose that still hung on a hook inside the cubicle.

A smile crept across his face as he pulled back into the blowing weather and headed toward the woman's address. The house had to be hidden, tucked in nicely behind the thick screen of trees, in line with all the other old, Victorian houses along Highway 257. In his mind, an image of her driveway entrance appeared, like a picture on a digital screen.

For some reason, it never occurred to him that her home would be one of the primary places they'd check when she came up missing. Logic apparently went out the window with Rose's handbag. Instead, the need to go there became sort of a compulsion. He had to go there. He just had to.

~

Kenny stood in the rain with the forest blowing wildly around him. His hair was soaked and slicked back. The cold water drenched him to the bone. He didn't care. His mind was consumed with both rage and fear. His daughter—his newly regained daughter—was in the hands of those putrid, depraved creatures. Kenny had to find her. He had to save her.

After spotting Hope's shoe in the muck, he'd rushed into the forest, following the trail left in the disturbed underbrush. At first, there were deep footprints where the beastly little vermin had slogged through the mud. Unfortunately, that trail soon disappeared because the thunderstorm sent water flowing briskly across the forest floor. Now, he stood still, breathing hard and unsure which way to go. Tomo and some of the others were following a few hundred yards behind him. They'd been calling out to him, trying to stop him, but he paid them no heed. Instead, he rushed headlong in pursuit—a pursuit that led him nowhere.

He felt it before he saw it in the darkness of the deep woods. It tickled his neck as it slithered by, swirling and twirling. Eventually, the specter took up a position directly in front of him, its red beady eyes level with his own. The rain fell through the phantom, and the wind had no effect. It appeared to be a mist, a black mist, oblivious to the elements. Kenny could see no mouth, but he heard its voice, high-pitched and abrasive.

"*Ahh, Kenny Burton, let me back in. I will direct your steps. Together, you and I, we will rescue your daughter and devastate those fallen ones. I know where they are, where they have taken her.*"

There it was. The temptation. The specter chose the perfect time and the ideal situation. All Kenny would need to do is let his defenses down. He knew the specter had the power to do what it promised, but he also knew the cost, the terrible cost. Kenny might save Hope, but without a doubt, he would lose himself, forever. There would be no recovery this time. No coming back. All that, and the evil spirit just might be lying—it probably was lying. Once it took control of Kenny's mind and body again, who knew where it would take him or what it would make him do. One thing was sure, it would include hurting people.

"*Kenny, Kenny. Even now, she sits in the cold, bound hand and foot, surrounded by those who wish her harm. They laugh at her. They taunt her. They tickle her neck with their shiny blades.*"

The lesser demon knew him well. It had fiddled around inside Kenny's head for over two years before finally taking full control. It knew his insecurities. It knew his sentimentalities. It knew the buttons to push, and it was pushing them hard. Slamming on them.

"*Who knows what sorts of terrible things they have planned for her? Torture, pain, a slow death. Maybe other atrocities.*"

Kenny peered back over his shoulder. The Adena men were

working through the brush toward him, though the mud and the muck were impeding their progress. Limbs were falling from the trees, broken loose by the wind. Lightning sizzled a nearby branch as the thunder shook him to the bone.

"Come now, Kenny. You're wasting time. We could go to her now. I know where she is. Together, we can save her. You know it's true."

As Hope's father stood there watching the specter swirling and undulating in the air before his face, he considered its words. It did know him, that much was certain. But he also knew it. It had shoved him into a mental corner and held him there while it used his body to nearly kill those he loved the most. If it hadn't been for his daughter's unimaginable courage, he would still be locked inside that mental prison. He knew the thing's power. He knew its tactics. And he knew that it was a master of manipulation and lies.

As the specter attacked his mind with a barrage of lies and promises, Kenny continued to search the forest for the trail. Frustration was building. Desperation was setting in, giving the lesser demon's temptations some grip on his mind. Then, there it was. How could he have missed it? The trail leapt out at him like a jack-in-the-box.

"Get out of my face!" he screamed before rushing through the phantom's swirling form as if it were nothing more than steam from a hot bath. "I don't need you. I can see their path clearly enough, and you're a liar."

On his heels, the Adena warriors followed, sloshing in the mud and slashing at the brush. The specter drifted off, biding its time.

~

There was nothing for Maggie to do. Too nervous to sit still and too scared to focus on anything specific, she paced. First, she looked through the front window at Calvin Churchill, sitting in his cruiser, parked on the cul-de-sac. Then she wandered into Hope's bedroom staring at the mirror, wishing her daughter home. Anni was in the kitchen. Cindy, Traci, and Teresa sat in the living room. Anni and Cindy seemed to be functioning in a daze, but Teresa and Traci did all they could to keep them occupied. Josh's and Danny's moms were as scared as she was, maybe more so, but they managed to keep calm. Maggie had no idea how. She was about to come out of her skin.

Calvin had come inside when he first arrived. The only thing they could tell him was about the wheelchair left in the middle of Basketball Court. No one had seen anything. They had nothing to go on, so neither did Cal. While he stood there, his radio crackled. He stepped out on the porch to get the details.

"It was Havener," he said as he stepped back inside. "It appears he also took Rose from the General. They caught his face on the security tape at the store."

Anni's eyes widened. "What? He has Rose too? Why?" She stood, a little shaky. Tears leaked down her cheeks. "I need to call Kevin. He doesn't know any of this yet." She shook her head as if in a daze. "I haven't called him. Why haven't I called him?" Anni jumped to her feet and fled into the kitchen, phone in hand.

Cindy, apparently realizing she'd neglected to call Roger, pulled out her phone. It shook in her hand as she tried to find the right buttons.

Calvin returned to his car where he sat watching the cul-de-sac, leaving the women in the living room.

Maggie paused, gazing at her neighbors before again pacing, wearing a path in her carpet. She slipped once more into Hope's bedroom, stopping to stare at the mirror. About to turn away, she froze when the surface rippled. "Hope?"

A head popped through. An ugly, angular, twisted grin on a yellowish-orange face. The creature glared at her. "Hello, lady," it said as its hands slid inside, gripping the edges of the mirror as if they were the edges of a doorframe. "I have come to visit for a little fun." It laughed as it began to pull itself into the room.

Maggie screamed. Groping for some sort of weapon, her hand found Hope's softball bat. She'd played as a girl, so she knew what to do with it. "Where's my daughter?" she screamed as she swung the metal club in a homerun cut. The wide metal end of the bat connected with the skull of the fallen elf with a clunk. Its eyes rolled up as its consciousness fled. The creature fell to the floor, out cold.

"Anni, Cindy, hurry. Find me some rope or duct tape or something. Quick!"

All the women met at the bedroom door, Cindy leading the way, Teresa tailing. "What. Is. That?" Cindy asked.

"Is that an elf?" Traci asked.

"I'll fill you in later. Right now, Cindy, find me something to tie this thing up with. There's some twine hanging on a hook out in the garage. Traci, get Deputy Churchill."

Both women sprinted away. That left Anni and Teresa standing in the doorway, looking over Maggie's shoulder, mouths open, hands shaking. The freckles on Anni's face were flushed.

"Does this have something to do with the boys being grabbed?" Anni stammered. "I don't understand what's going on."

Maggie, after weeks of one stressful situation after another, was further along the adaptation curve, so her heart went out to Anni. "No," she said. "This is different. I know about it, but it's different than the boys' situation. As soon as we restrain this thing, I'll fill you in." She stood over the little monster with the bat cocked, just in case.

Cindy returned. After tossing the twine to Maggie, she stood back against the doorjamb.

Maggie acted quickly. She spun multiple loops around the elf's bony ankles, then repeated the process with its knees. Just as she started on his wrists, Calvin Churchill stepped through the door.

"What the razzlesnatz is that?"

"It's a fallen elf," Maggie blurted. "Cuff the thing before it wakes up."

~

Still in the General, staring out the plate-glass window at the blowing storm and torrential rain, Jerry Steinkamp groaned. "Sheriff, how do we find this guy? He's got a huge head start. Havener could be anywhere in at least a twenty-mile radius by now." Jerry peered to the left, then the right, hoping that maybe Havener would drive back by.

Agent Franklin joined him at the window, staring between advertisements plastered to the glass. Lightning struck a large tree across the street. The lights flickered, the resulting boom rattling the bottles of beer in the cooler.

Rick remained behind the counter, teetering on the edge of despair. It seemed like every two weeks this little town nearly came apart at the seams. He rubbed his face with both hands, then slid them across the bristles of his close-cropped haircut.

"I don't know," Rick finally said. "Al had family here, but he's never really lived here himself, so he probably doesn't know the area all that well. On the other hand, he's had two weeks to plan this thing out." The sheriff stepped carefully through the debris of fallen cigarette packs and chewing gum scattered on the floor. "Havener wouldn't go back to the abandoned farm. He'd expect us to check it. That said, we need to cross that option off the list. Just in case."

Franklin glanced up at Rick who stood a couple of inches taller than both he and Deputy Steinkamp. "Well, then, he'd probably go wherever you think is the last place he'd go. Where would that be? Let's start at the end of the list and work backward."

"Ha," Steinkamp chuckled. "If it was me, I'd go to the old quarry. The one his aunt and uncle were using. He'd know about it from the news. He may have even visited it over the years, but he may think we'd not really consider it. Probably figures it's the last place we'd think to check on."

Rick stared out the window, considering Jerry's idea. It *was* likely that Havener didn't really know the area. He had no other property. The quarry sort of made sense. Yet, a pit was forming in his gut. Rick hated the quarry. If it was up to him, they'd drop a bomb on the complex and blow it off the face of the planet. The Hicks had used it as their personal killing ground. He'd almost died there himself. The idea of visiting it again filled him with dread— he hadn't been there since the investigation closed about a week after Hope's rescue—but now that it'd been suggested, Rick sensed the logic of it. The place was at least worth a looksee.

"Jerry, continue wrapping up here. Contact Rose's brother. Kevin's probably still down at the hardware store." Rick peered out into the storm again. "Unless he's been called home." He thought of Danny being snatched again. "Franklin, let's go check out that godforsaken, abandoned quarry."

As the storm continued to rage on, he and Franklin ducked out to Rick's cruiser, as if crouching through the rain would keep them dry. The wind blew the surrounding trees nearly vertical before whipping them back and forth. Lightning continued to flash all around. The resulting thunder shook the car. In the few steps from the door to the vehicle, everything not covered by rain gear was again soaked.

"Look!" Franklin pointed down Highway 257 toward the diner. "Those things are racing back toward the Quarry Pit."

Rick whipped around. Sure enough, a group of small beings— they looked like raggedly dressed kids—were rushing away from town, carrying overstuffed bags. Anders reached for his radio but remembered that Gator wasn't in uniform. The deputy didn't have his radio. Instead, Rick yanked his phone from his pocket, speed-dialed his deputy, while simultaneously throwing his car into reverse.

Gator answered as Rick pulled out into the flooded street to give chase. "*Sheriff, what's going on?*"

"The creatures are headed back your way. Make sure the doors are secure. I'm on their tail."

Franklin watched them run. "Those things are fast, even loaded down. Look at 'em go."

"*I see them,*" Gator's voice said through the speaker. "*They're running right at us.*"

Rick, with the help of the big Ford engine, gained on the miscreant elves. He was within fifty feet when the little thieves reached the diner parking lot. The large lights, still burning brightly despite the power outage in the diner itself, were supplemented by his own headlights as they reflected off the shiny aluminum siding of the restaurant. Rick skidded into the gravel lot and came to a sideways stop.

"*Rick, they're right here. They're coming for the diner!*"

Franklin exited the passenger side, pulling his weapon. Rick grabbed his service pistol and jumped from the driver's side door. "You, stop!" he screamed at the elves. "Stop, right there."

They didn't stop. They didn't even look back at him. Instead, the entire group, maybe a dozen in all, ran headlong into the side of the diner and disappeared.

Rick could see Gator through one of the large plate-glass windows. His eyes were quarters, and his mouth could hold a baseball. He raised both hands in the air as if to ask, *where'd they go?*

Rick shrugged and shook his head in response. He glanced at Franklin who stood there in the rain, staring at the diner. Water dripped from his ears and nose. Slowly, he holstered his gun. "Anders, you really do have a weird town here," he mumbled.

"Yes, I do." Rick returned to his car. "Come on. We need to find Havener before he hurts Rose or those boys."

After a moment, the speechless NSA agent turned away from the diner and crawled back into the warm Crown Vic. He sat silently as Rick retraced their path, cruising back into Cutters Notch. The silence was okay with Rick.

~

Mabel Robbins stood at the shack's aluminum storm door looking out over the rolling waters as the storm blew loose the few leaves left on the trees and sent them skimming across the lake's surface. The forest made popping sounds as the wind found weaknesses in the trees. Her left hand rested on the semi-automatic rifle leaning against the doorjamb. Robert joined her, gazing over her shoulder.

"It's crazy out there, Ma," Robert pointed out.

The old woman was reticent. "Yeah." Parker and Boyd were still playing cards in the space behind her. They'd been right earlier. She and her crew couldn't stay in this place. They should've left already. Eventually, someone would come snooping around, whether it be kids looking for a party spot or officials following up on some missed detail. They needed to clear out, sooner rather than later. Normally decisive, the disaster brought on by that Bray kid left her doubting herself.

Mabel was frightened and angry. Everything—her whole life's work—had fallen apart in moments. One lax move by her nitwit son allowed that teenager to escape. The result had been an avalanche of events culminating in their being holed up in this shack for the last two weeks. Despite her strong words to the others, she didn't really know what to do. A slight tremor shook her right hand. She pulled it in to her chest and held it there.

"Someone's comin' again." Robert pointed over her shoulder at headlights shining through the trees.

Mabel knew in that moment that she'd hesitated too long. She grabbed up the rifle, slammed the door, and ordered the lanterns doused. "Boyd, Parker, grab your guns. We got company. Once we deal with this, we're gettin' outta here."

~

Bayal had achieved his diversion. Hope remained bound in one of the few dry spots in the forest, right next to a warm fire. The Adena and the queen were apparently focused on her. Meanwhile, he and his ragtag army went back to the notorious Gate to Abandon, capturing a couple of Adena guards along the way. Despite the storm with its lightning and the blowing debris, he had to have that stone.

It pulled at him, drawing him like a bear is drawn to food.

Upon arrival, he stood before the massive boulder with his followers huddled around. It was mostly dry here. The rain seemed to gather upon an invisible shield above their heads and flow off transparent edges. Only water blowing in from the side reached close to the stone. Further down, the rain was somehow blocked from the ground by a rectangular depression surrounding the large rock. It stopped a few inches above the ground and flowed away. *Curious. Some sort of human structure.*

"Why is this huge rock so important?" one of his lieutenants asked.

Bayal ignored the question, rubbing his chin. The truth was he didn't truly know what he would find when he opened the gate, but he had his suspicions. Whatever happened here happened after he fled to the Abyss. Over the centuries he'd spent in the pit, he heard random stories from various specters about a battle held on this spot and the subsequent imprisonment of a creature in this place. All he cared about was the stone he knew the creature carried. Bayal yearned for the power that stone provided. He played dumb to the stories and plotted. He also knew the possessor of the stone wielded great power, and he meant to have it for himself. Again. "Gather around," he ordered, "and shove this rock away."

Bayal studied the boulder. It was large and heavy, but the elves were very strong. Twenty or so should be able to move it. "You there, grip that stone. You too, get in there and shove."

Despite their effort, the massive rock would not budge. He moved more elves into the effort, but still, it wouldn't give. "It is like something unseen is holding it back," one of them mumbled.

Bayal scratched his pitch-dark chin, rubbing a ribbon of red that ran along his cheek. He peered up into the maelstrom, considering the lack of water falling on his face, then glanced around at the rectangular shape of the dry ground. Only on the side facing the wind did the ground show moisture leaking in as if underneath the edge of an invisible barrier. *Of course. The humans must have secured it in some way within their realm.*

Across the close-cropped grass, Bayal could see another dry spot in the middle of the storm with rainwater flowing like waterfalls off another invisible barrier high above it. Shimmers hung within the space. There were several, but one was more prominent. It was oval, and large enough for an elf to pass through. "Keep working at it," he ordered. "I will return in a few moments."

Bayal crossed the open ground, ignoring the blowing rain, and peered into the shimmer. A human room for bodily relief occupied the space on the other side. Cautiously, he reached through the portal, pulling himself into the Human Realm. This was the first time he had crossed that barrier since re-emerging from the Abyss. In all previous occasions, he had sent his minions through. It was obvious the humans of this era were much more advanced than when he'd last visited their world.

As he pulled himself out of the mirror, he stood up on a stonelike basin. Across the room was what looked like a chair but with water pooled in the bottom. Yet another large oval stonelike basin occupied a niche in the opposing wall. As he'd traveled across the realm from the pit to this place, he'd peered through other shimmers and seen the humans using these various water sources. He found the practice odd yet efficient.

Art hung from pegs within the room. He pulled a picture down, looking it over before tossing it in the large basin. "Hmph. Strange place for decorations."

To Bayal's left, a wooden barrier hung on metal pins. He grabbed the edge; it moved back and forth. *Interesting*. He passed through the opening, stopping in a hallway to get his bearings. "The boulder will be to my left," he mumbled. More pictures hung in frames on the wall—very lifelike. As amazing as were all the new sights he saw, he didn't have time to gawk. He needed to move that rock aside before Agahpey caught on to his ruse, the native warriors returned, and before the sun broke through the storm clouds, trapping him in the Human Realm.

Hurrying through the human abode, he opened yet another wooden barrier on pins and stepped outside, finding himself on a large porch that stretched from one side of the human abode to the other. In front of him, another structure appeared through the blowing storm. A roof positioned on posts. The boulder sat unmoved beneath it.

Bayal darted through the torrential rain, again ignoring the debris being carried on the wind. He examined the Ancient Gate to Abandon as it appeared in this realm. "They have formed some sort of hardened stone floor and created a berm around the rock," Bayal bellowed into the cold, wet air. "I must bring my soldiers through and open the gate in this realm."

Quickly retracing his steps, Bayal called his forces to the shimmer and began to shove them through, one by one, until they'd all passed into the Human Realm. He left one near the stone basin to guard the shimmer against intrusion by his enemies.

Once they were all gathered in the pavilion, he pointed at the man-made stone barriers. "This stone floor and berm must be removed," he explained, barely containing his frustration. "Scatter about the human buildings. Find tools. Break this up and move that rock."

The fallen elves headed out into the weather toward the human structures. Bayal watched them enter the barn and break into a smaller shack. The sounds of their scrounging reached his large ears, despite the storm. In mere minutes they returned, carrying sledgehammers, smaller mallets, and some steel-bladed shovels. "Get to it," Bayal ordered.

~

Hope shivered despite the warmth of the fire. The guards crouched a few feet away at a second fire, murmuring to themselves and occasionally glancing at her with their large, angular eyes. She realized that by rushing headlong to save her dad, she had instead played into Bayal's warped hands. She'd screwed up royally and become Bayal's decoy. He wanted everyone to come searching for her, so he'd have time to take advantage of the distraction.

She struggled with her bindings, but the more she worked them the tighter they felt. Hope needed to get loose—to escape and warn the others. Wiggling and struggling with the bindings, her frustration and desperation grew with each passing moment.

"Can you not get free, little one?" The voice laughed into her mind.

Jerking her head upward, she saw the specter swirling and twirling before her. Its undulating shape shifted from broad to thin, short to tall, dark to darker. All the while, its red pinpoint eyes locked into her own.

"Your mighty bright aura doesn't seem to be helping you much right now." It cackled again.

Glancing at her captors only to see them laughing at her, she bared her teeth and growled deep in her throat like an angry bear.

The specter floated and danced around her as if to mock her inability to move.

"Get away from me!"

"*Make me.*"

The specter fluttered to the two guards for a moment. Both cocked their ears as if listening to a whispering child, then leapt to their feet and gathered their weapons as the entity returned to Hope.

"*Your father is rushing here as we speak. I just warned your elfin friends.*" The evil spirit laughed at what it had done.

Panic joined the desperation within Hope. She battled for control. "Why would you do that?" She screamed, fighting even harder against her bindings. Even as she asked the question, she knew the answer. The dark entity loved the chaos. The violence. The pain. It fed on it like a gourmet meal.

The specter cackled yet again. "*Oh, this is tasting good. The flavor of your desperation mixed with sheer panic is delectable.*" The lesser demon's red eyes flickered away briefly, then returned. "*He approaches now. This should be an absolute feast.*"

Her father came crashing through the underbrush. Snapping twigs. Breaking branches. Splashing steps. He was barging in, rushing headlong into a trap. "Dad, no! Stop," she screamed. Even as Hope yelled the words, she knew they wouldn't reach his ears through the roaring storm and the water rushing over the ledge above her head. She sat helpless, only a witness to what was about to unfold. Guilt grabbed the sides of her heart and squeezed. Whatever was about to happen was her fault.

~

The two fallen elves were ready. One had a sword. The other had a large knife. They'd taken up positions behind rocks on either side of Hope. The rain, pouring water, and thrashing limbs camouflaged their presence.

Seven

D ang it, Danny, my cast is soaked. Mom's gonna kill me."

"Really? That's what you're worried about right now?"

"Hmph," Rose added as she struggled against her bindings.

The three captives, each soaked to the bone, rolled around on the hard bed of the Ford pickup as Al Havener drove them wherever he was driving them. Danny began to shiver. He wasn't sure if it was due to the wet clothes in the cold air, or his usual dose of fear. Oddly enough, this time he thought it might only be the chill of the wet clothes. Something about jumping from the top of a one-hundred-foot silo had changed his perspective on survival.

As they struggled in the dark, Danny's eyes began to adjust. Little slivers of light leaked into the locked compartment around the edges. As his pupils dilated, it was just enough to allow him to see the outlines of the wheel wells. Eventually, the duct tape on his aunt's mouth took shape.

"Can you get the tape off her mouth?" Josh asked.

Danny's hands were bound, as were his knees and his ankles. He leaned toward his Aunt Rose's cheeks as to give her a kiss, but instead of a casual peck, he tried to grab the tape with his teeth. Missing the first time, he tried again. This time, he grabbed skin.

"Eeerrr," she groaned.

"Sorry." He leaned in one more time and snagged the edge of the sticky gray strip, giving it a jerk. It came free.

Rose spat a cloth from her mouth and gulped at the air. Then she hurled a series of expletives at the dark cover over her head in combinations that Danny had never contemplated.

"Wow," Josh said.

"Sorry," Danny mumbled again.

"I'm not cussing at you, Danny," Rose reassured him. "I'm cussing at that...that...Ugh," she groaned. "That man."

As the trio rolled around in the bed, a small amount of rainwater sloshed with each change of direction. Finally, the truck made a quick right, accelerated, then veered left before stopping. When it stopped, the rain pelting the bedcover stopped, too.

"We're at Floyd's Carwash," Rose announced. "Under one of the canopies."

"How can you tell?" Josh asked.

"I'm a good judge of distance and direction."

"What's he doing?" Danny asked.

"Probably thinking. Figuring out what to do. He pulled in here to get outta the rain so he can think. I'm guessing he had a plan when it was just you boys, but I was a spur-of-the-moment thing. After snatching me, he needs a new plan. He grabbed you for his revenge. He's grabbed me for some other reason."

"Why'd he grab you?" Josh asked.

Rose ignored the question.

After a moment, Danny broke the silence. "Aunt Rose, what are we gonna do?"

The woman wiggled to turn her body toward her nephew. Danny could feel the shift and he could sense her eyes looking at him in the dark. The stone necklace at her throat gave off a faint twinkle, and then a small glow rolled through the crystal. His aunt owned some eclectic jewelry, but he'd never noticed this piece. He found it a little mesmerizing. *I wish I could touch it.*

Josh was silent except for a few moans. Still recovering from his fall inside the silo, being tossed in the back of the Ford must have aggravated some of the recent injuries.

"I don't exactly know," Rose finally said. "We'll have to look for our opportunity and be ready to jump when it's time to jump." Danny could make out the outline of a forced smile on his aunt's face.

The pickup started to roll again. It turned left out of the carwash lot.

"He's headed back toward the General, the way we came." Rose flipped to her back.

Moments later, the vehicle slowed before turning to the right.

Gravel crunched under the wheels, and brush scratched the side panels. The rain, which had begun to drum the bedcover again as they pulled out, became more sporadic, as if the truck had pulled under the trees.

"Holy shinoly," she muttered, creating a more acceptable expletive. "Al's going to my house. He's probably gone through my purse, found my keys and address, and he's taking us there." She laughed. "He's gonna regret that idea."

~

Al watched the flashing blue lights from the General as he slowed the F-150 to turn right into Rose Flannery's driveway. It was a little risky passing this close to the scene where he'd snatched her up, but they didn't know what he was driving. It was even more risky taking his kidnapped victim back to her own home, but it was a compulsion he couldn't deny. Besides, a little risk got the heart pumping. Weirdly, an intense curiosity about where Rose lived had flooded his mind as he'd sat under the carwash canopy rummaging through her purse.

It amazed him how quickly the forest swallowed up the light as he steered along Rose's driveway. Considering the darkness of the storm and the thick underbrush, it was as if he were driving in the middle of a moonless night. The trees were thrashing violently up top, but the wind was less severe near the gravel trail as it wound through the oaks, maples, and sycamores.

He curved to the right then veered to the left. The drive seemed a mile long with all the curves. Suddenly, he emerged into a clearing, and there it was—the huge Victorian house with its massive portico, ornate trim, and an octagonal tower room jutting from the structure on the left. The architecture was intricate and breathtaking. Of all the ones he'd glimpsed through the trees, this one topped them all. *How does a convenience-store clerk afford this kind of place?*

The stained wooden front door with an oval glass window was aglow with light from a small lamp inside. Yet, he needed to see about a back entrance, something shielded from the road. The authorities might drive back here to check out the house. The truck needed to be concealed.

Continuing to follow the gravel driveway, he curled around the right side of the house, pulling up in front of a barn. A sheer rock wall jutted up beyond the treetops behind the rough wooden building. He could almost make out the top of the bluff through the angrily swinging limbs. Al climbed out and opened the barn doors. Empty. *Excellent.*

After moving the pickup inside, he left his captives where they were while he checked out the house. The backdoor was nondescript compared to the front. A basic wooden door with a rectangular glass panel. He fiddled with Rose's keys until he found the right one. The door opened to a mudroom. A staircase descended into darkness on his right—a basement. Al found a switch; he clicked it on. The stairs hit a landing halfway before turning left and dropping into more darkness.

Past the mudroom, he entered a kitchen. It featured a seventies-era motif—a green gas stove, orange countertops, and country-themed wallpaper accented with a flowery trim along the top of the walls. A small plate with scrambled-egg residue sat next to the sink with a coffee cup to keep it company. Two pieces of silverware jutted from the cup. As Al watched, one drip of water fell from the faucet. The sound seemed to resonate through the otherwise quiet house.

Straight through he found the dining room. An ornate wooden table with eight equally detailed chairs took up the center position underneath a small crystal chandelier. He paused to take it in. The place smelled a little musty. The floor was hardwood but with an Oriental rug stretching below the table. A large portrait hung between wall sconces on one end. The walls were a neutral color with dark wood trim.

The path of rooms turned to the right emptying into a massive entry foyer. He spotted the small table near the front door, the one with the small, lighted lamp. Above his head was another crystal chandelier—enormous, many times larger than the one in the dining room. Stepping near the door, he flipped a wall switch. The giant glass fixture bloomed to life revealing an oak staircase leading to a second-floor balcony. The steps were covered in reddish carpet with a Far-Eastern pattern.

Al was enjoying the exploration. He loved old houses and often dreamed of giant, ancient mansions with hidden rooms and secret passageways. This seemed just like his dreams, and he got a bit lost in the moment. A shiver traveled down his spine. He chalked it up to adrenaline.

Across the entryway were two massive, oak-pocket doors. Closed. He needed to see what sat beyond them. Al marched over and flung them open. He'd expected them to move slowly on old rollers, but instead, well-oiled, they clanged to their limits on each side. A touch of guilt struck him. He could hurt people with no regret, but he respected old houses.

Only a touch of light filtered in through the sheers and slightly opened drapes. Floor-to-ceiling bookcases surrounded the room with a roll-top desk stationed in a cut out. The ceiling was very high, so a ladder on wheels was set into the wall to slide along the shelves, giving access to the top rows of books. A large stone fireplace adorned the western wall. A sofa and side table sat before it.

"I wish I could stay here," he mumbled. His criminal mind began to contemplate ways to secure possession.

Returning to the foyer, he took the staircase two steps at a time. At the top, he looked right—a short hallway stretched out with doors on either side. Bedrooms. To the left, one door sat ajar at the very end of a hall that seemed too long for the distance covered. A touch of light leaked out. A long, narrow Persian rug led the way. Feeling a touch disoriented, he chose that direction. Its slightly opened door called to him.

Al stepped into the octagonal room, the storm raging outside. Limbs from the mighty trees brushed against the shingles. Overhead, a branch broke free, crashing to the roof with a thud.

Inside the room, Havener found himself in a small turret with a single window in one of the eight walls. A small, wooden table was positioned below a bright, detailed portrait of a Native American. *Amazing eyes. It's like they're looking right at me.* A sense of creepiness touched the back of his neck, and he shivered again.

On the lone table sat a small wooden box, nothing else. Another smaller version of the entryway chandelier hung over his head. He clicked it on. The crystals danced in the light with intricate shadow patterns flowing around the space. "Strange room. All this space for a painting and a box?" His voice bounced off the many walls, echoing in the nearly empty turret. "This is it. I'll bring 'em in here."

~

"Seems kinda stupid of him," Josh quipped. "Won't the police check your house when they find out you're gone?"

Rose was silent at first, considering. The house was her safe place, but it hadn't always been that way. Her first visit had terrified her, nearly killed her. Now, though, it was hers, fully and completely. Al Havener had made a crucial mistake. She knew it if no one else did.

Rose turned to look at Josh, the outline of his form was visible over the top of her nephew. "They might come here. But then again, they might not. This house has a way of making people forget it exists." She paused. "Unless it wants them to visit."

"Are you saying it's haunted?" Danny asked. His eyes grew as big as half dollars. Rose caught sight of the white around his pupils. "You're living in a haunted house?"

Rose hesitated. "I'm not exactly saying it's haunted." Then she added, "But it does seem to have a weird effect on people. It has a long, interesting history, but folks rarely notice it even exists."

Josh tilted his head up to peer at Rose. "Ya know, now that you mention it, I never knew this house was here until you bought it." He dropped back down before turning on his side toward Danny. "Even now, I keep forgetting you moved here. That is weird."

Rose quietly smiled. Thinking back to her first visit as a teenager, even then she was surprised when Minerva Woodstock had invited her to come work for her. She didn't know the house existed either until the old woman pointed at the driveway—clearly visible from the General's parking lot. It was like her vision automatically skipped by the place.

After that fateful first visit, she forgot about the house for long periods, only to recall it on the occasional times when she wore the necklace. Standing before the small wooden box, she'd fasten it around her neck and the house would come rushing back to her mind. It beckoned to her. It projected into her mind a sense of loneliness…aloneness. It was almost as if it was calling her home.

Finally, when some random official in some government office assigned it for an auction, it wouldn't leave her mind even if she wasn't wearing the strange piece of jewelry. It became like a nagging earworm, playing on a loop, until she finally decided to bid on it. As it turned out, she was the only one to show up at the auction, the only one to bid–a fact the auctioneer oddly failed to notice. It was as if all the other potential buyers had collectively forgotten to attend. She bought the place for a steal. *The house wanted me.*

Rose heard the house's backdoor open and close. The boys

squirmed next to her. Their captor opened the cover and lowered the tailgate.

"All right," he said. "I'm gonna pull each of you out. I've got the gun on you. Don't move unless I tell you, or someone's gonna get a bullet. Understand?"

"Yeah," the boys replied in stereo. Rose raised her head and smiled at the evil man, locking eyes with him. "Whatever you say, Al." She gave him a saccharine smile and winked.

~

Queen Hesed and her sons, along with Sacqueal, reached the Adena village to find it empty. A few fires were still burning in small, protected firepits beneath some of the homes. Fresh footprints were gathering water from the rain. The storm seemed to be intensifying with limbs breaking free of the trees. Some trees had even blown over, crashing into the forest.

"Where have they all gone?" she asked. Sacqueal grunted and shrugged in reply.

Smakal pointed toward a pattern of footprints in the muddy clearing. "It appears they have all gone in that direction."

Indeed, as Hesed studied the mucky area, she could see the flow of the trail. "Yes, and they were in a hurry. Perhaps, they know where Nozomi is being held. Gavin, lead the way."

The elfin entourage, accompanied by the sasquatch guardian, trudged off in pursuit of the Adena forces within the midst of the blowing tempest. The wind in the trees easily drowned out the noise of their feet surging through the muddy forest. Around them, lightning continued to strike; limbs continued to break free of the trees, becoming arboreal missiles striking with increasing fury.

~

Before finding Hope, Kenny smashed headlong through the underbrush. He didn't know where the dark specter had gone, and he didn't care. Its lies were tempting, but he knew them for what they were, lies. If Hope could be saved, it wouldn't be with the help of that evil spirit. Kenny would do it himself.

The big man was not a stranger to fights. When younger, he'd often fought in the streets of Muncie. Sometimes, he'd been the aggressor and sometimes he'd been the defender. He didn't always start the fights, but he always finished them. A couple of times, he got jumped while he was in prison—once in his cell and once at lunch. Neither occasion ended well for the other guy, or in the case of the attack in his cell, for the other guys. They'd crawled away, bloodied.

There. Ahead. The flicker of a fire. A voice calling out. Hope screaming something. Her voice pulled Kenny forward. Thorns grabbed his arms, his legs, his face. He didn't care. He'd nearly killed her himself under the influence of that swirling blackness, but she'd saved him. Now, it was his turn. He would save Hope.

The storm was raging. The trees doubled over. Broken branches became wooden projectiles. The rain fell like a high-powered shower through each break in the tree cover.

Closer now, Kenny could see the flames of the fire being pulled outward from the crevice where it burned. Hope squirmed, bound beside it. The light of the flickers danced across her anxious face. He read terror in her expression. Adrenaline surged in his arteries. "I'm coming, Hope."

Kenny didn't know if his new Adena family was still following him. He didn't care. Only thoughts of saving his daughter coursed through his mind. Anger. Fear. His face was wet. Rain mixed with tears. Pulling the large knife from his waistband, he burst through the last barrier of brush.

Hope was still screaming something at him. She sat alone. *They've left her all alone in the forest. She's alone and alive.* Joy hit his heart.

"Dad, no!" Hope screamed. "Watch out. It's a trap."

Kenny heard that. It took a moment for the words to register. He stopped short in a small clearing. Hope sat under an overhang, squirming by the fire. Rain poured off the ledge above her head like a waterfall, pooling in a muddy bog. The ground was broken up as if a herd of cattle had passed through. There was another fire nearby, unattended. As he frantically glanced around, two of her words registered in his mind: watch and trap. *Trap?*

Kenny stood ankle-deep in the muck. *Hope screamed something about a trap.* Rain drenched him, obscuring his vision. More tree limbs were blowing by. Movement to the left, to the right. *Elves.* Each small creature, armed with a blade glimmering in the firelight, marched toward him in the mist. Kenny held his own knife waist high.

Elves, Kenny knew, were very strong for their size and quite fast. He spread his arms and legs, preparing for their attack, the steel blade fitting well in his right hand. He didn't have to wait long.

The miniature-sized miscreants charged him. Like oversized mosquitos, they buzzed by, one behind and one in front. He parried the weapon of the one before him by bringing his own knife down, but the one that passed behind him used its sword to slice into the back of his legs. The sword's edge passed through his trousers and into the skin of his thighs. Fortunately, the cut was superficial. Still, blood trickled down the inside of his pant legs. It felt warm as it mixed with the rain.

They're too fast.

The fallen elves returned to their original positions, yet on opposite sides. They grinned at Kenny. One wagged a finger at him. The aura of their putrid-colored skin glowed orange against the dark, pulsating blue trees.

I need to get my back up against something. Kenny considered his options. He could duck under the overhang and back up against the stone wall, or he could locate a tree, putting his rear against the trunk. The tree would be a retreat. The stone wall would be near Hope. *I didn't come charging in here just to retreat.*

Before the elves drove at him again, Kenny splashed through the water falling from the stone above, dashing to the rear of the crevice. He was on Hope's right, back against the rock wall. The warmth of the fire in the natural alcove felt good, and it was free of the wind. The elves followed, stepping through the curtain of liquid, first one then the other, ninety degrees apart and thirty feet away.

"Now, you are trapped, human," the one to the left growled. The other one grunted out a laugh.

Kenny glanced at the knife in his hand and then at the bindings holding Hope. Carefully, slowly, he eased down meaning to cut her free.

"Do not attempt to free the girl," said the elf on the right.

"If you attempt it, we will kill her on the spot," stated the one on the left.

"They're lying," Hope said. "The elves are under strict orders from Bayal not to hurt me. I heard him give the orders. I'm just…this is just a decoy." She blurted the words in a rush. "He's using me to draw everyone's attention away while he takes the rest of his forces. They've gone back to the gate despite the storm."

While the elves threatened Hope, Kenny's eyes darted from one enemy to the other. Keeping his back to the stone wall, he ignored their threats and bent over, slicing through Hope's bindings in one swipe.

The two elves charged as one. Hope slipped out of the way. As Kenny turned back to face the fallen ones, they leapt at him with their blades flashing. He flung one off, then the other, but they kept surging back at him, steel edges cutting his flesh. Hope stood by screaming, unable to assist her father.

Kenny slashed and stabbed; he punched and twisted. Blood splattered. The elves snarled and cursed. Still, Kenny fought until his knees buckled. As he lost his balance, he managed to seize an elfin arm, twisting it around until it popped. The creature screeched in pain and jabbed his blade into Kenny's upper left chest.

The other elf was about to drive his weapon into Kenny's neck when an Adena spear struck the vicious creature square in the back. It fell over, the spear tip protruding from its chest.

Tomo leapt through the waterfall, Mala on his heels. The Adena leader grabbed the still-breathing elf and flung it out into the storm. As it landed, the rest of the warriors fell upon it. Then, Tomo knelt beside his wounded new friend. "Kenny Burton, where are you injured?"

"Pretty much everywhere," he whispered through gasping breaths.

Mala held Hope. The girl shook as tears streamed down her cheeks.

Kenny watched it all unfold as if outside himself, his eyes dancing from Tomo to the dead elf before him, then to the water gushing over the ledge and finally to his beautiful little girl. "I'm so sorry," he mumbled. His various wounds—the cut across the back of his thighs, the puncture in his chest—were taking their toll. There were more, many more. "They were so fast," he groaned. "How can they move so fast?"

Glancing down, he saw blood seeping from a wound in his gut. As his mind went there, he felt a deep, burning where he'd been stabbed. His head felt light. The firelight flickering off the walls gave him a whirling feeling. The world began to spin. Then, his mind fled.

"*You should have let me help you,*" the specter said into

Kenny's mind as everything else disappeared. *"Together, we would have destroyed those blasted little beings."*

Kenny no longer felt the pain. He was no longer locked in the here and now. Somewhere inside, he knew that he'd passed out. Though he may have escaped the angry burning of the punctures and cuts, he couldn't escape the reach of this evil spirit that doggedly continued to chase him. "Maybe we would have," he answered, "but at what cost? You would have my soul again. You would use me to do unspeakable things. No. I made my choice. I did what I came to do. Whatever happens to me, Hope is safe. Leave me now."

The specter didn't respond. Kenny drifted deeper and deeper until the darkness of his unconscious mind was swallowed up in a sudden bloom of light.

~

Hope leaned against Mala's side as the woman wrapped her arms tightly around the girl, pulling her in. Her dad lay slumped against the rear wall of the natural alcove. She could no longer hear the storm or the rushing waters. The sounds of the warriors, or even the voice of the kind woman trying to console her, were lost to her. All her ears would register were the groans, the mumblings, and the cries emanating from her father. *All my fault.*

So much blood. It seemed to come from all over him. Tomo was trying to stop it, stuffing cloths in various places even as the crimson liquid oozed over his fingers. The Adena chief called for others to help him.

Hope's eyes met her father's. They locked. Briefly. In that moment, she sensed him. She felt his love for her, his gratitude that she was safe. His eyes smiled through the pain. She wanted to hold on to that gaze, to force him to stay right where he was. He was trying to hold on also. She could tell.

Despite the struggle, her father's eyes lost focus. They rolled up under his lids as his head drooped.

Hope screamed. "No!"

~

Tomo called four of his warriors. "Carry Kenny Burton to our lodge. Mala, go with him. Care for him."

The Adena leader peered around. *Only two elves?* He was perplexed. He expected the whole bunch of them to be huddled out of the storm. Beyond the meager protection of the overhang, beyond the water falling from the rocks above, the forest was a violent thrashing of surging winds, blowing pellets of rain, and the debris of broken limbs. Occasionally, the sound of large trees losing their footing resounded above the storm's blasts.

"Where are the others?" Tomo asked, directing his gaze toward Hope as his men raised Kenny to their shoulders. "Do you know where they are? Where have they gone? Are they going to the gate in this storm?"

Hope wasn't listening. She tried to pull away from Mala as the warriors lifted her father. Yet, Tomo's wife kept her in a tight grip.

Tomo stepped into Hope's line of sight, stooping and taking her face in his hands. "Nozomi, please." The girl's blue eyes found his. She stopped struggling, though her eyes kept darting toward her dad. "I promise we will do all we can for your father, but I need you to listen to my voice. Can you hear me?"

Hope nodded.

"Do you know where the other fallen elves have gone?"

"Decoy," she muttered. "I was a decoy. They've all gone to the gate while you've been drawn here."

The realization of what she said crawled across his mind. A distraction. A magician's trick. Wiping one of his hands across his wet face, he left some of Kenny's blood on his cheek before standing up. *It may already be too late*. He cast his eyes into the forest. In the distance, an ancient evil waited to be released from its lair deep in Abandon. Perhaps it had already been released.

An elf rushed through the falling water. Gavin—his greenish aura glowed brightly from the effort. He paused only long enough to see the warriors struggling to balance Kenny between them, then turned his eyes on Hope. "Are you okay?" he exclaimed. "Are you hurt?"

Queen Hesed and her entourage followed Gavin into the protected alcove. Sacqueal needed to duck his furry head. "I heard what Nozomi said," the queen stated.

Tomo noted her large elfin ears.

"We must hurry before Bayal succeeds in destroying us all," she proclaimed.

"I posted guards," Tomo said.

"They have no doubt been captured," replied Hesed. "Bayal would have expected their presence."

Tomo gazed around, feeling defeated. His men had Kenny aloft. Hope, whom the queen referred to as Nozomi, was struggling to hold it together, still being constrained by Mala. The girl was shivering. Queen Hesed, her three sons, and her huge, hairy bodyguard stood near the water flooding down from above. His warriors waited in the rain. Tomo had failed to protect the gate; he had failed to protect his friend. His eyes dropped to his muddy feet.

"Tomo," Hesed broke through his thoughts, "it is not too late. We must hurry."

Tomo's wave of self-doubt passed. He raised his eyes again, lifting his chin. "Of course, you are right. Mala, see to Kenny. Save him." He knelt before Hope. "We will do all we can for your father," he said in a gentle tone. "Now, you must go home to your mother. We cannot protect you during the battle that is to come."

"I can't," Hope answered. "My dad—"

"Nozomi, dear," Hesed took the young girl's face with its bright aura into her hands. "Your father's life is in the hands of the Mighty One. All that can be done will be done. You must go home." Hesed turned to her sons. "Gronek, take Nozomi home. Return her to her room for sleeping and see that her mother knows she is there. Be sure she is secure before you return to me. Then join me at the gate."

Gronek reached out and took Hope's hand into his own. She peered at him, her face twisted with emotion, but she offered no resistance. As Tomo watched, Gronek easily lifted the girl, placing her on his back, then darted into the raging storm.

Tomo pulled his large knife. "To the gate!"

Mala and the men carrying Kenny hurried to the Adena village. Gronek with Hope on his shoulders darted toward Basketball Court. Tomo with his warriors, Queen Hesed with her sons and one large sasquatch, charged toward the Ancient Gate to Abandon.

Eight

S tanding in the old stone structure at the abandoned quarry, Mabel Robbins peeked past a dingy curtain into the raging weather. She watched the police cruiser slosh its way around the lake toward the shack. The car bounced in the deep, water-filled ruts, throwing waves of water to both sides. Her son, Robert, loomed over her shoulder, trying to see what he could see. Parker and Boyd, rifles in hand, were fighting each other for a view at another window.

She was sick to death of this dilapidated, hellhole of a hideout. Mabel found herself wishing she'd listened to her half-wit family and pulled out earlier. The place was moldy and musty. It stank of human sweat, tobacco, and vermin. Now, two cars had come by in a short window of time, and one of them a cop car. It seemed like her life was in a vise, and someone was cranking the handle. Suddenly, she knew what it felt like to be locked in one of her cages.

Outside, the lake resembled a small ocean with large breakers of water splashing in the wind. Debris from the trees flew across the view, careening into the turbulent surf. *Maybe they won't look too close at the shack in this storm.* It was a hope, anyway, but why else would they be coming out here in a storm? She felt her luck was about to run out. They'd been spared a bit earlier when that pickup cruised through, but eventually, if they didn't move on soon, someone would find them. It just might be now.

Lifting her AR-15, she checked to make sure it was ready to fire. "Check yer weapons, boys. If they stop and try to come in, we'll need to blast 'em. Then we'll dump 'em in the lake and clear outta here." Mabel heard clicks and mechanical movements. They were ready.

The huge oak that overhung the building brushed violently against the roof. The ceiling joists groaned in concert with the creaks and cracks of the tree.

The car slowly splashed past the front of the building, silhouetted by the grayness of the lake behind it. Rolling between the abandoned mining machines and the huge, rectangular stones stacked along the edge of the lake, the Ford Crown Vic turned right to cruise behind Mabel's hideout. Moments later, it reversed course and again began to traverse the rough, gravel-lined road in front of the building, slowly heading toward the mine exit.

Rick Anders was behind the wheel. *He's just gawking. He don't see nothing. Maybe we'll get out of this pickle yet.*

Just as she began to feel that glimmer of hope, a glow bloomed to her left, casting a light on the old, nearly transparent curtains. The old woman glanced over to see Boyd lighting a cigarette.

"You bloomin' idiot," she blurted.

Outside, the Crown Vic came to a sudden stop.

~

Agent Franklin and Sheriff Anders cruised in silence through Cutters Notch on their way to investigate the quarry. The streets were empty, but broken pieces of trees peppered their vehicle, pushed by the storm's swirling winds. After turning right onto the county road toward the entrance to the abandoned mine, Franklin found his voice again.

"You're new to this town, right?"

"I've lived here a few years now," Rick answered. "A little over three, I think."

"But you didn't grow up here, did you?"

Rick cut him a side glance as he maneuvered the narrow, winding road, keeping both hands on the steering wheel, his pale knuckles showing his stress level. "No. What are you getting at, Franklin?"

"Jim. Call me Jim. Can I call you Rick?"

"Sure."

Franklin turned slightly in his seat to peer at Rick as he continued. "Did you know this little nowhere town has a thick government file on it?"

Rick laughed. The car swerved around another curve as the wipers sloshed water and leaf pieces from the windshield. "Why would the government keep a file on sleepy little Cutters Notch? It's just a tiny, over-the-hill, Hoosier village." As he spoke, Rick's peripheral vision caught Jim Franklin crack a hint of a smile.

"The history in that file goes back nearly two hundred years."

"What?" Rick turned to look at the Fed. "Bull."

"No bull. Two hundred years of weirdness."

"There's no way that's true." Even as he said it, he knew it probably was true. If the previous two months proved anything, it proved Cutters Notch was anything but sleepy. Rick slowed the cruiser to turn into an overgrown drive. He pointed at the smashed weeds and the mucky ruts. "Someone's been down this road today."

Franklin pulled his weapon and checked its condition before sliding it back in its holster. "Any reason someone else might have come through here?"

The car began to bounce on the rough road. "In this storm? None that I know of. Besides, there's a locked gate up ahead."

Moments later, the two men found the gate closed, but the lock was missing. Rick swung it wide, soaking his parka in the process. They drove on into the forest surrounding the abandoned quarry, the headlights reflecting off brown oak leaves and barren tree limbs. The wind had continued to grow until even the largest of the trees swayed violently.

"So, this is where it happened?" They emerged beside the water-filled pit. "This is where the old couple were cutting up kids? Where Sheriff Dunlap nearly killed you?"

Rick stopped the car for a moment as he stared across the water at the small shack overshadowed by the huge, ancient oak tree. Even that massive tree was leaning toward them in the wind. *This place changed my life.* It occurred to Rick in that moment that sometimes the darkest of events can bring on glowing changes, that passing through the clouds makes the light of the sun seem even brighter. This old mine had almost been the end of the line for him, but instead, when Maggie stepped out of that helicopter, the joy in her eyes relit the fires of his heart.

"Anders?"

"Yeah?" he replied, glancing over at Franklin.

"You were somewhere else for a minute."

"No. Actually, I was right here. Remembering."

"This is the place where Sheriff Dunlap tried to kill you? Where the Hicks brought their victims?" He did little loops with his right hand in an urging motion.

"Uh, yeah. Not something I really want to discuss, though."

Silence again fell on the cruiser.

They drove along the rough road that wrapped around the lake and into the lot where all the mining work took place in another era, passing through broken down conveyors with flapping pieces of rubber belt and rusted heavy machines that were sinking into the earth. The huge slabs of limestone stacked along the rim of the lake looked like teeth pulled from a giant's mouth. The large ruts in the road filled with water and resembled miniature versions of the lake to their left.

Rick glared at the small white building as they rolled past. It looked cold and barren. *A couple sticks of dynamite would clean this place up.* The sheriff liked people and had a knack for getting along, but his hatred was reserved for certain places—places like this one.

"Look at that big, ole oak," Franklin quipped. "The wind is really whipping it, big as it is."

Rick was grateful for that huge tree. As much as he hated the little shack under its large limbs, his heart had attached itself to the oak. If it hadn't dropped one of its limbs at the exact right moment, he and the kids might still be stuck—and dead—inside that stone tomb where Dunlap had planned to put them. *Would any of us still be alive? It's been over a month.* Rick was sure none of them could have survived that long, and thoughts of how horrible that would've been often haunted his sleep.

"The wind up high must be really bad," Rick responded as he watched the giant oak twist. "It's hard to believe it could move the tree like that."

"I don't see that gray truck anywhere," Franklin noted as he shifted back and forth, gazing behind machines and into the piles of slabs.

"I'll pull around back. Maybe he stashed it, on the outside chance someone did come check out the place."

Rick felt queasy. He steered his Ford beyond the small, white stone building before turning around the corner toward the rear. There was the sloping, overgrown road he'd snuck down after he and Danny had found the place. No recent traffic there. Glancing toward the building, he spotted the corner where he'd crouched before rushing inside. As he reached the rear, his eyes were drawn beyond the huge trunk of the ancient oak to the piles of huge stone slabs. The one closest was supposed to have been his tomb.

"Nothing back here," Franklin said.

"I see some tracks in the mud, but it's impossible to see where they went or how long ago."

"Hey," Franklin exclaimed. "That tree's coming down." He pointed to the base of the oak; the roots were lifting straight out of the ground.

"Oh, Holy… That tree's been there for hundreds of years." Rick threw the Crown Vic in reverse and backed out to the open work lot. Jerking the wheel around and shoving the gearshift back to drive, he hit the accelerator to move the car further away. Franklin bent down and leaned over to get a better view.

Rick paused in front of the building, his heart wanting to take one more look at the old oak. *That tree saved my life.* He peered up at what was maybe the oldest tree in the surrounding forest. A sense of deep sadness came over him. It was for sure coming down—right on top of that little stone building.

Rick hit the gas. The great tree broke loose of its footing. Glass broke. A shot rang out. Something hit the side of the car with a thud. Then the tree smashed down upon the structure, completely obliterating it. The outer limbs slapped against the trunk of the Ford as they barely made it out of the way.

"Was that a gunshot I heard before the tree came down?" Franklin asked.

"I think so. I heard glass break, too."

The two men exited the vehicle into the pouring rain. Franklin sloshed through standing water to join Anders. There was a large bullet hole in the driver's side, rear quarter panel.

Rick returned his view to the destroyed building. "Someone was inside there. I think they took a shot at us."

Together, they carefully maneuvered toward the fallen tree, wind and rain in their eyes. Within moments, they found four bodies. Robert Robbins was pinned by a broken limb, a jagged edge extended through his torso and through Mabel's too. She was underneath her son. Boyd and Parker were smashed against the now broken stone, outer wall. No survivors. Their semi-automatic rifles were also pinned beneath the large oak limbs.

The men studied the scene. "Seems this tree saved my life again," Rick muttered.

As Anders and Franklin returned to the still-idling cruiser, Rick's radio crackled. "*Unit one, come in,*" Judy Steinkamp's voice clearly carried some urgency.

"This is one," Rick answered.

"*Sheriff, you need to get out to the Terrell place off Robbins Creek Road. It's a couple miles south of your place. Tim Terrell just got home and there're things tearing up his pavilion.*"

"Things? Some sort of animals? I have a situation at the abandoned quarry. Just found Mabel and her crew."

"*Not animals,*" Judy replied. "*Not people either. Terrell couldn't explain it. He said there are dozens of 'em.*"

"Roger that. Do we have any deputies we can send out to the old mine, the one where the Hicks took the kids? There's been an accident, a fallen tree. Mabel Robbins and her family are dead, pinned under the tree."

"*10-4. I'll get someone rolling.*"

Anders placed his mic back on its hook. Franklin stared at him. "Is this how it happens here?" Franklin asked. "Everything blows up at once?"

Rick grimaced. "Pretty much." He shifted into drive, and the tires spewed water as he bounced off the lot toward the access road.

~

Tim Terrell left Traci and his daughter, Teresa, behind when he took his son, Tony, on a father-son adventure to Indianapolis for the day. The plan was to venture into the big city, eat lunch at the famous Shapiro's Deli, take in the zoo, and maybe go check out the Indianapolis Motor Speedway. Recently, Tony had become interested in racing, and the track museum was open year-round.

They made it to Indy and were making a run through the zoo, watching the huge brown bears munch on watermelons, when Tim happened to check the radar on his phone. He saw the huge storm moving in a direct line toward their home. At this point, to his son's disappointment, he made the decision to hightail it back to Cutters Notch. Without calling ahead, they hit the road.

Rain started pelting the windshield as they passed through Bloomington. By the time they turned onto Highway 257, it was an all-out gully washer. The wind kept trying to shove them in a ditch.

The wipers were on full speed and couldn't keep up. Debris was blowing straight at them.

"Everyone's battened down the hatches," Tim remarked as they passed through Cutters Notch.

"Something's going on at the General," Tony noted as he pointed ahead to the left. "There's lights flashing."

They gawked as they rolled by and turned left onto Robbins Creek Road.

"Could you tell what's going on?" Tony asked. "It was cop cars, right?"

"Couldn't tell. Too much rain."

Tim swerved as a good-sized limb broke free, flashing across their vision just before the bridge over Robbins Creek. "Geesh, this is bad. Hope we don't lose the barn." After a moment, he added, "or the house."

Tony gripped on the hand strap over his window, pulling himself tightly toward the door before wrapping his other arm around the headrest. "This is scary, Dad."

"Absolutely scary." Tim's knuckles were white on the steering wheel. His arms were tense. Even his gut muscles were flexed. *I haven't been this scared since we moved that stupid stone*. He kept that thought to himself. No need to make Tony any more nervous. Besides, a little bit of a rough storm was nothing compared to a giant spider shaman trying to suck the life out of everyone he loved.

Driving slowly in the weather, they passed Basketball Court.

"Isn't that Mom's van back there?"

"Back where?"

"On the court. First house in on the left."

"Don't know. I don't dare take my eyes off this road."

"Well, I think it was. Wonder what she's doing there?"

"She probably had to take that girl home. What's her name? Hope? The one coming over this morning to hang out with your sister."

"Really?" Tony's voice became animated. "Hope Spencer was coming to my house, and you didn't tell me? She's like…famous! We should've stayed home." At the mention of Hope's name, all thoughts of the zoo and the motor speedway apparently fled from the boy's mind. "She's the most famous person in the whole town."

Despite the storm, Tim had to smile. Tony was a couple years younger than the Spencer girl, but his son was obviously smitten with her. *I remember that feeling.* Once, when he was in middle school, he'd had a crush of his own. His mind flashed back to the time he'd bought the girl an anonymous Valentine's gift. Tena was her name. He'd snuck it over to her grandparents' house, leaving it on the porch with a little tag that said it was from her "secret admirer."

After a couple of more minutes, they reached their driveway. Tim slowed even more to turn in. As their tires began to crunch on the gravel, he abruptly stopped.

"Dad, what's going on in our yard?"

Tim's driveway was a long one. It wound slightly downhill, past their old brick house and the lone sycamore tree before stopping in front of their garage. From his vantage point at the top of the hill, partially hidden by shrubbery, he could clearly see the new pavilion in their backyard.

"Are those people?" Tony asked.

"I don't know. If they are, they're awful little."

They looked like oversized ants standing on two legs. They were swarming around the large stone on the pavilion. One was swinging a sledgehammer, striking the concrete berm Tim had placed around the huge, old rock. The handle of the hammer was longer than the thing swinging it was tall.

Tim pushed the call button on his steering wheel. The system beeped as it was ready to take his command. "Call the Bowen County Sheriff's Department."

He gave the woman on the phone all the details. She didn't seem rattled at all when he'd said they looked sort of like people, but then again not really. "Some sort of small, people-like creatures," he'd said.

"Turn off the lights, Dad," Tony said. "They'll notice us."

Tim killed his headlights as he hit the system again to call Traci. Whatever those things were, he wasn't going to go down there to face them alone. His priority was protecting Tony.

~

Forcibly carried home, Hope bounced around on Gronek's shoulders as he darted along the trail through the forest, splashing through some puddles and jumping others. She was drenched, but that was the least of her concerns. Her dad was badly injured. *It's all my fault*. The guilt welled up inside her, and that one thought wouldn't leave her mind. *I just wanted to make sure he was okay, but instead, I've probably caused his death.* She said nothing to Gronek but berated herself all the way to her bedroom shimmer.

When they reached the portal, Gronek dropped her to the ground and stood before her. "Hope, please stay here with your mother. There is real danger, and we need you to be safe."

The rain camouflaged the tears on her flushed cheeks. Her heart was breaking. "Gronek, will my dad be okay?"

The elf grasped her shoulders and looked her straight in the eyes. "I truly do not know, but all efforts will be made to save him. Mala is a healer. She is very skilled and will do all she can."

"I need to go to him."

"Not now. Too dangerous." He shook his head. "As soon as the danger has passed, either myself or one of my brothers will come for you. Watch for us. I promise one of us will come as soon as we can."

Hope hugged her little friend before crawling through the shimmer onto her dresser, leaving the elf in the rain. Once she was inside her room, voices echoed from the hallway.

"Release me," a squeaky voice said. "I demand it. You cannot keep me here. I will not tell you anything more." The lack of contractions in the language helped Hope to recognize the voice as that of an elf. "If you do not release me, my friends will come for me. You will pay dearly."

Hope hurried into the living room leaving soggy footprints in the carpet. An orange-skinned, fallen elf was bound and sitting in one of their side chairs. The cushioned furniture looked oversized with the tiny humanoid occupying the space. The creature sported a large lump on the side of its head.

Maggie spotted her daughter, darted over, and enveloped Hope in a huge hug. Over her mother's shoulder, she saw Teresa and Traci in one corner. Cindy Gillis and Anni Flannery were sitting at the dining table. Cindy rose to her feet. A sheriff's deputy stood before the elf, his hands on his utility belt.

"Mom," she sobbed. "Dad's hurt bad. He may not make it. It's all my fault." She drooped within her mother's grasp.

Simultaneously, Traci's phone rang, and the deputy's radio crackled. Moments later Hope and Maggie were alone. The deputy had grabbed up the elf and carried him out. Traci and Teresa rushed out the door and sped away. Even Cindy and Anni seem to have disappeared.

"Where'd they all go?" she asked as she choked back more sobs.

"I think something's going on at Teresa's house."

"Oh, Mom," she exclaimed. "We need to get out there, too." Hope pulled herself together. "It's the Ancient Gate to Abandon. The fallen elves are trying to open it."

"But there's the storm, and you're so upset."

"I don't care. Come on." Hope grabbed her mother's arm, pulling her toward the door. "Grab the keys and let's go."

Hope somehow took her still-hesitant mother to the car. With the wipers fighting a losing battle with the rain, and the wind rocking the vehicle, her mom put the gear in reverse to back out of the driveway. Broken limbs and random lawn ornaments flew by, some striking the side panels and windows. A tree fell, smashing part of the fence around Willie Robbins' pasture.

Behind them, a gray Ford F150 pulled up, blocking them in.

Nine

After returning to his pickup parked in the barn, Al pulled each of his captives from under the bedcover of the truck until their legs hung off the tailgate. Josh yelped when Havener grabbed his cast. Rain blowing from the open door again soaked into their damp clothing. The kidnapper pulled a large knife from a sheath at his waist, clipping the bindings from their ankles and knees, but leaving their hands restrained behind their backs.

"Now, stand up." He held the knife at eye level so they could clearly see it. It was at least eight inches long. Lightning flashed, glaring off the side of the serrated blade. "Anyone moves too fast, I'll stick 'em."

A grin crept across his face. The only thing that could make him feel better would be the presence of that little punk of a blonde girl. *I'll get her, though.* She was on the agenda for the day, as well. *I'll go back for her.*

"Now, let's get inside," he ordered. "I'm sick of this freaking storm."

The boys looked frightened. *Good.* The one with the cast was grimacing, all his weight on one foot. *Excellent.*

"He can't walk," Danny blurted.

"Well, you two carry him then." Al shoved Rose to her side and slit through the bindings on her wrist. After repeating the process for Danny, he stood back, giving himself enough room to react should they make a run for it. He waved the knife, ensuring its blade drew their eyes.

Rose grinned at him. She almost seemed amused. It was unnerving. The woman had just been kidnapped from her work, bound, tossed in the back of a pickup truck, threatened with a large knife, and there she stood grinning at him. A twinge of self-doubt crackled across Al's mind like static electricity.

"What's so funny?" Havener asked Rose.

"Nothing's funny," she replied. The strange stone hanging from the leather string at her neck glistened. It was so green against her freckled skin, and it appeared to glow, draped there between the strands of her wet red hair. "There's nothing funny at all." Yet, she continued to smile, keeping her eyes locked on his.

It was a strange, disconcerting look. Even as she grinned, her eyes looked sad. Again, the self-doubt sparked in his brain. *I don't have time for this*. "Get inside," he ordered. "Now."

Havener stepped aside, motioning for them to move with the point of the knife. Josh looped his arms around Danny's and Rose's necks; they lifted him up so he could balance on one foot. With Al's urging, they sloshed their way to the house, tracking mud through Rose's backdoor. Across the threshold, with the other three passing on into the kitchen, Al turned to close the door. It was already swinging shut on its own. *What*? For a moment, Al was perplexed. *Air pressure. It's gotta be the air pressure*. When he turned back, the others were already in the dining room. He hurried to catch up.

"I'm sorry 'bout the mud on the floor, Aunt Rose," Danny said.

"Screw the mud," Al said as he moved past them. "It won't matter in a few minutes anyway. Get on through here and up the stairs." He pointed with the blade. "I like your house, Rose. I love old houses, and this one is so interesting."

"It likes you too, Al." The grin was locked onto the redhead's lips as if her cheeks had been pulled upward and then pinned down with tacks. "I hope you enjoy your visit."

"Rick's gonna catch you," Josh spewed through a groan. The boy wasn't grinning as he glared at the man.

It's a good thing that kid's eyes aren't loaded weapons. Al chuckled uneasily.

"Take them upstairs." The voice was in Al's mind, but he wasn't sure it was his own. He shook his head. He shook it again, as if trying to throw off a fog. *Imagination. This old house is creeping me out.* "Come on," he said. "Get moving. Up those stairs, then left." He continued to wave the knife around.

Rose, with Danny's help, moved Josh into the massive entryway. The giant chandelier blazed above their heads as they hobbled through. Carefully, they took the stairs one at a time.

Havener took a position behind them, prodding them with the knifepoint from time to time.

As they reached the halfway point on the staircase, Al paused, turning to take in the intricate woodwork. The oak banister, the cherry paneling, the walnut frames around classic pieces of art. It was all so beautiful. Inside, a desire to sit down on the steps and study the detail arose, tempting him to lose sight of his day's purpose. Again, he shook his head. Something about the house was mesmerizing. It seemed to pull at his mind.

~

Rose knew exactly where the house drew them. She couldn't help but be amused by the way it was toying with the man who thought he was the one in control. He'd lost control as soon as he drove within range of the big old mansion. The house liked Rose. She could feel its affection. It let her come and go as she pleased. However, she'd learned over the years that it didn't feel the same warmth toward everyone. It controlled who even noticed its existence.

Al Havener's knife blade poked her in the back, again.

"Ouch. Stop poking me. We're going as fast as we can."

Helping Josh up the stairs was precarious. He could only balance himself on one foot and had to dangle the other, which meant Rose and Danny needed to lift him up each step. She could see the grimace on her nephew's face. His ribs still ached, no doubt. Josh, on the other hand, was unusually quiet. She'd always known him as the loud, obnoxious one of the three. Rose could count on him for some juvenile entertainment every time the kids entered the General. Over the last few weeks, however, he'd changed. After his injuries in the silo, she only saw him if she visited Danny's house, but it was as if a dark cloud hung over him—unless Hope was nearby.

They reached the balcony overlooking the massive foyer and paused for a breath. Rose glanced at their destination down the short hall to the left. A small amount of light filtered through the lone plexiglass window. The wooden jewelry box she'd put back in its spot on the table underneath the huge portrait sat open, waiting. The Native American in the painting, some random artist's rendering of an indigenous chief, stared out the door in their direction. That painting, and the one in the dining room, belonged to the house. She didn't dare remove them.

Rose knew exactly how many people had been *taken* to that room with the box. She carried all their memories—the collective memories of thirty-seven of Minerva Woodstock's victims. Plus, she carried the memories of the one who took them, Minerva Woodstock, herself. She even carried the memories from the short life of Minerva's sister. Finally, she carried the fuzzy memories of the strange creature from whose arm had fallen the stone she wore at her neck. Thirty-five of Minerva Woodstock's victims had passed their memories on before dying in that turret room, most standing right before that box. Rose herself had almost been number thirty-six.

"Keep going," Havener growled.

They reached the room and Rose again paused briefly to take a breath. The air was better in the hallway. Inside, Rose and Danny carefully lowered Josh to the floor under the window, his casted leg stretched out before him. The rain had certainly ruined it.

"Sit down there next to your buddy," Al ordered Danny. "Bind their legs, so they can't move," he ordered Rose as he handed her some zip ties.

~

Al watched as Rose secured the boys with the zip ties. Even as he did, he felt watched himself. The small hairs on the back of his neck stood at attention. Clenching his jaw, he glanced around the small room, his eyes landing on the large painting above the box. The Native American's eyes seemed to be looking directly at him. *Maybe bringing them here wasn't such a great idea.* The thought fled, chased away as fast as it appeared.

Al shoved his paranoia aside. He was here for a job and a little side fun. Then he'd hightail it out of the creepy, old place to find the girl and end his obligations in Cutters Notch, Indiana. Suddenly, he felt a yearning for St. Louis, of all places.

The redhead finished rebinding the boys. They looked like scared little puppies huddling together under the window. He grinned. "All right, Rose, just step over here where I can see you better." Al motioned to her with the knife to stand in the middle of the room. He positioned her beneath the chandelier, another miniature version of the one in the grand entry.

Al hadn't decided what to do with Rose. He was an extortionist.

Add to that, he was an arsonist, an embezzler, and a murderer, but he wasn't a rapist. Never had he stooped that low, though he did like to look at pretty girls. Maybe he'd just sit for a bit and enjoy her beauty before making his blade her destiny. Al leaned against the opposite wall, thinking, considering. He weighed his own twisted sense of morals, allowing temptations to roll around in his brain.

"Stay under that overhead light so I can see you good," Al ordered. She complied and he motioned for her to twirl. "Do it slow, so I can really see you. Fluff your red curls out over your shoulders." *She is a pretty one.* Al was a touch conflicted. Taking Rose was a whim, a spur-of-the-moment decision. He liked her looks and wanted to see more. But now he'd have to kill her too. Al didn't really want to do that. Maybe he should take her home to St. Louis. *I could lock her in the basement.*

He liked how her red hair blended so well with her creamy complexion and the faint freckles covering her skin. She was a tad full-figured, but he liked that better than skinny chicks. Her lips were full too. *So much better than the thin, barely visible lips on some girls.* Al took in the shape of her eyebrows, the curl of her nose, the height of her cheekbones, and the way they slid down around her chin to her neck.

That stone.

The crystal on her neck caught his eyes, grabbing his mind and drawing it in. "Stop," he ordered. The room disappeared around him. All Al could see was the mesmerizing fluctuation of the gem as it shifted from green to blue to red, and then back to green again. No longer did he feel the eyes of the man in the portrait. The decorative woodwork drifted away. The small chandelier rose out of his field of vision. The boys, sitting silently against the wall, became an afterthought. Even Rose herself, with all her beauty, vanished. The only thing his consciousness had room for was the stone.

It was beautiful the way it floated above her throat. Even the leather string it hung from vanished. He wasn't big on jewelry. When he'd married, he only worn a simple gold band. These days, he wore only a relatively new Timex watch. Otherwise, bling wasn't his thing. However, Al absolutely had to have that jewel strung around Rose's neck. He had to. No question. No options. Not for his ex-wife. Not for his mother. Not for the girl of the week. No. He had to have that stone for himself. It drew him in and begged to hang from his own neck.

Slowly Rose began to turn around again, taking the gem in and out of his vision. "Stop!" She paused, slightly turned away. "Face me," he ordered. The beauty turned, looking him in the eyes. Peripherally, Al caught her gaze and her continual grin as if they were features of a far-off landscape. He ignored them. His eyes and mind were captured by the necklace. Havener stepped close to Rose. He could feel her breath on his neck, smell the faint aroma of her perfume. Al raised the knife until the point rested just under her chin.

"Please, don't hurt her," Danny begged. "Please."

The boy's pleas drifted as a faint voice coming from somewhere in the distance. The meaning was lost on his ears like the buzz of a distant mosquito.

"You like it, don't you?" Rose whispered. "Isn't it beautiful?"

"Yes," Al mumbled. "Yes, it is." *I'll take the stone. Then, I'll dispose of her and the boys. I can be satisfied when I have that necklace.* Slowly, he raised his right hand, even as he kept the knife in his left positioned under Rose's chin. He slipped his fingers under her red curls and reached around to the clasp. Fingering the tiny fixture, he managed to free it and hold on to one end. The leather string fell loose in his hand.

"It'll look good on you," Rose said. "Go ahead. Put it on. Step over to the box and look at it in the mirror as you place it on your own neck."

Yes. Good idea.

Now, oblivious to his captives, Al Havener turned his back on Rose, stepping to the wooden box on the lone table under the portrait. Somewhere in the distance, the boys' voices murmured, but they were somewhere else, somewhere far away. The mirror awaited. He had to see the glowing orb against his own skin.

After placing the knife on the table beside the box, he pulled the leather strings to either side of his face, connecting the ends at the back of his neck. *Yes, it's so beautiful there.*

As the clasp closed behind Al's neck, the stone drew back against his throat like a magnet to a piece of iron. It tingled. He fingered it to try to loosen it up, but it wouldn't budge. It was locked down, as with superglue. His mind began to spin. Memories poured from the past into the present, seeming to skip across his brain on a trip to a faraway land.

Recent memories and memories long forgotten arose before fading away as a mist dissipates in the warm summer sun. As he stood there, the visions grew older and older. The birth of his children. His wedding. The first man he killed. The time he burned down his teacher's house in high school. The other time, when he was ten and his own father took him along on a job to murder a rival.

The memories grew older still. He fell off his bike and broke his collarbone. He received that Tonka truck for Christmas at five years old. He was potty-trained at nineteen months. He was born.

He was gone.

~

Rose stood in the middle of the room watching Al Havener as he stepped over to gaze into the tiny mirror in the box. She encouraged him the same way Minerva had encouraged her victims, to put on the necklace and watch themselves in the mirror's reflection. It was how the process worked; Rose knew it had to be done, or he would kill all three of them. Still, the grin she'd been wearing evaporated. A sad sense of expectation replaced it. There was no doubt what was about to happen. In the memories she carried, she'd both experienced it and watched it many times, though she'd never before instigated it. Not only had it almost happened to her—it had, in fact, begun to happen before she fought back—but she carried the memories of all those to whom it had happened prior to Al Havener. Soon, she would carry the memories of what happened to him as well.

Ever since that day so many years ago, when she'd turned the tables on Minerva Woodstock, Rose had resisted the temptation to carry on the old woman's work. This man would be her first victim, but unlike Minerva's, he was not an innocent one. It was the only way she could save herself, her nephew, and his best friend. She was about to feel the process happen the way Minerva had done it, and the memory of this experience would be her own.

It started slowly. She found herself filling with anticipation. New memories began to trickle into her mind, memories not her own, joining the myriad of other memories she already carried there like an ancient, moldy backpack. She saw his children. She saw his fights with his ex-wife. Rose watched in horror as he killed and killed again. He grew younger, yet there was virtually no innocence there. He'd been raised in violence, tainted from an early age. Rose felt her own tears welling for his broken life.

Then he was a little child, learning to walk. He got an ouchy as he fell, scraping his knee. His mother held him, kissing the pain away.

Moments later, it was over. He was fully inside her. He wasn't *her*, but she was now him. She cried.

Before her, he slumped to the floor. The last of the air released from his lungs, and his bladder drained into his trousers. His blank eyes stared into the void.

Rose grabbed the knife from the table and sliced through Danny's bindings. After handing him the knife to finish the job and release Josh, she turned to Havener's corpse to retrieve her necklace.

"We need to get you out of here," she said even as she refastened the leather string around her own throat.

"You're different," Josh said. "Your hair changed."

"Yeah, your face, too," Danny added.

Rose glanced in the mirror. Her freckles had faded and were almost gone. Her red curly tresses were now straight and brown. *Interesting.* The age creases were gone at the corners of her eyes. Flexing her arms, she had new strength in her muscles. *Very interesting.*

"What happened to him?" Josh asked.

"Looks like he just keeled over and died," Rose answered. "Let's get you home."

Outside, the storm still raged. The sound of tree debris striking the house continued. The wind roared through the branches. Somewhere in the house, the wind whistled through a cracked windowpane. Rain pelted the octagonal room's lone window.

"How can we go home in this storm?" Danny asked. "Josh is already soaked."

She looked the boys over. It was true. Josh's cast would have to be redone. No doubt about it. Still, she needed to move them out of this room and out of this house. Stepping over to Al's corpse, she fished into his slightly damp pockets until she took hold of his keys. "We're gonna take his truck, that's how."

Five minutes later, with Al Havener's remains littering her turret room, Rose loaded the boys into his Gray Ford F-150 before speeding into the storm. The lights were still flashing on a lone cruiser as she passed the General. Jerry Steinkamp was holding down the fort inside the store. She ignored him and gunned the engine south on Robbins Creek Road.

"Look! Another deputy," Danny blurted as they approached Basketball Court. "Where's he going?" The cruiser pulled out of the cul-de-sac, headed further south, lights flashing. A minivan followed on its tail, wipers fighting a losing battle.

"I dunno," Rose answered as she turned the pickup into the tiny neighborhood. "Don't really care at the moment."

Spotting taillights on Maggie's car, she pulled up behind the vehicle. Realizing she was driving Al Havener's truck, she rolled down the driver's side window to wave at Maggie.

Maggie's reflection in the side mirror betrayed terror. It washed away, though, as she recognized Rose, despite the hair-color change. Maggie stepped out into the rain; her dark, curly locks already drenched.

"Where're you guys going in a rush?" Rose asked.

Hope jumped from the passenger side and rushed to Rose's open window.

"Hope! You're back," Josh gushed. A renewed smile swept across his face.

"The fallen elves are attacking the Gate in Teresa's yard," Hope shouted over the roar of the wind. Water was dripping from her ears, her nose, and her flattened bangs. "They're on this side of the shimmer. We need to get out there."

"What's a fallen elf?" Rose asked.

"Rose, please move your truck," Maggie urged. "I don't have time to explain."

"Gotcha." She shifted into drive as Hope stepped back. "I'll drop the boys at Josh's house and follow you out."

"We're going too," Josh demanded.

"Let's just follow 'em," Danny added.

Hope and Maggie returned to their car. Rose looped the cul-de-sac, moving out of their way. Maggie gunned the engine, backed out fast, and sped away.

Rose hesitated, peering toward Josh's driveway. She should draw the line and make the boys go home, but they wouldn't leave the truck willingly, so she made a split-second decision. Hitting the gas, Rose followed Maggie onto Robbins Creek Road.

~

Gator, still sitting on the floor of the diner holding Rhonda, was becoming antsy. Not that he didn't like holding the woman. In fact, the reality was just the opposite. He really liked it. Still, he didn't like missing out on the action or being kept in the dark—literally and figuratively.

Outside, the weather raged. In fact, in the time since the sheriff left with the NSA agent, it had only grown worse. Debris skipped down the road in a constant flow, everything from paper to strips of siding to large tree limbs. He watched as an old car fender flew out of the junkyard across the road.

Inside the Quarry Pit, the power was out, and the only illumination came from an emergency light mounted above the main door. The windows were flexing from the air pressure. He wouldn't be surprised if there was a tornado riding along with this late-season storm.

As he sat there holding the trembling Rhonda, her head leaning against his shoulder and her blonde hair falling across his chest, he felt the need to do something. To move. To act. To be out there where the action was. Instead, he was babysitting two weird corpses. Gator glanced at the one he'd taken down. So weird. The blood looked like puke.

Cynthia Sweet, to her credit, was no longer cowering in the corner. She'd regained her curiosity and had begun to take a closer look at the dead creatures, whatever they were. After crawling out of her booth, she bent down over the body closest to her, lifting one of the thing's hands for a closer look.

"Six fingers," she mumbled. "Hmm. Long angular nose and ears that come to a point. A yellowish-orange tint to the skin with a slight hint of green."

To Gator, her words sounded like notes. Then he saw she was speaking into her phone. "Who're you talking to?" Gator asked, taking a defensive tone. "I don't think you should be describing our scene before we've even started our investigation."

"I'm taking voice notes."

Despite the dead NSA agent nearby and the fact they could've all been killed, she was nearly beaming with excitement. "I've been looking for aliens my whole adult life," she said, "and now, here they are."

"Who said they're aliens?" Gator retorted.

"What else could they be?"

"I dunno, but I don't see no flying saucer. They looked like they came out from under the diner, so I don't know what they are."

"I think they're demons," Roger Gilles said, leaning over the counter with his large chopping blade in hand. "I ain't particularly religious, but they acted like demons."

"I don't think you can kill demons with bullets," Gator replied. "But, then again, what do I know about killing demons?" The deputy carefully slipped out from under Rhonda's leaning body, then lifted her to her feet. "Come on now, sweetie. Let's move you into a softer seat." He deposited her onto a nearby cushioned bench. "I need to call in and find out what's happening." Gator hit speed dial, and Judy Steinkamp picked up on the second ring.

"*Randal, what do you need?*" Judy was her terse self.

"I need to know what's going on. I'm isolated down here with no radio. Where is everyone?"

Judy didn't answer right away. The group standing around Gator was quiet, waiting for him to relay what she said. Lowering the phone, he hit speakerphone mode. "Judy?"

"*I'm here. Look, Gator, things have been happening fast. Rose was snatched by Al Havener. Seems he got the boys, Danny and Josh, too.*"

"What?" Roger Gillis exclaimed. He darted back to the kitchen.

"*Then Rick found Mabel Robbins and her crew, crushed by a tree at the old quarry. Now, everyone's rushing out to the Terrell place. Seems a large number of those creatures are out there doing something. I don't know what to make of any of this.*"

"Thanks, Judy," Gator said as he ended the call.

Gator peered around at the audience staring back at him. Everyone was watching to see what he'd do, except for Rhonda. She was sort of in a daze, gazing through the window at the storm.

Roger Gillis, cellphone in hand, came out from behind the counter. "I'm outta here," he announced. "I've got to get home." He didn't bother to grab a coat. Instead, he unlocked the door and rushed into the storm.

"Take me out there," Cynthia Sweet said.

"What?" Gator lifted his eyes to meet hers. She was bouncing on the tips of her toes.

"Like I said, I've been looking for alien life my whole career.

Take me out there. I want to see them."

With Roger gone, Rhonda in a stupor, and Cynthia itching to go, that left only the kitchen assistant, armed with a butcher knife standing guard with Gator. His heart was pulling him to the Terrell place, but his responsibility held him in the diner. He stared at the young man, thinking, deciding.

The assistant cook appeared substantial and confident. Gator didn't know him, but he had a large Marines tattoo on the side of one bicep. He sported the Marine haircut too. Maybe just out of the service. Their eyes locked.

"Go on, Deputy. I've got this. I was an MP."

Gator turned a slow three-sixty. Rhonda leaned against the glass, staring into the storm. She was the only one Gator was concerned about. They could lock the diner behind them.

"What's your name, son?" Gator asked.

"Nathan, sir."

"Okay, Nathan, can you take Rhonda home?"

"Yes, sir."

"Can you lock the place?"

"Yes, sir," he said again.

"You do that then. Thanks." Turning his attention to Cynthia, Gator added, "Sweet, you're with me. Let's all get outta here." Gator took another glance around as the Marine began to coax Rhonda to her feet, throwing a jacket over her shoulders. Blood splattered and pooled at each end of the restaurant. One dead NSA agent. Two dead creatures. One massive storm. Weird things happened from time to time in Cutters Notch. Always had. They'd been pinpoints in time that he remembered growing up. Still, this one made the pie and munched on it too.

Carefully, Gator stepped over a dead monster and took one more sip from his Mountain Dew. "Let's move," he said.

~

Bayal stood nearby and observed his followers. It was nice of the humans to construct the roof structure overhead to keep them dry, though it only marginally helped. The wind drove the rain horizontally, but at least it kept the worst of it out of his eyes. The water felt cool on his hot skin. He took off his outer armor to better enjoy the soothing effect. His mind drifted to a cold mountain stream. The cursed side effects of hiding in the pit were his burnt skin and the smoldering, scorching flesh beneath it.

The elves around him used the tools they'd found to break away the molded rock. As he stood watching, chips of stone flew in various directions. Periodically, chunks broke free before being tossed aside. They were making progress, albeit slow.

Some of Bayal's senior lieutenants stood under the roof with him. Another lucky few stood under the cover of the Terrell porch. The bulk of his followers suffered the attack of the storm with no cover as they gathered around the pavilion, dodging windblown arboreal missiles from the forest. Bayal pretended not to see their resentful glares.

The surrounding forest shifted violently, first one way, then the other. From time to time, lighting struck, followed by the sound of falling limbs or whole trees.

"Master Bayal," one of his servants said, pointing toward the crest of the hill beyond the house. "The humans have noticed us."

Peering uphill, he spotted the lone vehicle partially hidden by shrubbery. "So, they have. It makes no matter. Once we have the stone, they will have no power over us."

"Should we drive them off?" The lieutenant sneered, waving his sword.

"They are like ants. Drive one off, and three more will replace it. Let them witness our work. Imagine their fear, and let it inspire you." Bayal smiled at the much younger elf. His eyes fell on the blade his subordinate carried. It came at the cost of one the elf's companions. Still, he found no sympathy for the fallen one. He needed the likes of this one and the other followers to get to his stone. And they needed weapons to fight the necessary battles. A few deaths were the price of success.

Over the centuries, Bayal had inspired fear within the humans many times over. He'd enjoyed his forays into their primitive world. First, they reacted with fear, later with reverence. Soon, they bowed to him as if he had some supernatural power. *Oh, the gifts they gave me*. He'd grown fat with the luscious foods and spirited drinks.

Even so, life as a pseudo-god grew boring. He found himself giving them ridiculous orders for his own entertainment, just to watch them carry them out. At first, he ordered simple things—back flips, roll around on the ground. Their antics brought a chuckle. Then he progressed to ordering them to do self-humiliating acts such as cutting off their hair, carving up their skin, and using pieces of bone or rock to disfigure themselves. It intrigued and entertained him as they carried out his increasingly dangerous instructions.

Growing bolder, he called for violence. "Kill the people in the next village," he ordered. "Pillage their storehouses. Enslave their children." Finally, he reached the ultimate demonstration of his depravity—he ordered the tossing of their first-born children into sacrificial fires. The religion they created around his self-indulgence still amazed Bayal. It drew in many thousands of followers. He smiled at the memories.

"When I have the stone, they will worship me again," he mumbled. "They will have no choice if they wish to live." Turning to his dozens of soaked elfin devotees, he pointed at an area between the pavilion and the hillside. "Form a line of defense. We will allow the humans to observe, but do not let them approach."

As he watched the human-transport vehicle parked on the ridge, another one pulled up alongside it. It had flashing blue lights affixed to the roof. Then, more joined those two.

"It seems we are about to have a party," he quipped. Behind him, chips and chunks of man-made stone continued to fly.

"Bayal, you must stop." The voice roared over the sound of the storm and the slamming of hammers against stone.

The centuries-old false deity turned his eyes toward the human house. Queen Agahpey Hesed stood on the wooden porch with two of her sons. From around the corner of the house stepped the one called Tomo along with the queen's guardian, the sasquatch. They aligned themselves beneath the porch roofline, shoving his followers out into the rain. Additional Adena warriors emerged from the house, one by one, each carrying spears and blades.

At the top of the hill, more vehicles gathered, some without flashing blue lights, some with. Humans exited the vehicles, grouping at the crest of the hill where the long, winding path from the house ended. Urgency gripped Bayal. His ancient heart raced. Overhead, the storm was beginning to relent, the wind dying down. The cooling rain became a steady drizzle.

"Are you about finished?" he screamed at the elves hammering at the berm. "Move that rock!" Turning to Hesed, he added, "You cannot win, young Agahpey. Soon, I will have the power to take whatever I want from anyone, anywhere, regardless the dimension.

Soon, you will kneel to me."

"Master, the boulder moves," said a leather-jacketed, fallen elf.

Sure enough. Bayal turned toward the ancient rock to see a group of elves gathered to one side, pushing together. Slowly at first, the boulder moved, then slid aside.

"Quick! Open the gate," Bayal ordered as the disc below the boulder came into view—the Ancient Gate to Abandon.

~

Roger Gillis swerved into Basketball Court as he rode the bumper of his friend and neighbor, Kevin Flannery. He watched Kevin's Tahoe skid on the wet pavement, then followed suit in his Chevy Impala. Both men straightened their steering and gunned their engines in a rush to reach their wives.

As the husbands drove up, Cindy ran over and stood with Anni under the cover of the Flannery porch. The house blocked most of the weather, keeping them dry. They held one another. Kevin didn't pull into the driveway but rather pulled up along the curb, ready to speed away again. Roger parked and bolted across the grass. The men reached their wives together.

"What the hell happened?" Kevin blurted; the reddish tint of his face flushed to match his wife's complexion. "Have they found 'em yet?"

Roger stepped up to Cindy who was shivering in the cold air. He wrapped his arms around his wife, pulling her in. "Havener grabbed the boys," Cindy muttered. "He took Josh out of his wheelchair right there in the middle of the court in the pouring rain."

"Oh Honey," Roger whispered back. "I'm sorry I wasn't here sooner. There was a thing at the diner, and I didn't check my phone."

"Where have you been?" Anni demanded of her husband.

"The storm caused a leak. I was dealing with it. My phone was on my desk. I'm sorry." Kevin looked heartsick. "He's got Danny and Josh...and Rose? All three?"

"He has none of 'em now," Anni announced.

"How do you know?" Cindy replied, eyebrows raised.

"I haven't had a chance to tell you. I was watching through the window just now as Rose circled the court in a strange truck. She had the boys in the cab with her. They followed Maggie and Hope back out."

"Where were they going?" Roger asked.

"Probably out to the Terrell place," Anni answered.

"Who?"

"Traci and Teresa Terrell were over at Maggie's a little while ago," Cindy explained. "Crazy stuff happened. You wouldn't believe it."

"You'd be shocked at what I'd believe right now," Roger replied.

Cindy paused, looking at her husband with wide eyes. "Anyway, something's happening out at the Terrell place. It's south of here, off Robbins Creek Road."

Another police vehicle roared past, lights flashing and siren blaring. The blue lights reflected off the wet surfaces in the neighborhood.

"Let's go." Kevin retrieved his Tahoe keys from his pocket. "Let's head out there."

The four rushed from the porch to the waiting SUV with wind blowing rain in their faces and broken limbs crisscrossing the cul-de-sac. The drenched parents soaked the cloth interior as Kevin keyed the ignition. He spun the tires, gunning toward the Terrell homestead.

~

Kenny lay on his back on a straw pallet inside Tomo's and Mala's hut. A fire burned brightly in the center hearth causing shadows to dance on the curving, thatched walls. Wind howled outside, but the stone floor was dry. Theirs was one of the few shelters built on the ground, near the rock outcroppings where the soil gave way to limestone. Even lying so close to the flames and covered in blankets, the man shivered as he swam in and out of consciousness. Beads of sweat formed on his brow in his struggle at the boundary of life and death.

"Drink this," Mala said, lifting a cup of warm soup to his lips. Kenny forced a swallow before falling back. His eyes fluttered, a shadow drifted across his mind, and he found himself in another place.

He stood. Alone. The room was huge. Gone were the thatched walls and the howling wind. Gone were the dancing shadows from the warm fire. Light fixtures, hung at intervals on a marble ceiling, glowed brightly, but he couldn't see the walls. The room seemed to stretch indefinitely in every direction. Occasional white pillars held up the space. Kenny couldn't tell what they were made from—perhaps more marble.

"Come over here," a voice said. It sounded familiar as it echoed in the cavernous room. Turning in a circle, he tried to locate its source. "Over here," it said again. It was a man. He sounded close by.

Kenny turned slightly to his right, and there the man was just beyond the closest pillar. He sat on an L-shaped sofa with his feet kicked up on an ottoman, one arm draped casually on an armrest. He wore an Indiana Pacers cap and an unbuttoned red flannel shirt with a dark t-shirt underneath bearing a vaguely familiar logo. Faded blue jeans and a pair of leather boots finished the combo. Every piece looked familiar. Kenny had vague memories of each item.

"What do you want?" Kenny asked.

"We need to talk. We've got some things to discuss. Come over and sit down where I can see you."

"I'm not sure I want to."

"Are you going to be a coward now?" the man asked.

Kenny's ego overcame his hesitancy. He strode over, taking a seat opposite the stranger. It hurt to move. He ached in a few places—his side, his legs, other places. "Okay. I'm here. Now, what do you want?" The man's features were familiar, like the clothes.

"You're going to die."

"I am?"

"Yeah, so we need to iron out some things, you and me. We need to set some things to right."

"Who are you? And how did I get here? I can't remember. I was hurt…lying on a cot. Mala was trying to feed me. What's going on?"

"Are you a doofus as well as a coward? Don't you recognize me?"

Kenny saw it then. The clothes. The shape of the man's chin, his nose, his blue eyes. He was staring at himself. It was like a reflection in the mirror, one that could move independently. It was some part of him—a piece of himself from somewhere inside. Those blue eyes locked onto his own and stared him down. He found himself both exhilarated and terrified. "You're me?" Kenny asked.

"I am. At least I am who you were, and I'm still you at your core. We were one. Then we were broken. The question is whether I will be who you are yet to be."

"What do you mean?" Kenny was confused. He shook his head to clear his thoughts. It didn't help.

"You're still listening to it. The specter still pursues you, and you still allow it a voice."

"I've told it 'no' every time. I told it to go away."

"Yet, you still listen. You still allow it to make its case. It was listening that started your whole mess. It's time to make a final choice, the ultimate decision."

As Kenny's core spoke the words, the far side of the room began to glisten as dozens, maybe hundreds of figures dressed in bright white robes gathered. Their faces lacked pigment. Rather, they glowed with a pure light. Forming a line stretching into the distance in both directions, the figures sang softly among themselves. The sound of their voices carried the most beautiful notes Kenny had ever heard.

Another sound erupted—a scraping, skidding, scratching, strident sound. It came from behind Kenny, interrupting his enjoyment of the melodic voices. Turning to see what caused the obnoxious noise, he spied black-robed figures. Again, the faces lacked pigment; they lacked any light at all. They were pits of darkness in the shapes of human beings. Before them drifted specters, swirling and undulating. These figures, like their white-robed counterparts, formed a line that faded into the distance in both directions.

"You're still existing in a middle ground," his companion self said. "Sort of a limbo-land between choosing to be truly good and giving yourself fully to the evil still haunting you."

It was true. The purity and the beauty of the white-robed figures called out to him. Yet, there was something in the darkness that drew him there, as well. Even as he turned away from his pestering specter, denying it access, Kenny still interacted with the spirit, listening and then answering as it probed for a way inside his mind.

"Our time is short, Kenny Burton. You are the mind, and I am the soul. You must decide now. Shall we reunite and move toward the light? Or shall we remain lost in this limbo-land. A third choice will drag me with you into the dark oblivion. The light will come no closer. We must go to it. But the longer we linger here, the sooner the darkness will encroach. It will overtake us. You placed us here, and only you can fix this."

"Why haven't you dragged me over there? Just drag me away from the evil influence."

"I cannot go where you won't, but you can drag me wherever you please," Kenny's soul responded. "We're lucky you and I have this opportunity. Most don't have the chance." The soul lowered his gaze and shook his head. "As much as I would like to force you, I have the same limitations as those you see arrayed in the glowing white robes. They could easily overcome the darkness, driving it into oblivion. They could force themselves over us. Yet, they are also limited by choice, by freewill. See the glow above them; see how no darkness exists beyond their line?"

Sure enough, a brilliant glow as bright as the sun centered and floated just above the line of figures illuminating everything. No shadows existed anywhere within his field of vision. Even the robed figures cast no shadows.

"What you see are only the effects of the nearby presence of the one the elves referred to as The Mighty One. His love for us has granted us the freedom to choose him, and in his patience, he holds back his legions of pure light, waiting for us to choose. Eventually, however, the light will prevail over the darkness."

They both fell silent as Kenny contemplated what his soul had explained. It was a lot to take in.

"You are the key," Kenny the soul finally stated. "Choose the light or choose the darkness. You can't have it both ways. Either way, I'm tethered to you, so you will decide our fate for both of us."

Ten

A small crowd had gathered at the top of the hill overlooking the Terrell home when Maggie and Hope skidded to a stop behind Rick's cruiser. Teresa's dad stood watching events unfold in his yard below. Hope remembered his name to be Tim. The man held both Traci and Teresa, one in each arm. Their boy—*Tony?*—stood in front. Traci gripped the boy's shoulders. Deputy Calvin Churchill was also there. They stood together, staring down at the busyness happening in and around the Terrell pavilion.

Hope glanced at Cal's cruiser and saw an angry elfin face glaring at her. She glared back. As good as she knew Agahpey and her sons to be, these creatures were the opposite. Hateful, horrible beings. Hope had seen what they did to her father. Anger welled up inside. It was all she could do to resist the urge to take a large rock to the elf's face.

Rick retrieved a shotgun from his trunk. Maggie joined him as he closed the lid. There was an unknown man wearing a clear plastic poncho over a business suit standing on the other side of the car.

Rose arrived in the gray pickup with the boys and slid to a stop behind Maggie's car. Danny jumped out of the cab, joining Hope on the ridge.

"What's going on?" Josh yelled, still in the truck and unable to move himself.

There was no reason to try to keep the secret of the elves at this point. They were out in the open for everyone to see. "The fallen ones are down there," Hope yelled back. "Must be dozens of them. They're trying to open the gate."

"What gate?" Rick asked. "I don't see a gate."

More cars and trucks pulled up and more people gathered. Gator arrived with some unknown woman in tow, her wet hair matted to the sides of her face. Danny's and Josh's parents pulled up next. Hope ignored everyone. Her eyes were fixated on the black hole of an elf standing at the edge of the pavilion. She could see the red glow from the cracks in his skin. Her stomach lurched. It was that monster that left those two elves to attack her dad. She blamed him but mostly she blamed herself. It was her fault. She knew it. Still, Bayal provided a welcome target for her daggers of pain.

Hope was furious, angrier than she'd ever been before. Her hands clenched into wet fists. Now her father was badly injured, maybe dying, because that greedy elf wanted something he shouldn't have. She'd just gotten her dad back, just begun to feel the strong grip of his arms as he hugged her again. Now, she might lose him forever.

What could she do, though? This was no dark spirit she could run off with the light of her aura. No one could see that bright living light in this realm anyway. She had no weapon. All she had was her anger and the strength of her will.

The voices around her faded into the background. The people lost form in her peripheral vision. Everything in Hope's being focused on that evil creature holding court on the floor of Teresa's pavilion.

One voice broke through. It was familiar. Elfin. Queen Hesed. Movement caught her eye as Tomo emerged from the side of the sycamore tree near the house. The hairy form of Sacqueal followed. Agahpey Hesed stepped into view on Teresa's porch. Gavin and Smakal stood with her. More of Tomo's people joined them.

"Who're all those people coming out of our house?" Traci asked. "How'd they get in there?"

Hope knew, but she didn't care to answer. Behind her, Josh was calling from the truck cab. She couldn't make out what he was saying. It didn't matter anyway. Nothing mattered to her now but that dark elf down the hill.

Bayal's voice boomed above the abating storm, "Quick! Open the gate." He spun toward the queen. "You are too late, Agahpey," he bragged. "The stone will be mine." His laughter rose up the hill, carried on the wind.

It was too much. A final straw. Hope could take no more. "Bayal," she screamed as she surged down the driveway toward the melee. She had no plan. She had no weapon. Bayal needed to pay for what he'd done, and she intended to deliver the bill.

~

Before Hope sprinted away, Danny was standing behind her, looking over her right shoulder. He'd spoken to her a couple of times, but she didn't answer him. It was still raining, although it had slowed. Heavy clouds maintained their canopy in the sky. Down below, the elves were moving like ants around the Terrell pavilion. He'd never been here before, but he assumed the Ancient Gate to Abandon must be in the center of their group, under the pavilion roof.

"What can you see?" Josh asked, still in the cab of the pickup. With his ruined cast on his still healing leg, he couldn't get out without some help.

The adults nearby were murmuring among themselves, trying to come up with some sort of plan. A woman Danny had never seen before approached with a deputy and stood next to Rick. She had a huge smile and seemed almost hypnotized by the events unfolding below. Another stranger stood on the other side of the sheriff. He wore a suit and tie beneath a clear plastic parka. The stranger didn't seem nearly as excited as the woman. He kept his right hand inside his jacket.

Another vehicle pulled up nearby, gravel crunching. His mother called his name. Danny turned to look.

In a flash Hope screamed, "Bayal!" She took off, running headlong downhill toward the swarming elves. Danny didn't think. He didn't consider consequences. Gone was the boy whose feet always seemed nailed down. Gone was his youthful timidity. Present was a young man whose friend was rushing into danger. Ignoring his mother's call, Danny followed. He didn't scream a name. He simply screamed and ran headlong in pursuit of his friend.

~

Josh sat moping in Al Havener's pickup truck. When they'd arrived, Rose jumped from the driver's seat and Danny jumped from the passenger seat, leaving him alone to watch the action through the rain-soaked window.

Scooting over behind the wheel, he lowered the driver's side window, stretching and leaning out to get a better view. Mostly friends, family, and neighbors were standing in his way.

His cast kept inhibiting his movement. Rose had moved the seat way up, and the stupid cast holding his leg together kept snagging on the steering wheel. Josh reached down, found the adjustment lever, and gave himself some more room.

"What's going on?" he yelled at his friends. Hope answered but barely glanced back at him. Something about fallen elves and the gate. He barely heard her over the rain and everyone else's murmuring.

Josh's nature was one of action. He'd literally jumped through dimensional portals for Hope. Being intensely curious, he couldn't stand to be in the back. Hope was upset, and he wanted to be by her side. Watching her from behind, he saw her clenched fists, the set of her shoulders, and the way she was focused on whatever was happening down below. The frustration and sense of helplessness at his situation were more than he could bear.

Lately, despite their boyfriend/girlfriend status, they'd seen less and less of one another. Sure, she'd spent time with him as he recovered, but she'd also split her time in the Arboreal Realm, visiting her dad. Hope and Danny had returned to school. She had homework. Now, she had a new friend, the girl who lived in the house down the hill, Teresa.

Am I jealous? Josh did a quick assessment. *No. I just miss her.* He considered the question again. *Well, okay, yeah. A little.*

She, Danny, and Josh had been nearly inseparable for over a year, but ever since the Hicks snatched her, and he and Danny nearly died trying to save her, their relationship had gone to a whole new place. His connection to Hope was special. He was in love, and it seemed she felt the same. Josh knew he had to share her, but he didn't want to.

The gathered crowd included deputies, Rick, the family who lived in the house, and a couple of other people Josh had never seen before. They were watching, talking, considering what to do. Then Rick retrieved a shotgun from his trunk.

As another vehicle arrived carrying his folks and Danny's parents, the crowd began to stir with more interest. "What's happening now?" Josh called. No one responded. He pounded on the steering wheel in frustration.

Suddenly, Hope screamed and disappeared down the hill. "Hope!" Josh yelled desperately from inside the truck. "Where're you going? Hope, no!"

Danny rushed after her. Maggie gave chase, as well as Rose. The balance of the adults hesitated, calling after them. A few moments later, Rick, his companion in the suit, and the other deputies joined the pursuit.

Without thinking, Josh opened the door of the truck. He needed to follow, to help, to protect. Instead, he fell to the ground, dragging his casted leg behind him, and landed in a muddy puddle. He couldn't get up on his own. As the dirty water seeped into his already damp clothes, he lay there, sobbing and pounding at the mud in frustration.

No one noticed him lying there until his parents rounded the truck. Cindy called out in shock, and Roger lifted him from the mud as Anni and Kevin followed the others down the hill. Josh wrapped his arms around his father's neck, sobbing into his shoulder. "Dad, I'm useless," he cried. "I can't do anything. I'm freaking useless." Then, stretching his neck, he scanned the area below to find Hope. "What's going on? Is Hope okay?"

Roger carried Josh to the crest of the hill. They peered down in time to see Hope and Danny slam into the line of fallen elves. Apparently, the unexpected charge of the human teenagers took them off guard because most simply moved out of the way, and the ones who didn't were knocked to the ground. Maggie with Rose on her heels followed the kids through the hole they'd made in the elfin line.

Hope stopped in front of the one named Bayal. Clearly from her body language, she was screaming at him. She was in mid-tirade when a burst of white surged from the center of the pavilion obliterating the roof, sending wooden shrapnel flying before spreading evenly in all directions. A massive web formed a fibrous cocoon-like bubble covering everything, including the house, for a couple of hundred feet. The edge of the enormous cocoon ended midway up the driveway, fully enveloping everyone and everything.

Rick, the suit man, and the deputies were left standing before the huge white dome, weapons dangling uselessly in their hands. Kevin Flannery stopped short, but Anni's momentum threw her into the sidewall of the cocoon. She stuck there briefly before Kevin pulled her free.

Hope, Danny, Maggie, and Rose were gone.

~

Dargo and Dorcas shivered in the cold air as they circled the area above the storm clouds, searching for the correct location. Their leafy tunics and elfin armor provided little protection against the cold upper atmosphere. Dargo had no doubt that his battle-ready force of elves in the armada following them were suffering similar fates. Streams of mist flowed from the undulating hooves of the flying reindeer as they dragged the troop carriers along. Below them, the storm raged on, though the edge of the storm was beginning to move through. The end of the maelstrom was in sight.

"The storm is finally beginning to move away," he said.

Dorcas, her shoulders covered in a thick blanket, glanced over the side of the carriage down toward the waiting earth below. "Yes. I see it. Do you think we are near?"

"Absolutely. Perhaps one more loop and we will locate them."

In silence, they made the additional circle, far above the forest, above the passing storm. They were in the Arboreal Realm, so they bore no concern for human detection, though the storm affected both dimensions. Dargo peered over his right shoulder, inspecting the following forces in their respective carriages. All were safe. All were in line. All were ready.

"I hope we are not too late," Dorcas whispered, just loud enough for Dargo to hear with his large ears. "I could not bear it if our queen is lost."

"And Gavin?" Dargo gave her a slight smile.

"Yes, and Gavin." She smiled back, nervously.

Below them, the storm continued to move to the northeast. They made yet another loop, and their view of the forest cleared. Many great old trees had been blown over. The storm contained a tornado because its path of fallen trees was obvious.

"I believe we are very near," Dargo noted. "I need to get my bearings."

"What is that?" Dorcas pointed beyond Dargo as he banked the carriage to the left. "It is like nothing I have ever seen."

From the ground rose a perfectly round dome of white material covering an area roughly a quarter of a mile in circumference. A large sycamore tree extended through it and wore it like a dress to a grand ball. At a spot nearby, a human-made trail skirted the dome, leading toward one of the human points of devastation they called a town.

Dargo studied the object. It looked soft and interwoven like a massive spider cocoon. He followed the human trail and noted the large sycamore tree. His heart thudded in his elfin chest. "We are too late," he moaned. "That is the gate, the Ancient Gate to Abandon. I do not know what has created that dome, but I know it is not natural. I believe the gate may have been opened."

Dorcas sucked in air, covered her mouth with her hand, and held her breath. Dargo brought the carriage down, landing it on the nearby human trail, his warriors following suit. They gathered on the ridge overlooking the centuries-old stone and stared at the strange, webbed containment. There remained a mist in the air, the fresh smell of ozone. Dargo adjusted the strap draped over his oak-leaf tunic so that the sword rested over his left shoulder.

He spied movement near where the dome met the earth—humans. From their clothing styles, he gathered they were Tomo's people. "Hey there, Human," he called down to the nearest one, a woman. "What has happened?"

Turning, the woman spotted Dargo and ran to join him on the hilltop. As she reached him, she fell to her knees, bringing her face just below his. "Our people are trapped," she explained. "We were being pulled through a shimmer, one at a time. Your fallen one, Bayal, was trying to open the gate in the Human Realm. We were entering to defend it. All at once, the stone moved aside, the lid lifted, and darkness spewed from the open hole." she bellowed. The woman fell further to the ground, sobbing. "Tomo and our people," she cried. "They are all lost."

Dargo withdrew his sword, moving past the woman. He raced downhill and quickly approached the webbed dome. His troops followed, drawing their swords as they moved. As the director of security approached the webbed containment, he swung the blade over his head, bringing it down in a slicing motion. It bounced off the webbing and flew from his hands. No effect.

~

Kenny sat on the sofa, a deep red one, made with some sort of plush fabric. Resting his head back, he stared up at a white ceiling that at one moment seemed very low and close, but the next seemed to go on far into the distance. He leveled his gaze again, darkness to one side, light to the other, and stared at his own soul. "I don't like the darkness," he said. A feeling like squirming worms started on his face, wriggled down his neck, and settled in his stomach. "It scares the hell outta me."

"Yet, you and I both know you're drawn to it," Kenny's soul replied. "It pulls at you. It tugs at you. It gnaws at your desires. It will have you unless you fully reject it—once and for all. Otherwise, it will have us both."

"But...how? How do I reject it? I already told that dark swirling thing to leave me alone."

"How did our daughter overcome it?"

Kenny was thinking about that, remembering that horrible battle and the bright light of Hope's aura. Then something struck him on the shoulder. It jarred him, knocking him forward. Turning his head about, he saw nothing. "What was that?"

On the other side of the sofa, Kenny the soul was fading, like an image projected on a white surface as someone turns up the lights. "Where're you going?" The image faded, faded, faded until it disappeared. Then something struck him again.

~

"Kenny Burton, wake up."

Kenny's eyes fluttered open. He tried to jerk upward, but Mala used her strong hands to push his shoulders back down. "What? Who? Where am I?"

"You were dreaming, muttering in your sleep," Mala said. "That is no matter. It is time for you to have more soup, and I need to check your wounds."

The big man relaxed, dropping back to his cot. Groaning, he gingerly moved his hands to touch the bandages. "I hurt so bad. So many wounds. Am I going to die? He told me I was going to die."

Mala ignored Kenny's question. She didn't like his chances. "Drink this soup. It will help some with the pain." Holding the soup in her right hand, she lifted his head with her left. She smiled thinly as he slowly sipped the liquid meal.

As he finished and lay back, his eyes moved around the ceiling of the hut. They grew large. Fear floated in his pupils. Turning her head to follow his gaze, she saw why.

Mala bolted to her feet. She gazed into the flickering shadows of the thatched ceiling. Swirling around above their heads was a particular shadow, one not created by the dancing light of the fire. It moved independent of the others, twirling and shuddering. Two red eyes appeared from time to time, looking down on Kenny as he groaned.

"You are not welcome here," Mala stated to the fluttering darkness. "Go away."

In this realm, she saw these evil spirits from time to time. When she did, bad things usually followed. Others could hear them speaking, something she'd never experienced herself. Mala was fine with that. She didn't want to hear their horrible words. Turning her eyes to Kenny, she noticed his furrowed brow and the grimace across his mouth. He squeezed his eyes shut and clenched at the blanket, pulling it to his chin like a little boy.

"Go away. Please, go away," he mumbled. "Leave me alone."

As Mala watched, the twirling specter floated down, hovering just over Kenny's wounded body, aligning his red eyes with Kenny's face. The man's semi-conscious struggling intensified. He pulled his shoulders inward, kept his eyes jammed shut, and pulled his knees up into a fetal position. From somewhere deep inside, the roar of a scream built and built until it exploded into the room.

"NOOOOO! Leave me. Leave me now. Leave me forever."

The specter jerked back and paused as if to consider Kenny's words. Then, it glanced at Mala. Its malevolent red eyes drilled into her brown ones. Mala didn't back down. Finally, it darted upward, exiting through the smoke vent at the pinnacle of the ceiling.

Mala leaned over Kenny as she sat next to him again on the cot. He seemed to be resting easier. His legs extended, his clenched fists now relaxed and opened. Kenny's furrowed brow and grimaced mouth softened. A slight smile formed above his chin. "Kenny Burton, you won that fight. Now, fight to stay with us. You hang on to your life."

~

Rick stood at the edge of the unnatural white structure. Shortly after the fibrous dome formed, seemingly from nothing, the others joined Rick, the deputies, Agent Franklin, and the Flannerys. Roger carried Josh carefully down the hill. Almost thirteen years old, he was a handful to carry, mostly bone and muscle, and the cast flopping around. The day suddenly calmed as the storm relented, though a layer of clouds blanketed the sun. Nothing made a sound.

Cindy Gillis reached out, placing her palm against the white surface. "Sticky," she said. "What is it?" She noticed Anni picking pieces of white from her face, arms, and shirt.

"A giant spiderweb," said little Tony Terrell, standing next to his father and peering up at the group of adults.

"He's right," Tim acknowledged. "They've opened the gate, and he's escaped again."

Everyone turned to face Tim and Traci with Tony standing by. Teresa moved near Josh to console him as he rested his head against his father's shoulder. The boy stared off into the distance.

"What are you talking about?" Rick asked. "Released who from where? And what do you mean by 'again'?"

"You won't believe us," Traci quipped. "It's crazy weird." She glanced at Tim. He returned her look. "And terrifying," she added.

"You'd be surprised what we'd believe today," Gator stated. "Weird or not."

Cynthia Sweet stumbled. She dropped to a nearby rock.

"What is it?" Franklin asked his associate. "Are you okay?"

"Look," Cynthia replied, pointing at the giant web. "Something large and black is crawling around on the inside of that thing." Even as she spoke, two football-sized black orbs passed in front of them beneath the semi-transparent white wall.

"Spiders," Teresa spoke up, turning away from Josh. "The shaman has brought his minions with him. There may be hundreds of 'em in there."

As they watched, more large black spots skittered across the inner surface of the dome.

"Shaman?" Calvin asked. "Like some native witchdoctor?"

"We need to get away from here," Tim Terrell said. "The shaman is hundreds of years old. He was a medicine man who got caught up in magic. Long story short, he concocted a spell that left him half man and half spider. He's gone mad. I don't understand it all, but it seems an angel rescued the tribe he was attacking and locked him in a chamber underground. They call it Abandon. The rock on my pavilion covers a hole that is the gate to the chamber. Once he's done with the people inside, he'll break through with his army of dog-sized spiders and come for us. We need to get away and find reinforcements if we're going to survive."

The group was speechless for a few seconds, staring at Terrell. It was Rick who broke the spell, taking charge. "Everyone. Go back up that hill," he ordered, pointing with the shotgun. "Let's put some distance between us and whatever this is. Get moving, now."

"But our son's in there!" Anni cried. "Kevin's sister, too."

Rick peered at the distraught mother, compassion flooding him. "Anni, I know. So is Maggie and Hope." Rick's own eyes welled up.

At the mention of Hope's name, Josh sobbed.

Noticing Josh for the first time, Rick suddenly realized that he'd seen Danny and Rose rushing down the hill after Hope. They'd been kidnapped. "How'd you escape from Havener?" he asked Josh. "Where is he?" He searched the hilltop to see if the man was standing up there, as unlikely as that seemed.

"He's dead," was all Josh could choke out.

The strain of carrying the boy was showing on Roger's face, but he kept his arms locked around his son, bracing his feet on the inclined surface of the gravel driveway. He leaned his head against Josh's, the tendons in his neck standing out from the effort.

Rick returned to the issue at hand. "We need to put some distance between us and these creatures, so we can get some perspective and make a plan. Come on now. Let's move."

They regathered in front of Rick's cruiser on the hilltop. Rick leaned on the hood of his car; the others grouped around him. Cynthia Sweet joined them but kept her eyes down the hill, staring at the strange white structure. A mist lifted from the forest canopy, but a light drizzle kept it fed.

"We really need to get as far away from here as we can," Traci Terrell stated. "We've seen this thing. It almost killed our whole family. It will kill us now if we stay here. When it's done in there, it'll come out here. It'll be looking for more."

"We can't leave our people to die," Gator erupted. "C'mon, we have to help 'em. We have to."

"You should call the National Guard," Agent Franklin suggested.

"And tell them what? What would be my reason?" Rick asked. "A giant spiderweb has spewed from the ground, and its creator, a hundreds-of-years-old witchdoctor is threatening our whole community? They'd laugh me down in a heartbeat. Probably hang up on me." The sheriff peered at the NSA agent. "And before you think you'd have any more luck, you should think it through. We need to warn folks nearby and in town, but for now we're on our own." Rick turned to his deputies. "What weapons do you have in your cruisers?"

"I have a Remington 12-gauge shotgun," Calvin replied.

"An AR-15, two full clips," Gator answered.

"Excellent," Rick said. "Bring 'em out. I'll take the AR." He handed his shotgun to Agent Franklin. "Give the other shotgun to Kevin here. You two go on back to Cutters Notch and start an evacuation. Stop along the way and warn Willie Robbins. He'll be the first one to go if this thing gets past us."

"What do we tell folks?" Gator asked, concern on his face. "People here are stubborn. They'll want to know why."

"I dunno," the sheriff replied. "Put your heads together and make something up. Call Judy as you go. Have her summon the other deputies to give you a hand. Also, retrieve some more firepower from the weapons locker at the office."

"You got it," Calvin replied.

"Excuse me. Pardon me." Someone was speaking from outside their huddled circle. A gap formed in the group. They all fell silent, turning to the sound of the new voice. A voice that was both pleasant and yet commanding. The aged frame of Clarence D'Angelo stepped gingerly through the space, using his cane for support. A slight smile graced his light brown face. Tiny droplets of water rested in his close-cropped gray hair. Stepping over to Josh, still lost in his sense of grief and uselessness as he clung to his dad's neck, Clarence stroked the boy's hair. "Young man, no one who is a great friend and has really great friends is useless. You have some very special friends, and you have been wonderful to them. They need you and you need them. You'll see."

He glanced at Teresa, his golden eyes sparkled, and he winked, then he stepped away and turned his gaze on Rick. "Hello, Sheriff," he said, crossing in front of him. "Excuse me, please." The old man edged past the big lawman and through the rest of the gathered crowd before continuing his course downhill toward the giant web. His gait was slow, measured, and careful on the steep, graveled slope.

Rick watched him go. He felt like he was watching an accident about to happen as the man limped down the gravel path, the cane poking into the earth with each advancing step. Still, he couldn't move. Stunned, his feet locked in place.

"Who was that?" "Where's he going?" "Shouldn't we stop him?"

The questions peppered Rick's ears. Recovering from the surprise, he called after his new neighbor. "Hey, Clarence? Stop. It's not safe."

"I'll be fine," he called back, waving with his left hand. "Don't worry."

"Stop him, Rick," Cindy urged. Others in the circle echoed the sentiment. Yet, no one moved. It was as if a malaise had fallen over them, freezing them in place. Rick wanted to pursue the man, but he couldn't remember how to make his legs move. Collectively, they were locked in place, staring down at the old man as he approached the giant spider enclosure. "We should go get him," Tim Terrell said. Still, no one moved.

As the group watched, Clarence arrived at the base of the cocoon. Pausing, he reached out, seemingly testing its surface with his left hand. It stuck slightly, and he pulled it back, examining residue on his palm. Then, he turned toward his audience and smiled, a twinkle in his eye. Raising his cane high over his head, he brought it down in one smooth stroke against the thick, impervious webbing.

Eleven

When Hope charged downhill and drove headlong through the line of fallen elves, she had no real plan. She wasn't thinking—only reacting out of her anger—being driven by the guilt she'd shifted to Bayal. Hope had been consumed with the idea that she'd brought this on her dad when she'd recklessly rushed out. Somehow, though, between being returned to her mother and their frantic drive to the Terrell homestead, she formed a new narrative. This wasn't her fault at all, she tried to convince herself. The fault belonged to that evil elf standing below within Teresa's pavilion. He'd amassed the fallen ones. He'd engaged Tomo's people, her father included, in his attempt to retrieve what he wanted. He'd captured her. Finally, he'd left those two miscreants with her, the ones who attacked her father. Fury had overtaken any rational thought, and off she went in search of revenge.

"Bayal!" She screamed as she slammed into the elfin barrier. The fallen ones weren't seasoned warriors. While all elves are faster and stronger than humans, most of these minions were simply discontented rabble. Elves who had fallen out with the Elfin society. Instead of slipping through shimmers to gather useful discarded items, they slipped in and swiped booze. They drank human alcohol and felt sorry for themselves. Their leader preyed upon their personal dissatisfaction, turning them into a ragtag gang of pretend warriors. It seemed they didn't know what hit them when the young blonde human girl charged, bursting into their circle.

Those elves she didn't knock off their feet backed away to give her space. Bayal turned his red-streaked, char-skinned face toward the angry teenager. A grin creased his chin. "Ahh, the party becomes more interesting," he quipped.

"Nozomi, no!" Queen Hesed's voice carried across the crowd.

Hope ignored her, keeping her eyes on the burnt elf.

"Your guards nearly killed my dad," Hope raged. "And for what? You want to come here and move a boulder over? Well, you've got your stone. Your boulder is moved. And because of it, my dad may die." She stood there, fists on her hips, lecturing him but unsure of her next move.

"Oh, you impetuous, young human," Bayal said, "this boulder is not the objective. It is not the stone I seek. No, no, no. I seek the special stone, the jewel, that the shaman bears on…" He paused as the lid was lifted from the ancient gate. The fallen ones lifting it away jumped back as a deep, dark hole revealed a pulsating blue glow. Stale, dark air escaped with a whoosh followed by clicking sounds—thousands of tiny tapping noises, growing louder and louder and louder.

Danny appeared by her side. Hope glanced back when Maggie placed her hands on her shoulders from behind. Rose stepped up beside her, opposite Danny. Then, literally, all hell broke loose. A white fibrous fog erupted from the opened gate, surging upward, smashing through the pavilion roof, and throwing wooden debris in all directions. The fog expanded, creating a dome that enveloped everything. The walls came down beyond the house, into the forest, and halfway up the gravel driveway. The white silken barrier blocked the storm, leaving the space in dull gray light.

The blue glow from the open Gate to Abandon intensified. It illuminated the interior of the webbed dome as the click, click, clicking sounds grew louder and louder.

The fallen elves, including Bayal's key lieutenants, retreated and joined Queen Hesed and the Adena people on the Terrell porch, wrapping themselves around the base of the house. Hope and her entourage moved with the others and took up a position in front of the queen. They all faced Bayal as the ominous noise continued to intensify. Something was coming.

Bayal, left standing alone, faced Hope and Hesed. "So, my army has deserted me?" he asked. "No matter. I am about to claim what I have come for." He laughed. "All your striving, Agahpey, and I am winning anyway. Your army did not arrive. You are powerless to stop me now. I will have my stone and then I will rule both the Elfin Realm and the Human Realm. Nothing and no one will be able to stand in my way."

The ancient dark elf's eyes locked with Hope's narrow gaze. He smiled at her, and it sent a chill crawling up her spine. His eyes seemed dead, like holes to nothingness. "Young one," Bayal addressed Hope, "I have seen your aura of life, and I will take it first." He smiled again, but there was no affection in the expression, only a greedy hunger. Bayal lifted his eyes, refocusing on the queen. "Then, I will have yours, Agahpey. I will take your memories of the years I have missed as I languished in that dark place."

"Mother, what stone is he speaking of?" Gavin whispered. "He has taken control of the boulder already. Is there some other stone?"

Hope could hear their conversation, but she kept her eyes locked on Bayal. Beside her, Rose tried to shove Danny behind her to protect him, but he kept pushing forward to be next to Hope. Around them, the fallen elves huddled together, shivering with fear. Tomo, now on the porch with the queen, was conferring with his warriors, telling them to prepare their weapons.

Hope glanced at Gavin standing with his mother. A dagger hung from his belt. Edging over as to speak with him, she snagged the weapon and charged a few steps toward Bayal. "You need to die, you evil monster!" She flung the blade. As if in slow motion, it flew end over end until it struck Bayal in the shoulder, buried to the hilt.

Hope turned to the others gathered on the porch. "What are you waiting for? Get him!" Then she turned back, meaning to rush the elf headlong, only to be stopped in her tracks as hundreds of large black spiders surged from the open gate. They poured out like muck from an overflowing sewer.

Danny grabbed Hope's shoulders, jerking her back. Rose wrapped her arms around both teens as Maggie stepped in front. Hope, breaking from Rose's grasp, grabbed her mother, pulling her away. Around them, Adena warriors and elves alike screamed and huddled with their backs against the wall. Some fled into the Terrell home, locking and barricading the door.

The arachnids, as large as beagles, skittered out of the hole, three or four at a time. They rushed up what was left of the pavilion, charged to the outer edges of the webbed dome, then climbed the side walls. Some hung from strands attached to the ceiling. Within seconds, spiders were all around. They carried black abdomens with red stripes. Dead, beady eyes the size of baseballs glared hungrily at the assembled humans and elves.

Bayal, for his part, didn't move. He grinned as the force of spiders scampered around his feet, forming a line three arachnids deep between himself and their likely victims near the house. The creatures seemed to pay the dark elf no mind, ignoring his presence. He chuckled, the knife handle rising and falling as he laughed, dark liquid trickling from his wounded shoulder.

The blue pulsating light from the open gate intensified.

Tomo bellowed instructions to his people. "Adena warriors, raise your spears and blades. This is our purpose. This is why we are here. We must defend both ourselves and our families. The shaman arises. Fight for those you love."

The array of elves, fallen elves, Adena warriors, and modern humans pressed together. Bayal took a couple of steps back from the hole. As he did, the shaman slipped out into the stale, cocooned air, revealing his half human, half spider form. Rising on his rear legs to over seven feet in height, he displayed the pulsating blue streak in his bulbous abdomen. His humanoid face grinned widely between the sharp mandibles that grew like deadly hooks out of the sides of his jaw. The ancient, evil abomination threw his two human hands together in a clap of joy. "Ah, here we are again," he exclaimed, "and what a meal I have before me."

Bayal, seemingly shaken himself by what he saw, stumbled to the side, gripping one of the surviving pavilion corner posts.

"I'm incredibly hungry," the shaman announced. "It's been a while since my last meal. In fact, my last one wasn't very satisfying." The human spider darted into the assorted spectators, grabbing a hapless fallen elf. He quickly enveloped it in what looked like a web sleeping bag before hanging it upside down from the crown of the webbed dome. After stepping back to examine his work, the spider shaman used his mandibles to puncture the elf's throat, allowing the victim's blood to drain into his open mouth. The whole horrifying action took no more than thirty seconds. Finished, the giant arachnid gave a loud sigh.

"Who is next?" Oversized eyes bulging from his human face darted from person to elf to person. "Where is that young girl of faith I met during my last excursion? Is she not here?" His vision settled on Hope. "Who is this one?" Moving a few steps closer, he leaned toward the girl for a better look as the crowd pressed further back. Hope stood her ground, though terror had a stranglehold on her throat. She could hardly breathe.

"Ashtor, leave her," Bayal said. "She is mine."

The shaman turned to Bayal. "Someone is here who knows my real name?" He skittered away from the terrified crowd for a closer look at the dark elf. "Bayal, is that truly you?"

Tomo whispered to Queen Hesed. "I am confused. How can they know one another?"

"I heard rumors," Hesed replied, "when I was a young elf, of a fallen human who consorted with Bayal. We thought they were only stories because he never made an appearance. It seems they were more than childish fables."

"It is I," Bayal stated to the giant arachnid. "I am glad to see you again, although this form you take is distressing. What happened to you during my long absence?"

The man-spider stepped back and, using his human arms, gestured across his body—the almost human head to the bulging, bulbous abdomen. "This?" He laughed loudly. "This is the result of my own foolishness. But I intend to make the most of it. I will feast on the flesh of all. The world is my dinner table, you might say." The shaman examined Bayal in return. "Your form has changed, as well. It appears as if you've been roasting over a fire." Again, Ashtor laughed. "Perhaps, you are a little too well done."

"I spent two millennium in the pit near the core of the Earth," Bayal explained. "*Her* father's work." He pointed to Queen Hesed. Turning his attention her way, Bayal addressed her. "Agahpey, where is your father? Why is he not here with us at this little reunion?"

The queen with two of her sons flanking her stepped forward to reply. "Bayal, your brother was wounded badly in his last battle with you and your forces. He did not survive."

The dark elf stared at Hesed for a long moment. Then his eyes dropped to the ground at the news she'd provided. "That is unfortunate. Unfortunate, indeed. I did not wish that."

"Nevertheless, you brought it upon him," Hesed snapped.

Bayal took a deep breath. "Ashtor, I've come to free you and collect the stone I left in your possession when last we met. You are free. I ask now that you return the jewel."

Ashtor laughed hysterically. He laughed a long time. All the while, Bayal stared at him until eventually the gaze became a glare.

"Why is this so funny?"

"Because, my old friend, I do not have the stone. I've not had it since I was entombed in that dark well below. It fell from my arm as I was forced inside. I appreciate the freedom. I truly do. For that, you will be spared, but I cannot return your jewel."

"You will spare me?" Bayal shouted. He stepped toward the shaman. "Spare *me*? I have been your friend for thousands of years. We have pillaged villages and swayed the hearts of entire peoples together, and now you flippantly promise to spare me?"

Ashtor ignored Bayal's rant. Grinning, he lifted his pincers at an angle to his face. "Bayal, in this form I have power beyond any you have ever experienced. And a hunger that is unimaginable. Even now I can barely hold back the desire to string up and drain the full lot of our audience. For me to spare you is a great kindness."

The beast turned his attention to the array of humans, elves, and the lone sasquatch. "Where is the girl of faith from my last visit? I was hoping to see her again." He moved back and forth before them, examining each until his bulbous eyes locked onto Rose. Again, the creature grinned broadly.

"Bayal," he said as he turned to face his one-time friend, "I no longer have the stone, but it is here. Look! It dangles from this woman's throat." He pointed one long, slender, hairy spider leg directly at Rose.

~

Kenny opened his eyes, but it hurt to move. After attempting one lame effort to turn over, which fired a spike of agony up his left side, he remained still, and stared at the thatched ceiling with the smoke hole in the center. Physically, he felt weak and in tremendous pain, but inside he felt clean, almost pristine, for the first time in his memory. Smiling, he tried to take a deep breath. Pain again shot from several wounds as his chest expanded to take in the air, tearing the congealed cuts. "Ow," he groaned.

Mala attended him. Sitting carefully on the edge of the cot, she swiped a warm cloth across Kenny's forehead, staring deeply into his eyes. "Your soul looks renewed, yet you must eat some more. If you do not, you will grow weaker."

Kenny shook his head. It hurt too much to lift himself even to slurp the soup. He gazed back into the Mala's brown eyes. "I hurt so bad," he whispered, "but on the inside I feel so good." He attempted another smile. "I feel clean again."

"Yes, yes," Mala replied. "The evil shadow is gone now." She spooned some of the soup and held it to his lips. "Please. You need to eat so your body has the strength to heal."

He parted his lips, allowing the warm broth to flow into his mouth. It tasted good and it whet his appetite for more. Kenny tried to lift his head from the pillow, attempting to pull himself onto his elbows. Sharp jolts again rippled through his large frame, and he collapsed back to the bedding.

"Let me feed it to you with a spoon. You stay down and rest easy. There is no rush."

Kenny nodded, resigned to the much slower process. It tasted incredible and felt even better as it flowed down his throat. A new feeling overwhelmed him. Gratefulness.

~

Mala managed to spoon about half the bowl before Kenny nodded off. His eyelids grew heavy; he stopped responding to her prodding with the utensil. Placing the clay bowl and wooden spoon on a side table, she peered down at the big man as he slept. She felt some worry lines form crinkles across her forehead. Despite the changes within, his wounds were many and terrible. Much blood loss. His skin was pale and cool to the touch, sometimes hot when the fever struck him. She could sense him growing weaker despite the soup.

Mala's concern for Kenny was only eclipsed by her concern for her husband. Tomo had rushed off into the battle to protect that dreaded rock they were to guard. As leader of the Adena people, he had no choice, but it still sat heavy upon her heart. After his previous brush with the demon held underneath the gate, she harbored many nightmares of what could happen to Tomo.

She knew the histories, the stories handed down from generation to generation. Mala understood the obligation they had to prevent the opening of the gate. Still, she yearned for a time when she could have her husband's undivided attention. He'd been the love of her life since she was a young girl, and that affection had only deepened with age.

One of the village children rushed in from the common yard. "Mother Mala," the girl loudly called, pausing to wipe her wet feet on a mat.

"Shh," she answered. "You will wake Kenny Burton. He needs his rest. Why have you returned?" she asked in a hushed tone.

The child, a young girl with dark hair that hung to her back, tiptoed to Mala's side. "Something strange is on the horizon. We have seen an army of elves pass over in carts pulled by flying reindeer, and a large white dome has formed over the Gate to Abandon."

Mala leapt to her feet, rushing outside. Crossing the clearing from their spot along the side of the ridge, she viewed over the treetops to the area where the stone kept the gate closed. Instead of the beauty of the forest, a fibrous dome of white enveloped everything, mixing with the trees, and blocking any view of the spot they took so much care to guard.

Her heart sank with despair. The evil shaman had escaped again.

~

After dropping Hope through the shimmer into her bedroom, Gronek had sprinted off through the pouring rain and the blowing trees toward the ancient gate. He was fast, but it was still a long run with numerous storm-related obstacles demanding detours—fallen trees and large pools of water. It stopped raining as he darted through the forest. When he finally emerged on the hillside above the gate, he was shocked to find the huge dome of webbing and an army of elves hacking away at it with their swords and blades, seemingly to no avail.

He recognized some of the elfin crew. They were from his mother's home in the southern forest. He spotted Dargo, the minister of security, and Dorcas. A sense of relief swept over him. "Ahh, reinforcements have finally arrived." Still, he did not see his mother or his brothers anywhere among the forces.

Gronek trotted down the hill to join his fellow elves. "Dargo, it is so good to see you," he shouted as he approached.

Dargo paused his hacking, turning to see who called to him. "Gronek, my prince," he said and briefly bowed, dipping his forehead to the hilt of his sword. "You are here and safe. Are you alone?"

Gronek ignored the question. Brushing aside the formalities, he responded with a question of his own. "Where is my mother? My brothers?"

"We are trying to gain access," Dargo said, his eyes turning toward the monstrously huge dome. "Yet, we cannot seem to cut through to reach them."

"They are inside? What is this thing?"

Dorcas approached. "One of Tomo's people claims it is a giant spider's web. Their people are inside. I have just been informed that the queen and your brothers are also trapped within the cocoon. The Gate to Abandon has been opened."

Gronek pulled his own blade and joined the others hacking at the fibers. He sliced and poked and chopped, but nothing penetrated the webbing. As with the blades of the other elves and the Adena warriors, his blade seemed to have no effect. The webbing repelled the force of each swing.

Above them the cloud cover was thinning. More light was filtering through. A mist of fog hung around the base of the dome as it met the forest.

As they chopped at the impenetrable barrier, elves in the middle and Adena to each side, a murmur arose behind them. A bright shining light began to drift down the hillside toward their position— a sliver at first, then more of a pillar as it neared. Gronek was the first elf to notice it. He pulled at Dargo's sleeve to grab his attention. When it neared, they moved aside.

"Is that—?" Gronek whispered.

"I am not sure," Dorcas muttered. "It is surely brilliant. It could be."

To each side, the Adena all took a knee. They bowed their heads and covered their eyes. Suddenly, Gronek found himself kneeling. The elfin forces all found their knees.

The light reached the edge of the dome, pausing where Dargo had stood. A flash slashed out from the bright, hovering column of light. It caused a rift in the webbing. A gap opened in the structure. The sliver of brilliant light slipped inside.

Gronek thrust himself at the opening, but as he reached it, the gap closed, resealing itself as if nothing had happened. The elf stuck to the surface from face to feet. Dargo and Dorcas peeled him away.

"We must get inside," he bellowed, chopping furiously at the web. His flurry of strokes left no mark, no damage at all.

~

Teresa, Hope's new friend, stood with her mother among the

group of people gathered on the gravel driveway that led down the hill toward where her home stood enveloped in the shaman's domed web. Like the others, when Clarence D'Angelo passed through their group on his journey downhill, she'd been initially shocked into inactivity. He moved slowly and carried a cane. The man was obviously old. She didn't understand what he could be thinking. Then, she'd caught sight of his golden brilliant eyes, and he'd winked at her. Immediately, she recognized the old man for who he really was. "Mom, I know him," she said as he trundled away.

"Know him? From where?"

"From here. He's been here before. He looked so awesome and so different then, but I recognize his eyes." Teresa wrapped her arms around her mother and gave her a tight hug. "It's going to be okay," she whispered. "You'll see."

As they looked on, Clarence reached the edge of the giant structure. Pausing only for a moment, he glanced back up the hill toward the group and smiled. He raised his cane in the air, slamming it down on the impenetrable webbing. The blunt object sliced through the fibers more easily than a new blade on a hairy leg. A gap opened, and the old man slipped inside.

Rick and the others eventually found their feet and raced down the hill, but the gap sealed up behind the old man. When they reached the spot, there was no sign, no mark, no crease to show that there had ever been an opening.

"What just happened?" Rick asked. "How'd he do that?"

"I dunno," Franklin muttered.

Teresa approached, placing her hand on the side of the web, and she chuckled to the point of giddiness. "It'll all be over soon," she said. "You'll see."

Twelve

Rose, already terrified, felt a new wave of terror rush through her as the spider shaman pointed one of his arachnid legs toward the jewel she wore at her throat. She fingered the tingling stone reflexively. She'd long wondered about the origins of the strange piece of jewelry that she'd violently inherited from Minerva Woodstock. Rose still didn't have a clear picture, but she now knew that its history was older, darker, and more dangerous than she'd even imagined.

Bayal's eyes turned toward her, locking in on the string dangling at her neck. As the attention was thrown her way, the Adena warriors instinctively stepped back further. Rose found herself isolated, standing alone before the ancient, grinning elf. The pulsating red glow showing in the cracks of his blackened skin brightened and intensified. The knife Hope had thrown still bobbed up and down in the creature's shoulder with trickles of black blood oozing around the wound.

Danny stepped in front of his aunt. "You stay away from her!" Hope joined him, despite her mother pulling at her shirt. Together, they formed a teenage wall of defense.

"Seize the woman," Bayal ordered. As he spoke, more blood drained from the wound in his shoulder. The members of his horde, however, were still in terror of the dog-sized spiders scurrying around on the ground, crawling on the woven walls, and dangling from oversized strands of webbing. They refused to move. Instead, they fell back among the Adena forces, seeking to disappear behind the taller humans.

Seeing he would receive no assistance from his fallen ones,

Bayal addressed Rose directly. "Woman, you have something that belongs to me. I have waited long and traveled far. All that you see here today was done so that I could retrieve what you have resting on your throat. You must now return what is mine. I will have it."

Her knees wobbled, and Rose gripped a post on the Terrell's porch. She rested her trembling left hand on Danny's shoulder and whispered into his ear. "You need to step aside, Danny. There's nothing you can do to save me. Don't get in the way."

"Aunt Rose..." Danny stammered.

"You've suddenly become quite the brave young man. I'm proud of you." She smiled weakly, turning his face toward her own. "Let me face my fate."

"No," he screamed.

"Enough of this," the shaman stated. A flow of silk surged from Ashtor's curled abdomen, striking Danny in the chest, splatting from his chin to his groin. The shaman jerked the silver strand, pulling the boy from the porch and wrapping him quickly within a silken cocoon. Danny now dangled from the rain gutter. "Another morsel for me," the giant arachnid quipped. "Bayal, retrieve your precious jewel. I wish to continue with the next course of my feast." He laughed, an odd insectile chatter.

Danny struggled, unable to break free. Hope tried to go to him, but Maggie held her fast, wrapping both arms around her from behind.

Another shot of spider silk emerged from Ashtor's abdomen, striking Rose in the chest. Jerked, she flew from the porch into the clearing between the assembled crowd and the two vile beings, Bayal and Ashtor. Landing on her knees, Rose glared at the elf and the arachnid. Her newly straight, now-brown hair hung loosely on each side of her face. The air in the space smelled fetid, and nothing moved. Everything went silent.

A bird, one that had been hiding in an enveloped tree, flew from its refuge, seeking a better spot in another tree. Everyone's eyes were pulled toward the sudden noise even as one of Ashtor's creatures snagged it in midair, then cocooned and hung it nearby.

"You want the necklace?" Rose blurted. "Well, here it is," she said, lifting her chin. The strange stone glimmered in the dull light. "I won't give it to you willingly, though. If it's really yours, you'll have to come take it."

Bayal's eyes locked onto the crystalline light below her jawline. She felt the attractive power it emitted, snagging his attention. The ancient elf's eyes glazed as he inched toward her.

"I have waited so many centuries to regain this precious prize," Bayal murmured. "You have no idea of the power you possess."

Along the edge of the Terrell home, the assembled assortment of Adena warriors, both fallen and royal elves, and one sasquatch stood silent as Bayal advanced on the kneeling woman. The burnt elf moved slowly, apparently relishing the experience.

"Mother, what will happen when Bayal retrieves the stone?" Gavin asked.

Rose heard the question, creasing her lips into the slightest of smiles. She accepted her fate.

"I fear we will all perish," Hesed replied. "This is where we end. Perhaps your brother will survive us. Perhaps Dargo will protect him. The battles will be many, and they will be furious."

Bayal stepped before Rose. Reaching down with his charred right hand, he took her left, lifting her to her feet. The sparkle of the jewel reflected in his coal black eyes as they stared at her necklace. Up close, the pulsating red crevices in his skin seemed to glow from a source deeper than the creature's small body occupied. "I have missed you so," Bayal almost whispered to the crystal. "Now, I need your power to restore myself to my full glory. Once you are safely around my neck again, I will drain the life force from my kin and my minions, and you will remake me into what I was in the prime of my youth." A huge smile stretched across his face, cracking the charred skin as his smile spread. Red light glowed through the new fissures.

Ashtor tried to slow his one-time friend. "Bayal, I do not think you should act too hastily. If she carries the crystal safely and does not give it to you willingly—"

Bayal was not dissuaded. Reaching out, he snatched the necklace from Rose's neck. The leather string released with little force. Rose stood calmly; her stare was unwavering as the elf fumbled with the leather ends. He lifted it to his own throat, tying the leather behind his head. When the stone neared the elfin skin, it snapped into contact. Rose's eyes rolled back, her irises buried behind her eyelids. Dropping to the ground in a seated position, she supported herself on her hands and leaned her head back. The life essences began to flow.

~

When Bayal spied the stone unexpectedly hanging from the woman's neck, his mind flashed back to the time eons ago when he'd first acquired it. He was a rather young elf at the time, only just beginning his forays into the Human Realm, seeking treasure, soaking in the accolades from the simple people, and stoking his ego. His skin, now charred as black as coal, then was still smooth and clear and green.

Bayal walked along a river, the one called the Euphrates. The sky grew darker as the sun set red in the west. He had been in the human domain for over a full day, risking what elves typically did not risk—discovery.

Ahead, he saw smoke and the glow of a fire. He didn't expect to find people in this remote place, so he crept carefully, staying hidden behind the scrub bushes. Incense filled the air. Rhythmic chants met his oversized ears. There were no words—only incomprehensible utterances and guttural sounds.

Slowly, he poked his angular nose through the foliage until he could see the source. One human woman sat in the clearing, her hair fanned out around her head like a lion's mane, floating on the wind blowing across the fire. A breeze blew in his face, carrying the exotic smells the woman created as she tossed various herbs into the burning wood. The flames leapt with each injection of a new substance. A full moon was rising on the horizon beyond the human female.

On a flat rock positioned between the woman and the raging fire sat a strange crystal. Its light snagged Bayal's eyes. He felt drawn, called even. As the woman waved her open palms over the colorful stone, Bayal slipped from his hiding place. He approached silently behind the witch as she continued her magical intonations, pulling his blade as he strode. "I will have that stone," he whispered into her ear as he laid the blade near her throat. "It calls to me, and I will have it."

The woman relaxed in Bayal's grasp. Her hands ceased to wave. The smoky incense glowed in the firelight. "Take it, elf," she calmly answered. "The stone chooses who it will. If it chooses you, it will be yours. If not, you will soon reside inside my mind." Then she laughed, an almost hysterical cackle.

The woman's reaction disconcerted Bayal. He expected a fearful timidity, or perhaps a terror-filled submission, but the laughter screamed a confidence that gave him pause. "Where did you acquire that rock? Does it hold some power?"

The firelight danced off the crystal facets, giving it a living, mesmerizing glow of fluctuating hues. The greedy elf could not move his gaze away. The more he peered at it, the more he knew it was destined to be his.

The woman did not immediately answer, letting the stone have its effect.

"I asked you a question. Answer me now. Where did you obtain that stone?"

"It once rested in the crown belonging to an ancient king, a king that reigned for decade upon decade in times of old. When he finally died, they say he lived to be hundreds of years old. The crown was buried with him. I retrieved it and plucked the stone from the headpiece myself. If you want to know its power, by all means, pick it up. Study it." A grin slipped across her darkly tanned face. Her skin was smooth and soft, like a young girl's skin resting on a hag's face.

Gripped by the hypnotic colors flowing from the strange jewel, Bayal briefly lost track of his captive's presence. His grasp loosened slightly, and she took advantage of his momentary lapse, tearing herself away. As she jerked, her neck brushed against the blade at her throat. The sharp edge did its deadly work, slicing cleanly into her flesh, cutting the artery that carried her lifeblood.

At first, she didn't realize her mistake, dancing away and laughing. Then, she looked down to see her tan woven tunic covered in the warm red blood gushing from her wound. She grasped at her neck, shock spreading across her formerly grinning face.

Bayal had not intended to kill the witch. Murder was not yet in his soul. He only coveted the stone. "What has been done cannot be reversed," he muttered to himself. Reaching down, his six-fingered right hand wrapped itself around the glowing rock. As it touched his skin, it fastened itself against his flesh, and his mind began to swirl. The force of the visions knocked him to the ground.

A flood of memories invaded his mind. He could see through the witch's eyes as she gazed at her own reflection in a pond. Bayal saw her with her mate; he experienced the memories. Indeed, he saw her with several mates, experiencing each one. The elf watched as her vision danced around various fires—some with sacrifices, human and animal. Bayal saw her mixing powders and potions. Immediately, he knew the recipes. Her knowledge was his knowledge. It all rushed at him, and he realized the essence of the woman—her memories, her knowledge, the sum of all her experiences—now rested within his mind.

Even more memories swam into his brain. Ancient ones. He experienced lying on a bed in agony, badly wounded, fading. Before that, he was on a battlefield swinging a great sword. Blood. So much blood. His army fighting a sworn enemy—his brother, a neighboring kingdom. The leader of his army, his friend, lay on the ground before him, missing his hand as blood poured from his wrist. Someone's head rested near his elbow.

Again, the memories, or rather the king's memories that now were his own, washed backward. He remembered a great feast. Then, a dimly lit bedroom in candlelight. His wife was there. She was beautiful. He loved her. The king's emotions were his emotions.

Backward. Backward. Backward. Finally, he remembered being given the strange jewel. It was set in a golden crown. A soothsayer from the East, from the ancient lands, handed it to him. There, the memories ceased and Bayal slept.

When he finally awoke, he found the witch lying in the dirt, her body desiccated into a brittle state. He touched her arm, and it fell from her shoulder. Her bones, covered in gray skin, looked like sticks covered in delicate fabric. Bayal felt younger, though. Wandering to a nearby stream, he peered down at his reflection and was surprised to see a mane of human-like hair sprouting out around his head, his pointy ears protruding from each side. His normally long, pointy nose had a rounder, more human look. He was taller.

As the years went by, he used that stone to garner power and wealth. The humans feared him. His fellow elves rejected him, although some came to follow him. He drained the lives of many men and women as the mood struck him. Each time, he felt more invigorated, more youthful. Eventually, the humans, out of fear and compliance, brought their children to him. He would drain their life force, then burn them on the fire, growing younger and stronger with each sacrifice.

Years went by. Centuries. His own kind reviled him and fought against him, but he would retreat to the Human Realm to enjoy his power and the spoils of his greed. He traveled the world, duping the human inhabitants. Bayal made connections with other greedy false gods who also enjoyed the control of hapless humans. He met the strange Ashtor on one such trip. They were rivals, yet they developed a mutual respect.

Suddenly, the world shifted. The Mighty One, the God who was not false, shifted the landscape. From Bayal's experience, and the experience of all those whose memories he had absorbed, the Mighty One had never interfered with the course of events. He let those who would be mastered by such as himself fall under the control of whoever wished to take the reins of power. But all at once, that changed, and the True One interjected himself, causing humankind to see through the facades of those who were false.

From then on, Bayal was on the run, hunted and desperate. He found Ashtor planning his own escape to a land far to the west across a great sea. Bayal joined him, traveling with the human witchdoctor. Eventually, he left the stone in the care of his pseudo friend, being careful to instruct him never to touch it to his skin, and then he fled to the pit. There, he bided his time, plotted his return, and baked in the furnace at the world's core.

Finally, after centuries of waiting, plotting, and planning, there it was, his greatest treasure, hanging from the throat of a simple human female. Mere inches from his grasp. His stone. The mesmerizing facets, like sirens, called to him. He would have it back.

"I have missed you so much," he said to the crystal as it dangled against the woman's faintly freckled skin. She put him in mind of the woman from whom he had first taken it. Ashtor muttered something in his new insectile voice. Bayal ignored him.

The charred elf snatched the stone from Rose with his right hand. Lifting the leather strings, he hung it from his own throat. Immediately, the stone clung to his skin. The woman fell away. Power surged into his mind. He thought about how he would use it to pull the life force from all those present, restoring himself. The charred one would again be young and vigorous. Bayal would rule both the realms of men and the realms of the elves. Gone would be the charred skin and the red fissures. He would be strong, and all would be at his feet—even this Ashtor abomination.

"All will bow to me," he shouted and turned toward the spider shaman. "If you kneel now, perhaps I will spare *you*." But those assembled under Ashtor's webbed dome were not kneeling. Instead, they appeared shocked. Their eyes were saucers, and their mouths hung open.

"Are you hearing me? Bow! Bow, now."

"Bayal, you have had a long run," Ashtor said. Though insectile, the words sounded sad to Bayal's ears.

It made no sense. *I will drain Ashtor first*. He would gain the shaman's knowledge of the dark arts. Angry, he tried to turn toward his one-time friend but found he could not. Instead, his vision locked onto the face of the human woman before him. Bayal's blackened eyes met her sparkling blue ones. She grinned at him.

Then he felt it. The reversal of fortune. Her life force was not flowing into him. Rather, his life was flowing into her. All his history. All his knowledge. All his plans. They were flooding out of him. Pouring into this simple human specimen.

"But...the stone...It chose me."

Rose continued to smile. "It's changed its mind."

~

Rose lurched as the flow of life energy surged into her. It hit her like an avalanche, yet it lifted her skyward when it connected, thrusting her own consciousness into the ozone layer. It was akin to a firehose being snapped onto her brainstem and the valve opened wide. She could see nothing but the endless inpouring of images, feelings, and knowledge. Once, when she was ten or eleven, her mother had taken her to Niagara Falls where she'd been mesmerized by the waters surging over the cliff faces, crashing on the massive rocks below. Now, her consciousness was those rocks, and Bayal's thousands of years of life were the surging, slamming waters. She was drowning, choked out by a sea of new knowledge.

Her eyes snapped open, wide as walnuts. She could see the past and the present simultaneously. In her mind, the months and years passed by in flashes, images in a video set to fast-forward. In the here and now, Bayal fell to his knees in agony. Frantically, the fallen elf gripped at the stone as it clung to his neck. He clawed at it, scratching, gouging out hunks of his own skin, yet the stone remained.

Rose squeezed in a thought of Minerva Woodstock, the way the incredibly old woman had ended up a pile of bones and dust inside her clothing. Before her now, the transformation was even more horrifying. First, Bayal's charred skin flaked away leaving a glowing red dermis. His clothing sagged from his frame when the fire-colored flesh peeled and sloughed off. Gaps opened in his cheeks. Rose could see his teeth break loose, falling through the holes. His nose and ears dried up and fell off, turning to dust before hitting the ground.

A slight breeze briefly stirred the stale air inside the spider cocoon. It blew across from Rose's left. As it struck the ancient elf, the balance of his skin drifted away in a cloud, eventually coating the far side of the webbed structure. Bayal's bones crumbled as they struck the earth. In the end, nothing was left of the evil elf but his leather jacket. The knife Hope had hurled still poked through a hole at the jacket's shoulder. Rose's beautiful, dangerous crystal lay nestled in the fine bone dust gathered in a pile on the liner inside.

Rose collapsed. Her eyes rolled back in her head. Everything swirled around her, inside and outside her mind. The world was humming. Then, darkness.

~

Hope stood in front of the throng on the crowded Terrell porch, watching the horror unfold. With each shift in the action, the elves and Adena alike would either murmur or gasp like spectators at a tennis match. When Rose was singled out by the shaman, whom the evil elf called Ashtor, Hope was convinced Danny's aunt was doomed. When the woman fell to her knees, Hope half covered her eyes as tears leaked down her cheeks. She was unable to look and yet unable to look away. Suddenly, though, Hope's heart leapt when the tables turned and Bayal's greedy desires literally bit him in the face.

"What's happening to him?" Danny asked. "He's crumbling to pieces."

Hope didn't respond. Instead, she jerked free of her mother's grip. She believed that, like Rose, she carried a unique power. She'd been told about her super-bright aura, seen it on her own arms during her visits to the realm of the elves. She'd used it to drive off the evil specter to save her dad. Now, she needed to face up to this giant man-spider. Her aura, though not visible here in her home realm, may be the only chance for her friends and her mother. And every minute this dragged on was another minute lost between her and her father.

Spying the undulating light of Rose's jewel lying in the dust, Hope had an idea. *If I can fling it at the monster, maybe it'll suck him dry too.* Carefully, she edged toward the crystal.

Ashtor laughed. "I warned you," he said to the residual dust of his one-time friend. With his many legs, he skittered toward the crowd. They drew back in terror, and he stopped short, laughing again. The whole thing seemed a game to him. He was toying with his prey like a barnyard cat might play with a captured mole, batting it from side to side, letting it go only to catch it again.

Hope glanced at Queen Hesed. She and her sons were as terrified as the rest of the assembled warriors and fallen elves. Gavin stood in front of his mother, trying to protect her. Sacqueal loomed in front of them both with his swords drawn, but fear shone in his eyes. His huge, hairy arms trembled even as they wielded the weapons. A dog-sized spider dropped on a strand from the porch roof right in front of the sasquatch. Sacqueal expelled a sound that was between a roar and a scream before using one sword to slice through the spider's abdomen. The creature fell from the web in two pieces at his feet.

"Hope, get back here," her mother called to her. "Get back from that thing!"

Hope peered at her mom. She'd never seen that look on her mother's face, even when her dad had been terrorizing them. What she saw was the face of abject horror. Maggie tried to grab Hope, but an Adena warrior held her back.

"Please, Hope. Please come back here." Maggie begged her even as the man held her firmly in place.

"Hope," Gavin shouted. "Back away. Please." Then, he added, "Sacqueal, protect her."

The terrified sasquatch, as mighty as he was, glared desperately at the prince. Despite his fear, his loyalty prevailed. He only hesitated a moment. He roared and started forward.

"Stop!" Hope screamed, throwing her left hand up. As if hit by an invisible force, Sacqueal hesitated.

Facing the spider-shaman again, Hope glared at him, willing daggers to fly from her eyes. The monster still paced before his audience, paying her no mind, pausing only long enough to drain the fluid from the abdomen of his fallen pet. His other spiders scurried here and there on the walls and the webs, apparently holding back until their master gave the final word for their own feast. Hope glanced at Rose. The woman seemed to be recovering from her ordeal with Bayal, reaching slowly forward, her fingers edging along the ground toward the strange necklace.

Hope darted out and stood over the glowing jewel on the leather string. At this, Ashtor took notice, finally turning his oversized eyes in her direction. He tapped his protruding mandibles in anticipation.

Reaching down, Hope took care to pick up the necklace by the leather strip from which it dangled. She held it up before the creature.

"Give it to me," Rose weakly instructed. "Don't touch it."

"Do you mean to use that rock as a weapon against me, girl?" Ashtor asked with a sneer. "Do you think me as stupid as my former elfin friend?" Angling slightly toward the onlookers, he scanned his assorted future victims still on the porch. His eyes landed on Maggie. He pointed one arachnid leg. "That is your mother, is she not?"

Before Hope could respond, a stream of silk surged from Ashtor's abdomen, catching Maggie square in the chest. The shaman jerked her from the porch, pulling her directly into his grasp. Holding Maggie captive, his pincers moved in and out just above her head.

"Even if you manage to touch me with that stone," Ashtor hissed, "I will still have time to sink my pincers into your mother's throat. She will soon be nothing more than a dry sack of bones."

The life of her mother or the lives of everyone? An impossible choice. She saw what touching the jewel had done to Bayal. No doubt, based on Ashtor's reaction, it would likely do the same to him. Yet, if she even tried to move it close to him, he'd kill her mother. If she threw it, she could very well miss. No, she would almost definitely miss. She needed to get in closer. Even if she tried, her mother would die, but if she didn't try, everyone would die.

Glancing at the odd crystal dangling from the string in her hand, the shifting colors captured her eyes. All at once, she couldn't pull her vision away. It called to her. Hope longed to hang it around her own neck, as she lifted it higher.

"Hope," Rose bellowed, still sitting in the dirt. "Don't look at it. Turn your eyes away. Quick, give it to me. I'm the only one who can safely hold it."

"Perhaps, it will let me—" she mumbled. Slowly, she lifted it, taking the other end of the string in her left hand. "It's calling me."

"Nozomi!" Hesed called, stepping out from the huddled crowd. "Look at me, Nozomi."

Hesed's use of Hope's nickname broke the trance. Peering at the elf queen, she lowered the necklace. Still, the dilemma remained. Her mother was still in the shaman's insectile grasp, the likelihood of everyone's death still imminent.

"Take the knife at your feet and cut a piece of leather from Bayal's jacket," Ashtor instructed. "Wrap the stone in the leather and bring it to me. If you do, I will spare both you and your mother."

"What about everyone else?" Hope asked. "Will you let us all go?"

The human spider laughed from deep in his abdomen. Maggie shook in his grasp. "Of course not. But I will release your mother, and I'll spare you both."

"He lies," Tomo said. "He always lies."

"Shut up," Ashtor hissed at the Adena leader. "Do as I say, girl. Do it now, or I will drain your mother before your very eyes."

What do I do? Hope's mind was racing. *If I rush him, he'll kill my mom. If I throw it, I might miss. If I give him the stone, everyone dies but me and mom...unless he's lying. He's probably lying.*

Hope's reasoning came to one inevitable conclusion. No matter what she did, if she didn't get that stone against his hardened arachnid exoskeleton, everyone was going to die. Everyone. She looked longingly at her mother, then scanned the assembled faces, human and elf alike, gathered on the Terrell porch. Her gaze paused at Danny's fearful face. She thought of Josh and hoped he would be okay, that he'd survive. Her dad came into her thoughts last. She loved him so much. He'd just come back into her life, and he was suffering in pain somewhere at this very moment—unless he'd already died. A sense of deep loss welled up inside, carrying with it a large bubble of righteous indignation. None of this was fair. None of this could stand. She would do something about it. She would end this.

Gathering up the leather strings until the jewel rested in her palm, she locked eyes with Ashtor and charged. "I will end this," she screamed. Even as she rushed at the creature, she felt the pull of the stone as it began its insidious work on her lifeforce.

Somewhere nearby, Rose bellowed a mournful, wolf-like howl.

Thirteen

Kenny again found himself sitting on the sofa across from his own likeness. The white-robed figures were still gathered in a line behind the portion of him that sported the flannel shirt. Their eyes shone like sparkling diamonds. Glancing over his shoulder, he saw the dark figures still arrayed as well. Specters fluttered over their heads and weaved in and out of their torsos. He shivered before looking back to see soul-Kenny reading a book.

Lowering the tome, his likeness peered back at him. "Here we are again. Have you figured it out?"

"Figured what out?"

"How Hope managed to defeat the specter."

"I've been told that she 'loved' me back. I don't know what that means, but it's what Tomo told me."

"Yes, she did love you back, but not with the ushy-gushy, touchy-feely kind of love. There was more to it." Soul-Kenny closed his book and rested it on his lap. He cocked his head at an angle. "Do you understand yet?"

Kenny stared at his own soul, thinking. He gazed at the assembled line of people glowing with white light. The aura that brightened the space behind them bloomed ever brighter and seemed to have moved closer. Then he thought about that battle Hope had with the darkness that'd controlled him—how she threw herself at it. She'd risked it all for the chance to free him. After a few minutes, Kenny finally spoke. "She loved me with a reckless abandon, a no-turning-back, all-bets-are-off, win-or-lose sort of love. A love that drove her to act selflessly."

"Now you're on the right track." Soul-Kenny sat up. Placing his boots on the white marble floor, he leaned forward. "You did that today, too."

"I did?"

"Yes, you did. You proved you're capable of that level of love. It's the reason we're allowed to have this talk—the only reason, despite the darkness that you struggle to resist."

Suddenly, the pain returned. He felt it on his calves, his thighs, his back, sides, and arms.

"Your love for Hope drove you to risk it all to save her. You dared to die so she would live."

He remembered how he'd stood there in the rain and watched Hope bound by the fire. Those freaking little elves moved so fast with their flashing blades. All his thoughts were about how to save her, regardless of whatever happened to himself. "I guess I did."

"No guessing. You definitely did." The soul motioned toward the assembled bright ones with their melodic voices. They were singing. Kenny almost recognized the tune. "If you choose the light, it is with that same sense of all-bets-are-off, reckless abandon that you must make that choice. Anything less will leave you with the dark ones. Will leave *us* with the dark ones."

Kenny rose. His likeness rose, as well. He turned his back to the ones adorned in the white robes, and as he did their song faded. His eyes took in the dark, undulating forms of the multitude of black-robed, empty-faced beings beckoning for him to come to them. Their harsh tones rose in his ears. Three faces appeared in the crowd. The face of Jim Pickle, the school janitor who gave him his first taste of beer. He'd kept a thermos in the basement of Roosevelt Elementary School. There was Janice Drysdale, the thirty-something neighbor with whom he'd crossed a barrier at fifteen. Finally, Rance Raymond's face materialized. They'd been best friends until they were both sixteen. Rance kept a stash of stuff in a box up in the attic access above his bedroom closet. Stuff to look at and stuff to swallow. He'd died so young. It hurt to see him standing over there in the darkness.

All three of those faces represented turning points. Choices. Decisions.

Turning back to the brightness, more faces appeared. Grandma Burton. She'd held him when he cried. She took him to church. Encouraged him to do good things. Mary Ellen Siler, his fifth-grade teacher, who'd loved his artwork and helped him with his math homework. She smiled at him now, so sweetly. Mr. Payton, the owner of the corner store down from his house. He let him work off the value of the stuff he stole. The man caught him but didn't call the cops or his folks. Instead, he gave him a job. Kenny loved that old man.

Choices. Decisions. Before, he'd chosen badly. Now, it was time to choose what was right.

Behind the assembled bright ones, the glow blossomed. Golden spikes emanated from the rays of light in each direction.

Kenny stepped forward.

~

Gator and Calvin sped away from the web dome to start the evacuation of Cutters Notch. The balance of the assembled ragtag bunch stared at one another. Roger deposited Josh onto the hood of Kevin's SUV. Franklin inspected the shotgun, checking the shells, pocketing more.

Rick watched them, then turned to review the giant cocoon as seen from the hilltop. Despite what Teresa Terrell had said, a sense of hopelessness gripped the man. This was beyond any training he'd ever had at the Police Academy. They don't teach you how to deal with the invasion of dog-sized spiders hiding in a web larger than a house.

"Hey," Kevin Flannery exclaimed. "I have a chainsaw in the back. Just tuned it and sharpened it for a customer. It ought to penetrate that web."

Rick peered at him grimly, doubtful. "Get it and let's go."

Kevin was pulling the cord to start the small engine when the peak of the webbed dome opened and began to dissolve across the top and down the sides.

"They're coming out!" Cynthia Sweet screamed.

~

Dargo, Dorcas, and Gronek paused, exhausted. To each side, the few Adena warriors that were not trapped inside continued to hack, to no avail.

"We are not even making scratches," lamented Gronek. "I have not cut a single strand."

Dargo grimaced. His green aura had turned orange from the effort. He said nothing but returned to his hacking.

Dorcas stood back, hands on her hips, examining the monstrous structure. Sweat drained from her angled face, and one drop hung from the end of her nose. Suddenly, the blade slipped from her fingers. She gasped.

"What?" Gronek asked.

Wearily, Dargo stepped back with her, following her gaze.

The giant dome was falling in on itself, seeming to dissolve as it went.

One warrior screamed. "The shaman is coming out," he yelled, backing away. He turned and fled up the hillside. The other Adena followed him.

~

Even as she palmed the stone and charged at Ashtor, Hope felt the jewel beginning to pull at her consciousness. She would not be an exception. It would drain her just as it drained Bayal. Not knowing the history of how the bewitched crystal worked, an image of herself disintegrating into dust flashed across her mind. Still, she had no choice. It was the only way, her best chance to connect the rock directly to the shell of the monster looming over everyone.

"Hope, no," Maggie bellowed, squirming in the monster's grasp.

Ashtor drew back, his legs flaring out. "Get her!" he screamed at his spider minions. They scattered instead. Large spiders skittered away in every direction, scaling the dome's sidewalls.

Hope didn't know what to expect when she reached the shaman. She only knew what she'd seen. The stone had somehow killed Bayal, drying him to dust. Ashtor was clearly both enamored and fearful of the jewel. Inside, the crystal was draining her, sucking the energy and the memories from her mind.

Rose grabbed both sides of her own head, screaming, eyes bugging out. "No! I don't want these."

Slamming into the giant man-spider, Hope wrapped her arms around the beast, pressing the palm of her hand with the odd jewel flat against the hard shell of the creature's lower back, above his bulging abdomen.

Ashtor wailed in pain. "Get it off!"

Yet, it wouldn't come off. Hope tried to remove her hand, leaving the stone against the creature, but it was stuck to the stone. And the stone was stuck to the beast. Their fates were now linked. One of the shaman's hairy spider legs tossed her lower torso in the air, but the crystal held her in place.

Maggie bellowed, still held in the shaman's grasp, the soft skin of her arm touching the hairy skin of one of the shaman's human arms. She slammed her free hand against the side of her own head as the power of the stone began to drain her as well.

Rose's screams intensified. She rolled on the grass in pain, her legs flailing in the air.

Ashtor's arachnid appendages swung wildly in every direction; his pincers snapped in and out. He staggered back, then reversed course, careening forward. Hope's feet dragged across the ground. The muscles in her arm that was fastened to the shaman's carapace were fighting desperately to stay connected to her shoulder.

The many memories of Hope's short life flew through her mind. A favorite rattle as a toddler. Swinging on the swings at Heekin Park. Ice Cream on her chin. Riding on her daddy's shoulders. Her mother's waffles. The smell of her grandmother's perfume. Danny and Josh when she'd first met them. Tears leaked from her eyes as she swung there, still attached to the shaman's shell.

"Enough!"

Everything stopped. No more screams. Ashtor ceased stumbling. The memory stream froze in place. All eyes swung toward the voice. A figure walked toward them. An old man. Close-cropped, curly gray hair. A walking cane. Hope's new neighbor.

As he moved, he began to change. First, he grew taller. His skin began to glow, and his eyes appeared as bulbs of golden bright light. The short hair on his scalp lengthened until it became a mane of shiny gray locks. Muscles in his arms and legs bulged beneath a flowing white tunic. The figure swung the walking cane above his head, and it extended to three times its original length, flattening into a brilliant broadsword.

Hope watched him approach, mesmerized by the transformation. She forgot about the tug at her mind. The flow of memories had evaporated. *Wings? Do I see wings?* Indeed, she did. Large white wings extended high above the approaching being's head, their tips nearly touching the peak of the dome.

"It's an angel," Danny stated, the wonder evident in his voice.

Murmurs of "bright one" slipped out from among the assembled elves.

The sword flashed toward Ashtor and Hope. The angel directed it deftly between Hope's hand and the shaman's carapace, breaking the bond of the magic stone. Hope fell away, landing on her backside. Ashtor stumbled toward the destroyed pavilion. Maggie fell toward the porch, completing the triangle.

The angel lifted the blade into the air. The stone with its undulating colors hung from its tip; the leather strips wrapped around the sword's edge. "This despicable creation has caused enough trouble," the angel stated. He brought the sword down, then flipped it upward. The jewel flew free. As it descended again, the angel swung his mighty sword in a sweeping arc, hitting the stone mid-flight, shattering it into a million dust-sized fragments. They sparkled as they disappeared into the turf, then faded into oblivion.

Turning in a circle, the angel assessed the scene. His gaze fell first upon the assorted beings on the porch—humans, sasquatch, and elves alike. As he continued to peer around, he paused at Rose. She stared back, mouth agape, eyes huge. He smiled at her before continuing. Finally, the bright one's glare settled upon Ashtor with his spider minions now gathered behind him.

"Ashtor, you have forced me to return once again. You do not learn. For centuries, you have suffered the consequences of your evil choices, but you refuse to change. I grow weary of your pitiful ambitions. Return now. Return to the pit. Return to the depths of Abandon and take your pets with you."

The spiders went first. They skittered across the grass, crossed the concrete floor of the destroyed pavilion, and surged into the tunnel to Abandon. Slowly, Ashtor backed his way to the gate, seemingly hesitant to depart, yet terrified of the brilliant angel before him.

"Have I no other choice?" Ashtor asked. "Is there no other place?"

"That is not for me to decide. You will have your day before the Mighty One soon enough. You should dread that day. For now, begone."

Ashtor slipped through the gate, descending from view toward the chamber of Abandon.

Turning his gaze toward the peak of the dome, the angel pointed his sword. "You also have caused enough pain."

Hope peered toward the web-woven ceiling. Suddenly the air began to stir, and a dark undulating shadow appeared. Normally invisible in the Human Realm, the specter materialized before her eyes, its red eyes the size of half dollars.

"You will also now find tormented rest in the depths. Go. Now!"

The specter swirled downward as if caught in the flush of a toilet. As it reached the gaping pit, it paused. *Was that an agonized face that appeared around the red, pinpoint eyes?* Then, it dropped inside.

The angel retrieved the cap plate, lifting it as if it were nothing more than a coffee saucer and placed it back over the hole. Before replacing the large boulder, he ran his sword tip around the edge of the gate cover. The rim began to glow as it melted, then bonded with the marble base. Finally, the bright one stepped behind the cap rock, shoving it back into place with one hand.

With all threats removed, the angel turned his eyes on those remaining. The elves, sasquatch, and Adena all knelt before him.

Seeing the others kneel, Danny dropped to his knees. Hope, Maggie, and Rose were still sitting on the grass between the porch and the angel.

"Get up," he ordered. "Do not worship me." Everyone stood.

"Queen Agahpey Hesed," said the angel, "I will leave you to deal with your fallen ones. I trust you will see that they cause no more mischief."

The queen bowed quickly. "I will see to it, bright one."

"Tomo, you will continue the vigilance of your guardianship. You and your people."

"We will," he replied softly, averting his gaze.

The bright one then turned to Rose. "Rose Flannery, while you have carried the stone without causing any harm to innocents, you can carry it no longer. The weight of bearing something so powerful holds dark temptations. Eventually, you would have fallen prey to its potential. You will retain the memories now embedded in your mind. Use them to do good, lest I need to return."

The redhead-turned-brunette nodded quickly. "Yes. Yes, I will."

Finally, the angel peered at Hope. She shifted before him, gazing into his brilliant eyes, the gold color swirling around his pupils. "Hope Spencer Burton, your memories remain your own?" he asked.

"Yes," she responded, "I think so."

"Very good." The bright one smiled at her, revealing teeth that sparkled like diamonds. "Hope, your acts of selfless love have been noticed. Your consistent choices to give at all costs and to risk yourself for the benefit of others have wide-ranging effects on those you encounter, your father included. Take heed that your inevitable grief does not turn your bright aura dark."

The bright one then raised his sword until the tip punctured the peak of the web's dome. It began to disintegrate from that point. His tasks complete, he turned and walked toward the forest, changing as he went, until once again he was simply an old man with a walking cane. As he reached the far wall, he turned back, winking one golden eye. As the webbed sidewall fell before him, he disappeared into the trees.

Fourteen

When the webbed walls fell, Hope rushed to squeeze her mother in a tight hug. Danny joined in. Then Rose. Rick and the others on the outside made their way down the hill.

The sun came out, deactivating the shimmer through which they'd entered, and Queen Hesed, her sons, and the fallen elves found themselves trapped in the Human Realm. Their long-held secret existence, already in desperate jeopardy, dissolved like sugar in hot water.

Hesed attempted to find cover, ushering Sacqueal and all the elves into the Terrell home even as Cynthia Sweet and Agent Franklin entered the scene. Despite the effort, Hesed didn't make it through the door before being spotted. The Adena warriors fled to the forest. Tomo disappeared around the corner of the house toward the huge sycamore tree. The queen was left standing on the porch behind Hope, Maggie, Rose, and Danny as the lone visitor from the Arboreal Realm.

The Flannerys gathered around Rose and Danny. Rick made a beeline to Maggie and Hope. The Terrells examined their destroyed pavilion. That left Franklin and Sweet gazing at the elf queen.

~

Cynthia Sweet's mind, mesmerized by the presence of Agahpey Hesed, filled with questions. Immediately before her stood a being not from this world wearing a crown woven with golden-coated nuts and pinecones. Adorned in a tunic of gold-painted magnolia leaves, the being had pointy ears, a long, angular nose, a light green complexion, and six fingers on each hand.

Sweet was awestruck. "Where are you from?" Cynthia asked. "Do you understand my language?"

Franklin stood beside her, reticent but taking it all in.

Hesed smiled. "The land you call Kentucky."

"The hell you say," Franklin quipped. Sweet shushed him.

"How can that be?" Sweet pressed. Kentucky was a beautiful state, sprinkled with horse farms and partially dense forests, but well-populated and definitely part of this world.

The being peered at Franklin with large, dark eyes. "Who are you? Are you a scientist or some other investigator? Are you from the human government?"

"He's an investigator," replied Sweet. "I'm Cynthia Sweet, a scientist and a researcher from SETI."

Hesed laughed. "I see now. You think me an alien from outer space. Perhaps you think that you have finally found your proof of extraterrestrial life?"

"You know of SETI? Are you not from outer space? From some other world?" Sweet tilted her head to one side.

"No. I told you. I am from Kentucky."

Gavin and Smakal stepped out of the Terrell home, joining their mother. Gavin stood to her left, Smakal to her right. Their green-tinted skin, pointy ears, and angular noses clearly visible in the late afternoon sunlight.

"We live here," Gavin stated.

"Right here in Indiana," Smakal added. "We are Hoosiers," he said with a smile.

Cynthia fumbled in her bag for something to write on. "How can this be?"

"You look for life from outer space," Hesed said. "We are from what might be termed by some humans as 'inner space.' Our world is a parallel dimension. We refer to it as the Arboreal Realm. It is primarily populated by plants and trees, which generally exist in both dimensions simultaneously but dominate there."

Agent Franklin pulled his phone from his pocket. He lifted it to eye level, intending to take a photo. At Hope's urging, Rick stepped over to block his shot.

"I need to document this," he complained. "We need a record of this event."

"I don't think I'll let you do that," Anders stated.

"But I have to. I don't have a choice. My partner's dead."

"Make something up," Rick said.

"You are with the government, correct? What is your role, young man?" Hesed asked Franklin.

"I'm a senior agent with the NSA, the security arm of the United States Government."

"Very good." The queen smiled at the man. "Give my regards to your president. I have not seen him since his inauguration."

"You know Presi..." Franklin fell silent, staring.

"Of course. I travel and meet all the new presidents. I liked Benjamin Franklin a great deal, though he was never a president. Perhaps, he was a relative of yours?" Hesed cocked her head to the side as she spoke to Agent Franklin but didn't wait for his reply. "I was quite fond of Abraham Lincoln, too. Such a tragic end. He was from near here, you know. The United States presidents, they have their little book of secrets. You will find that my people and I are in that book. You would do well to keep that secret, I think."

"But..." Franklin fell silent again, then he slowly backed away. His face grimaced as he likely began inventing the short story that would become his report.

Gavin leaned over, whispering into Hesed's ear. She smiled and nodded.

"Cynthia Sweet from SETI, would you like to visit our realm? Do you have any obligations that would prevent you from taking a small journey into our dimension?"

Sweet hesitated only seconds. "I would be honored to accept. How do I go there?"

~

Rick, noting Danny's and Rose's presence nearby, stepped over. "Where's Havener? How'd you escape?"

"He's dead," Rose answered. "In my house."

"What happened?" Rick pressed. A frown spread across his face and his forehead crinkled. He looked away in thought. "Where do you live? I can't ever seem to remember."

"Havener wanted my necklace," she answered. "He took us to my house, to one of my upstairs rooms, and..." She paused, as if considering how to explain. "Well, he grabbed my necklace, and a few moments later he fell to the floor and died."

"He just fell over and died?" Maggie asked. "Just like that? Weird." She gave Rose a telling look and the hint of a smile.

"That's what happened," Danny confirmed.

~

"I have to go to Dad," Hope blurted. "He's hurt bad." Approaching Queen Hesed, she interrupted the elf's conversation with Cynthia Sweet. "Agahpey, I need to go see my dad. How do I get to him?"

"My dear Nozomi, the sun is shining again. The shimmers are closed until nightfall. I am sorry."

"There must be a way. I have to get to him before it's too late." Hope's arms stiffened as if they were baseball bats attached to her shoulders. Her fingers curled into fists. She fidgeted before the queen, eyes darting to the forest, then to the house, and back to the forest again.

Hesed examined the sun's angle in the sky. It hung just above the treetops on the western horizon. "When the sun drops below the trees, we will watch for the shimmers to reappear. It will not be long."

"Hope? Are you okay?" Josh interjected.

Hope turned to see Josh in the arms of his father. Roger seated his son on the top porch step, Josh's ruined cast extending out over the wooden planks. "I wanted to run down here, but I'm useless in this cast."

"Oh, Josh." Hope dropped to her knees and wrapped both arms around him, pulling him tight. "My dad's hurt really bad. Fallen elves with knives cut him up." She sobbed into his shoulder, and he held her close. "I need to get back through a shimmer. I need to go to him. I need to save him. I've got to."

Hope's mind raced. At first, she'd been skeptical of all the amazement of the elves over her aura in the Arboreal Realm. What's the big deal if her arms had a bright glow about them? Then, all the sudden, she could come and go through the shimmers all by herself. She beat back that dark specter, freeing her dad. Finally, she was able to pull Josh back from the brink of death. Her father had lost so much blood as the Adena warriors carried him off—she saw it now in her mind's eye. Hope had to go to him. She had to use this apparent power she carried.

Danny sat on the top step next to her. The three friends were together again. "You'll get there," he whispered. "You'll see."

~

"You look weird," Tony Terrell said to Smakal. "You've got

Vulcan ears and a Pinocchio nose."

The elf smiled back at him. They were eye to eye. "Yes, I do, and I have six fingers on each of my hands." He held them up for Tony to examine.

"Wow," the boy said, "that's kinda cool."

~

The balance of the afternoon unfolded slowly for Hope as she waited for the sun to sink below the tree line. Rick, Maggie, Anni, Kevin, Roger, Cindy, Rose, and the Terrell family met Queen Hesed along with Gavin and Smakal. Rick called off the evacuation of Cutters Notch, recalling Gator and Calvin.

Gator retrieved Agent Franklin, giving him a ride back to the diner to deal with his partner's body. Roger Gillis loaned him an extra set of keys to the Quarry Pit. Jerry Steinkamp was assigned to assist Gator in securing the bodies of the fallen elves, also still at the diner. They wrapped them in blankets and transported them to the Terrell property so that Queen Hesed could take them back into the Arboreal Realm.

Rick told Calvin that Al Havener and Mabel's crew weren't going anywhere this time, so they could simply wait.

Hope continued to lean against Josh on the Terrell porch. The shadows lengthened, and the sun dropped behind the trees.

~

Lights came on inside the Terrell house. Smakal rushed outside to Gavin and his mother. "The shimmers have activated, and the portal is open," he announced. "Mother, Gronek is on the other side with Dargo and Dorcas."

At the mention of Dorcas, Gavin raised his large eyes toward his brother and smiled. "Dorcas came? She is here?"

"Yes, brother, she is." Smakal smiled back and winked.

Gavin didn't hesitate. He shoved past his brother into the house, wiggling his way through the few Adena warriors still hiding inside, and rushed to the large bathroom mirror. Before anyone could ask him what he was doing, he jumped on the counter and flung himself back into the Arboreal Realm.

Gavin stumbled as he landed, then glanced up into what was the most beautiful face in the world. Sheepishly, he stood, brushing off his leafy tunic. "Uh, Dorcas, you are here." A smile wrapped its way around his face until it nearly touched his pointy ears. "You came here?"

The female elf gave Gavin a warm smile in return. "I am and I did." She hugged him, holding him for a long time.

Hope appeared through the nearby shimmering portal, landing beside Gavin. "Which way to Tomo's village?" she demanded.

Gavin pointed up the hill. "Veer to the left at the top of the hill. It is about a mile straight through the forest. Look for where the stream has a small waterfall. Their village is close by in a clearing and sits at the base of a sheer cliff."

The girl didn't reply. Instead, she sprinted up the hill.

~

When Smakal announced that the portal had opened, Hope pulled away from Josh, looking toward the Terrell door.

"I have to go to my dad," she exclaimed, clambering to her feet.

"He's going to be okay," Josh offered. It was all he could think of to say. Before his rushing mind could come up with anything more, Hope fled into the house, leaving Josh sitting helplessly on the top step.

"Where's she going?" Maggie asked.

"To her dad," Josh answered.

Maggie followed her daughter. Josh and Danny watched her squeeze into the crowded house.

"I want to go," Josh said to Danny. "I need to go with her." People were around, but no one was paying them any attention. All their parents were standing in the ruined pavilion examining the boulder with the ancient carvings on top. "I'm so freaking worthless right now."

Danny shrugged. "You're not worthless, but there's nothing we can do. We can't go through the shimmer from this side. Only Hope can do that."

Josh whipped around toward his friend, realization in his eyes. "Hope can do it. That's right. But so can the elves. One of 'em could carry me through. Where's Smakal?"

"I am here," the elf answered nearby.

"Josh, you can't walk," Danny pointed out. "How would you go anywhere once we're through?"

"I could carry him," Smakal offered.

Danny nodded. "I forgot how strong you elves are. It could work."

Smakal glanced at his mother, the queen. She nodded her approval.

"Quick. Help me through before anyone notices." Josh eyed his parents, making sure they were still distracted.

Deftly, the elf lifted Josh from the step and placed him on his back. Josh wrapped his arms around Smakal's shoulders.

~

Danny followed Smakal as the elf carried Josh into the house, slipping through the crowded space. Traci Terrell was busy in the kitchen, filling glasses of lemonade for the thirsty native warriors. Sacqueal was crowded in there, too. He had a plastic bag of walnut pieces and was munching the broken nut morsels.

A voice drifted Danny's way from the direction of the backdoor as they approached the bathroom. It was Josh's dad. "Where'd those boys go?" Roger Gilles asked.

"We need to hurry," Danny urged.

They found Maggie staring at her own reflection in the mirror, her right hand pressed against the glass. "She went right through. I couldn't stop her, and she jumped into the mirror like it was a pool of water on the wall."

"Excuse us, Miss Spencer," Smakal said.

Before Maggie could respond, another elf burst into the room, coming through the mirror from the other side. He looked dangerous with his dagger in one hand and a sword swinging from a sheath at his waist. His oversized eyes darted from face to face.

"Dargo," Smakal exclaimed. "It is very good to see you."

"Likewise, my prince," the minister of defense replied. "Is your mother safe? Where is the queen?"

"Mother is through there. To the left. She is safe and well. However, she will need your assistance in dealing with the many fallen ones. There are also dead ones to retrieve."

Dargo rushed into the house. Smakal hopped on the sink and jumped through the portal, still carrying Josh. Danny followed the duo onto the sink but was stuck on the human side. He placed both hands on the glass, willing himself through. Just as he was about to resign himself to being left behind, a six-fingered hand slipped through the glass, snatched him by the collar of his shirt, and jerked him into the Arboreal Realm.

Danny landed in the grass on his hands and knees. As he rose, he found himself nose to pointy nose with Gavin. "Thanks," the boy said, "but did you have to jerk me so hard?"

Gavin seemed to process it for a moment but apparently decided to ignore the question. "Daniel, this is my...uh...my friend, Dorcas." The elf was smiling broadly.

"Hello, Daniel," Dorcas said. "I am pleased to meet you. Gavin has told us much about you and your friends."

Danny stumbled to his feet. "Nice to meet you, too," he said, sticking out his hand to shake. Dorcas took his hand into hers, smiling sweetly. He couldn't stop fidgeting. Over Gavin's shoulder he spied Smakal carrying Josh up the hill. At the top of the hill was Hope darting away. Gavin and Dorcas followed his gaze.

"Are they rushing to Hope's father?" Gavin asked.

"Yes."

"Climb on, my friend. We will follow."

Danny didn't hesitate. He now remembered that night when the elves carried them through the forest. Their physical power was amazing. As Gavin turned, Danny draped his arms around the elf's neck and wrapped his feet around the small creature's waist. In a moment, they were in pursuit up the hill. Dorcas trotted easily alongside them.

Fifteen

Hope carried two agendas. She would find her dad and she would save her dad. She'd done it before with Josh, and she planned to do it again with her father. The beautiful blue pulsating aura of the fall forest in the Arboreal realm was only a blur in her vision as she raced along. Cresting the hillside, she crossed what in her own world was Robbins Creek Road and surged into the forest on the other side. Thorns grabbed at her arms. Leafless branches slapped at her face. Fallen limbs and the uneven surface of the forest floor made running treacherous. Pools of water from the recent storm filled low spots, making her divert or splash right through.

She leapt. She slapped. She ducked. She slogged. Mostly, she ran. And ran, and ran, and ran. Using her youthful legs and athletic lungs, she rushed as fast as she possibly could to find her father. The more she ran, the more she blamed herself. The more she blamed herself, the more desperately she ran, Bayal's guilt shifting back on herself.

I caused this. She told herself that same line again and again as she sprinted through the barren trees. *If I'd only followed Gavin's instructions, he'd be safe now.* Each time she emotionally flailed herself, she surged again into more underbrush. She wasn't following a trail; she was cutting her own.

All the other issues of the past few weeks were now behind her. The Hicks were in jail. Havener was apparently dead. The Ancient Gate to Abandon was again sealed and safely guarded. Bayal was no more. Josh and Danny were safe. Her dad was the only one in jeopardy. Saving him was all that mattered. Guilt and trying to save him were the two main thoughts fighting for domination in her mind.

She found the stream as it wound through the woods—swollen

and rushing from the rain. Since it was fall, the leaves had dropped to the forest floor. With only a few still hanging on, she had a clear view ahead. Hope ran alongside the flowing water, jumping on rocks, traversing fallen trees, avoiding mud bogs until she could hear the rush of falling water.

Hope emerged from the trees to see a beautiful, sparkling waterfall. Mist circled the bottom, and whitewater rushed across boulders at the top, thirty feet above her. The water pouring across the ledge overhead was hidden under the canopy of sycamores with their mottled gray and white trunks pulsating with a blue aura. The trees stood like guardians around the pool at the bottom. She paused, getting her bearings, peering around for the clearing where the village would be found.

There. Through the trees to her left. Hope darted along a trail leading from the waterfall to the native village. The path was wide, well-worn.

Within moments, she stood in a courtyard of sorts. A large stone circle sat in the middle with the ashes of recent fires tamped down by the rain. Here and there, puddles of water gathered in low spots. Simple homes rested among the branches. A few with earthen walls and thatch roofs covered in deerskin stood along the base of a rock face. There were tables here and there with assorted chairs. Twine was strung between trees. The tiny village was quiet, no one around.

Smoke drifted from the roof peak of a house directly across the clearing. That had to be Tomo's home. Looping around the fire ring, Hope rushed across the courtyard only to be met by Mala stepping outside.

Tomo's wife looked wise and majestic as she blocked Hope's path into her home. Small wrinkles at the corners of Mala's sharp eyes accented her tan skin, and her high cheekbones flowed to a smooth chin. The woman's aura was the tone of warm caramel. She stood eye level with Hope, carried a towel, and greeted her warmly, yet with no smile.

"Your father sleeps," she stated. "I have done all I can for him." She shook her head as she stared at her own feet. "I cleaned and dressed his wounds. There are many and they are deep. He has lost much blood and is very weak. I fear that he is crossing to the next life."

Hope began to push past the Adena woman, but Mala gripped

her shoulders. "Hope…" She paused, staring deeply into the teenager's blue eyes. "You must prepare yourself. Oh, dear…" She paused again, turning her eyes downward. "It will be hard." A tear slipped down along the line of her nose.

Hope stared back at Mala, her mouth clamped shut, its corners quivering. This woman did not know the power she carried. Finally, Hope managed a few words. "If I can go to him, I can bring him back. I've done it before." She paused, then added, "I have to try."

Edging past the older woman, Hope heard others approaching the village from the waterfall. She paid them no mind in her determination to right the wrong she'd caused.

Once inside, Hope's heart fell. Her father lay on his back on a cot along the right-side wall, covered with a colorful blanket pulled up to his chin. Only his arms and his face were uncovered. His aura was faint, ebbing, a slowly fluctuating glow of white light. Every few moments, he took a deep breath.

Hope sat on the edge of the cot, taking one of his large hands in her own. Glancing to the door, she saw Danny enter alongside Smakal with Gavin on his heels carrying Josh on his back. Another female elf she didn't recognize accompanied them. Hope smiled weakly before turning back to her father.

"Dad," she said as she leaned close, kissing his forehead, "please be okay. I love you. Stay with me." Hope carefully placed her head on his chest and sobbed. "Don't leave me." She willed her aura to do its magic.

Mala pulled a wooden chair nearby, and Gavin placed Josh so that he could sit close to Hope. The boy took her hand. Danny stood behind her, lightly rubbing her shoulder.

"I just got you back. You've got to be okay." With all her heart and mind, she drove her aura to meld with her fallen father's essence. She wished her own strength to become his.

~

Kenny, still in the strange room of light and darkness, with his soul-self now standing behind him, stepped over to examine the assembled crowd of white-robed onlookers. On the verge of a final decision, he felt drawn toward the source of the light that bloomed over their heads. His mind continued to sort through the myriad memories flooding into his consciousness. Every loving moment in his life was coupled with every bad decision. The bright memory of riding on his own father's shoulders—the same way he'd carried Hope—as they walked to Heekin Park was followed by the dark memory of his angry words in the driveway after his dad found his stash in the garage. Images of stealing from his mother's purse when she wasn't looking came on the heels of visions of her cooking beef and noodles in the kitchen as he sat and joked at the table nearby.

Kenny smiled at those good memories, grimaced at the bad ones, but they were all soon washed away by still others. He stole money from his dad's wallet while he napped on the sofa. He screamed at his mother, telling her he hated her after she wouldn't let him run the streets with his buddies. He snuck out late, stole a car, and spent much of the night in the juvenile detention center. On they went, first cheering him, then deflating him.

He remembered laughing and joking with his teenaged friends in Muncie. It was fun stealing the car. It was a blast racing it down Madison Street, laying rubber and power-braking in parking lots. Kenny liked guzzling beers under the moonlight at the reservoir. The darkness tugged at him. It was almost like fingers grasping at his sleeves, pulling him away from the golden glow toward the darkness at his back.

It seemed Kenny had always felt that tug. He'd been taught right from wrong, yet the wrong always seemed more fun, more entertaining, more adventurous. Kenny had laughed at the goody-goodies, the ones who always followed the rules, the losers.

Eventually, memories of Hope surged into his mind. He saw her eyes as she looked up at him helpless from the trunk of his car. Those eyes were a mixture of fear, longing, and deep, deep sadness. They ripped his mind away from embracing the darkness. After all, it was the darkness that drove him to create that pain in his daughter. It was the tug of the darkness that made him listen to the specter, eventually to engage the evil spirit, then open the door and let it in. It had nearly driven him to kill the only person who still loved him. *I don't want to be that person anymore*!

Before him, the long line of white-robed figures parted. Another figure stepped into the gap—the form of a man dressed in a golden robe. Light in the form of pure power burst from every surface, incredibly bright, but somehow it didn't hurt Kenny's eyes. The individual approached, his hair swaying, the golden glow giving the appearance of a lion's mane.

The figure neared and his eyes came into view. They were no color Kenny had ever seen before—bright, crystalline, piercing. He felt the gaze of the man's eyes, streams of energy surged forth, entering his own pupils, bouncing off the back of his skull. Still, it didn't hurt. It didn't feel invasive. Rather, it felt like a warm embrace, the touch of a long, lost love. Not demanding. Not coercive. Only inviting.

The man's arms extended, and his hands opened as if to encourage Kenny to embrace him.

The golden man peered toward the floor near Kenny's feet. Kenny's eyes followed. There was a step there—a clear line that must be crossed.

"It's your decision," Kenny's soul whispered into his right ear, having followed him to the spot where he stood. "*Our* decision, actually, but one you need to make for us. I go where you go."

Kenny knew his choice. He'd made the decision already. He simply hadn't acted on it yet. The assembled dark figures receded behind him, dropping into the shadows of his past. Returning his eyes to the power-enveloped visage before him, he felt so unworthy. "I've made so many mistakes," Kenny said. "Horrible choices."

A golden arm raised, waves of light-energy flowing from every surface. The brilliant image extended his index figure until it touched Kenny in the middle of his chest. The residual darkness hanging on to his heart fled away from the touch. Kenny felt it leave. All that was left was his choice to lift his foot and take the step forward.

"Dad, please be okay. I love you. Stay with me."

Hope's voice echoed in the massive hall. Kenny cocked his head, lifting his ear to hear better. A deep longing for Hope hit him like an ocean breeze on a hot summer evening. It felt good but it called him away.

Kenny momentarily looked away from the stunning image. A sense of guilt rose behind his longing for Hope. Refocusing on the golden man in front of him, he expected to see disappointment. Yet instead, he sensed compassion, understanding, and patience. A singular thought entered his mind, driving all others away.

Go see her, hold her, and love her one more time.

~

Hope closed her eyes, feeling her father's massive chest slowly rise and fall. "Please, God," she whispered. It was all she could think to say. Her family wasn't religious. Her mother's parents were, but their influence had always been at a distance. She didn't know how to pray. If there were special words, she didn't know them. "Please."

Hope felt her daddy's whiskered cheek, stroked his oily hair. It had grown out some in the last couple of weeks. He didn't move. His skin felt cold, clammy.

Someone took her left hand. Josh. She squeezed his fingers and gave him a weak smile. He returned it just as weakly. A tear dribbled to his chin. Danny stood behind her. She felt his fingers squeezing her shoulders. Her friends were doing all they could to support her.

The light in the room was low. Shadows flickered on the walls from nearby candles. The sun had fully settled in for the evening.

"Is there anything else we can do for him?" Danny asked. Hope knew he was speaking to Mala. "If we could get him back to our world, maybe we could rush him to a hospital."

"There is nothing else," the Adena woman replied. "His wounds are severe, and we could never move him to a shimmer without causing more harm. It is in the Mighty One's hands now."

Releasing Josh's hand, Hope raised herself up and grabbed her dad's shoulders. "You come back to me," she shouted. "I love you, Dad. Come back. Come back now!" Turning her eyes toward the ceiling, she added, "Send him back. Please send him back."

A hand fell on her right arm, a large hand. "Why are you shouting?" Kenny asked, the words slipping slowly out. He smacked his lips. "I'm thirsty."

Danny clamored for a cup of water while Hope joyfully hugged her dad, kissing his cheek. "I thought you were gone," Hope said between kisses.

Danny held a small tin cup, placing it near Kenny's lips so that he could take a sip. The man took it, downing the cool water.

"I'm only back to see you, to say I love you one more time." The man's eyes rose to the ceiling like he was looking at something a million miles away. A large smile creased his face. "I can't stay, though." He paused, staring into her eyes. "I love you, pumpkin." Kenny pulled in a deep breath, grimacing at the effort.

Hope was shocked. Disconcerted by the mixed messages of his words and his smile, she found herself at a loss. Then, her guilt came gushing out. "It's my fault. If I'd only listened to Gavin and stayed safe at home. I did this to you. Dad, I'm so sorry." Her aura turned red with shame.

Kenny refixed his eyes on his daughter; he took her hand. "Sweetie, this is not your fault. I was lost. Almost completely. It was you, your love, that dragged me back from the darkness. If it hadn't been for you, I'd be rotting in a cell because of that evil darkness. Instead, you saved me, honey. Now, I'm healed from that dark existence. Thanks to your courage and your love, I've chosen the light." He took another breath. "It's calling to me now."

Hope pulled her hand from his and framed his face with her palms. She was at first confused, then realized that he meant he was dying and that he accepted it, even embraced it. "What? No. Please don't die," she moaned. "I need you. Stay with me."

Kenny smiled again. "Sweetie, we all die eventually. This is my time. I know that. And you don't need me. You have your mother. Your friends." His eyes shifted first to Josh, then to Danny.

"You're not gonna die. You can't die. Not now. I'm here now. See my bright aura? I'll use it for you."

Danny stepped back, standing with Mala, tears streaming down his face. Josh sat quietly, his hand stroking Hope's shoulder as she slumped over her father. Outside, the night swallowed any residual daylight while inside, shadows continued to dance on the walls from the candles and the fire burning in the center of the room.

Kenny wrapped his large hands around Hope's soft, freckled cheeks. Her aura was blooming even more brightly than normal but with a red tinge from her anxious heart. His own aura was soft but had become pure white. Their merging life forces combined to dispel the shadows in the otherwise dark, candlelit room.

"I am going to pass, sweetheart. I've seen the light on the other side. It calls to me with love and hope and forgiveness. Please don't mourn for me too long," Kenny said. "For the first time, I feel clean and fresh. I can see truth with new eyes. I was broken and evil, but I've been made whole. Lean on your mom. Lean on your friends." He turned toward Josh. "Son, take care of my little girl."

"I will," Josh choked out.

"Dad, I can't lose you."

"You're not losing me. I'll be watching and waiting for you." Tears flooded from Kenny's eyes, slipping from the corners and trickling down to his ears. "Hope, it's beautiful over there." He smiled again, taking a deep breath before his vision lost focus. As the air slipped from his lungs, his hands fell from Hope's cheeks. Kenny crossed.

"Dad? No, Dad, no, no, no." Hope collapsed onto her father's chest, sobbing violently.

Coming near, Mala knelt beside Hope. Slowly, the woman pulled her into a hug. All sense of awareness evaporated as the pain overwhelmed her. Together with Mala, Hope rocked back and forth, lost in her grief.

~

Gavin carried Josh with Dorcas at his side as two Adena warriors carried Hope home. Distraught, the girl's legs wouldn't carry her. She couldn't bring herself to walk. Mala and Danny walked along beside her, holding her hands. Smakal brought up the rear. Once they reached her portal, the warriors carefully passed Hope through, placing her on her own bed.

The house was dark. Maggie had not yet returned home. Gavin and Danny helped Josh pass through, then Danny followed. The warriors and the elves departed leaving the boys sitting on opposite sides of Hope's bed, chatting softly as their friend slept.

Sometime later, Maggie stepped into the dimly lit room. She leaned over her daughter on the bed, taking in the tears that streaked Hope's cheeks.

"Kenny?" Maggie asked, glancing at Josh.

Josh nodded and lowered his eyes. "He's gone."

"Oh," Maggie whispered, tears glistening her own eyes.

Danny stood. Maggie sat next to Hope, caressing her daughter's cheek, sweeping her long, blonde hair away from her eyes.

Hope awoke. "Oh, Mom," she wailed, throwing her arms around her mother. "He died, Mom. My daddy's dead. I couldn't stop it. I couldn't save him."

Maggie held her little girl. Josh and Danny stayed nearby as their friend again lost herself in grief.

~

Hope again slept fitfully as nearby, Josh and Danny whispered in the dark. Maggie reluctantly left her daughter to fix some snacks in the kitchen. A dim nightlight illuminated the room leaving shadows in every corner. No moonlight filtered through the bedroom window, but the light from the hallway reflected off the large mirror on Hope's dresser. The bedside clock read 10:06 P.M.

"I'm worried about her," Josh said. "I can't imagine how I'd feel if I lost my dad."

Danny was nodding. "Yeah, I keep thinking the same thing."

"I don't know what to say."

"Me either."

"Say nothing." The voice came from the back of the room. The boys turned to find Queen Hesed standing on Hope's dresser in front of the mirror. "Be there for her. She will share her heart with you when she is ready."

The boys stood as the elf queen leapt nimbly to the floor before them. She smiled, her head cocked upward to meet their gazes. "Not bad for a two-thousand-year-old elf woman, huh?" Hesed said nothing more. Instead, she rounded the end of the bed and sat next to Hope. The girl opened her eyes but remained still, as if she couldn't move.

"My sweet Nozomi, you have suffered such a terrible loss." In much the same way as Maggie had done earlier, the queen used her hand to brush Hope's hair from her face. "My heart breaks for you. I lost my own father to Bayal's treachery so many years ago. I understand your hurt."

"It's my fault," Hope confessed. "I should've listened to Gavin when he told me to stay home." Tears welled again as Hope stared into Hesed's eyes. "He'd still be here."

The elf queen's face lost its softness. The set of her jaw hardened. "Listen to me now and listen well. Nothing about this is your fault. Nothing. You must understand, Bayal brought this disaster upon you. The guilt is his. You were driven by your love for your father. Your concern for him drove you to seek him out. It was that same love that rescued him only a few days earlier. Never regret loving and acting on that love. Never."

Hope's jaw clenched in response. Her eyes narrowed. All the pain, all the loss, all the fear, all the horror—everything that had happened to her over the last month found new ground to stand on. Every emotion boiling just below the surface of Hope's conscious mind suddenly burst forth. Anger overrode every other feeling. She knew what she'd done. She knew she'd failed. Most of all, she knew it was her own fault, and no one was going to tell her differently. Not her friends. Not her mother. Not even the queen of the elves.

Hope shoved Queen Hesed away, causing her to stumble into Danny's arms. He caught her awkwardly, lifting Agahpey to her feet. Hope rose on her bed, glaring. "You say it's not my fault. My dad, he said that too. He said my love saved him. You say the same thing. Well, apparently it was my love that also killed him, so screw my love and screw you. I loved my dad to death. Right down into the grave. I loved him so much I got him murdered. So, to hell with my love and to hell with you. To hell with everyone!"

The girl shot daggers with her eyes. Her fists balled up and her teeth clenched. "Get out. Everyone. Agahpey. Danny. Even you, Josh. Get away from me before I get you killed too. Get out and leave me alone."

Maggie rushed in from the other room. "What's wrong? What's going on?"

"Get them out, Mom. Everyone out. I want to be alone. I'm never loving anyone or anything ever again."

Sixteen

Two weeks passed. The bodies of Mabel and her family were retrieved from the destroyed quarry building. Al Havener's corpse was removed from Rose's upstairs room, which no one could quite remember doing after the task was completed. The bodies of the two fallen elves were sent back through a portal to the Arboreal Realm. Lastly, NSA Agent Franklin concocted a convoluted story of how his partner had died heroically trying to stop a robbery at an out-of-the-way diner somewhere in southwestern Indiana.

Rose fed details of the Havener crime family to Rick who passed them along to the FBI as coming from a confidential informant. As a result, raids were made in the St. Louis area, taking down multiple illicit schemes. Rick asked Rose how she knew those things, but all she would say was that Havener's lips were loose before he died. She then returned to her life managing the General and living in her own personal, haunted old house.

Gator finally asked Rhonda on a date. He'd been wanting to for about twenty years. She smiled, smacked him on the shoulder, and asked if he wanted some more Mountain Dew. Later, she slipped him a dining receipt with a little note written on the back: "Pick me up at 7 tonight. XOXO." There was red lipstick also, kissed right onto the paper.

Cynthia Sweet called in a leave-of-absence to SETI. Leaving all technology behind, she slipped into the Arboreal Realm and traveled to Kentucky, where she spent a long time visiting with the queen and learning about the history of the elves.

The realtor sign was again in front of Earl and Faye Hicks' house. When asked, the realtor said he knew nothing about a Clarence D'Angelo having bought the place. As far as he knew, it'd been on the market all along. There was no evidence of the old codger in or around the house, except for an old copy of a Charles Dickens novel with curled edges found on one of the kitchen counters.

Life in Cutters Notch returned to normal. The fall traffic dropped to a trickle as the leaves found their resting place on the forest floor. Business at the General slowed, and Rose spent a lot of time filing her nails and reading the latest Dean Koontz novel. Occasionally, she reached up to finger the mesmerizing crystal at her throat only to be reminded that it was long gone, smashed into a million dust-sized particles by the sword of an otherworldly figure. She still carried the memories, though—the memories of all of Minerva's victims, Minerva's memories, plus the memories of Bayal, the evil elf. Rose even knew the history of the ancient king from whose crown the witch had plucked the jewel. All in all, it was a heavy load. Gray hairs began to appear in her newly brown tresses.

~

Maggie fixed dinner for Rick on the nights he wasn't working. She liked cooking for him. He teased her about fattening him up, but he obviously loved every minute of it.

For each meal, Maggie made a tray for Hope and set it on the girl's dresser. Sometimes she nibbled a little and sometimes she didn't. Overall, Hope secluded herself, unwilling to engage with anyone in her grief.

The door to Hope's room remained closed. At night, she kept her lights off so the portal in her mirror wouldn't activate. She refused to see Josh or Danny, and she barely spoke to her mother. Rather, she withdrew into her own painful world, coming out only to go to the bathroom. Hope had showered only a handful of times, mainly when Maggie put her foot down and demanded it.

Maggie was at a loss as to what to do. The idea of some sort of institutional stay had crossed her mind. She kept praying that her little girl would come back to her.

Every day, Danny would wheel Josh over to Hope's house. At first, they asked to see Hope, and were sent away disappointed. Then they brought cards, which Hope refused to look at, and flowers that Hope wouldn't allow in her room. Maggie collected them all on the dining room table. After each trip across the cul-de-sac, the boys returned home, both dejected and worried.

Fourteen days after Kenny's battle with the fallen elves and subsequent death, Maggie called each of the boys to invite them to dine with her and Rick. She cooked up a large pot of beef with homemade noodles accompanied by buttery mashed potatoes and green beans, adding some fresh yeast rolls to top it off. The wonderful smells permeated the house. It was Hope's favorite meal.

With the aromas wafting through the rooms, Maggie tapped on Hope's bedroom door. "Sweetie, can I come in?"

"Okay."

Maggie cracked the door open, surreptitiously waving in the aroma of beef, buttery noodles, and fresh rolls as she entered. "Can I turn the light on?"

"No. Keep it off."

"Honey, I've made your favorite meal—beef and noodles. I've even made some of Grandma's yeast rolls."

"Okay." Hope had taken to one-word replies. She sat up against her headboard with her hair unkempt and drooping across her shoulders. Dark circles ringed the underside of her bloodshot eyes.

"Honey, I'd like you to come out to the table and eat with us tonight. I'm serious."

Hope didn't answer at first. Rather, she dropped her gaze to the blanket covering the lower half of her body. Eventually, she shook her head—a quick back and forth.

"Please. Rick will be here. Josh and Danny, too."

At the mention of the boys, Hope jerked her head up to meet her mother's eyes. Even in the dim light, Maggie could see her daughter's tears welling up, the yearning there. After a moment, Hope shook her head again. "I can't do it. Close the door, Mom, before the light draws the elves through my mirror."

Maggie stepped back from the bedroom, lightly pulling the door closed. Her own tears flowed again as they often had over the previous two weeks. She'd given up on mascara. As she plodded back to the kitchen, she addressed the empty house, "What do I do?" It felt like she was at the end of a long hallway with no doors to walk through, nowhere to go.

As a distraction, Maggie busied herself setting the table and placing the food in serving bowls. The doorbell rang. Carefully, she placed the large container of mashed potatoes on the table, tossed down a dishtowel she was using as a potholder, and hurried to the front door. Josh sat there holding a bouquet of red carnations and smiling up from his wheelchair, his new cast extended out in front of him. Danny stood behind him with a silly grin.

Maggie stooped and kissed Josh on the cheek. The boy blushed. "Come on in," she said. "Dinner is almost ready. Rick will be here any second."

Danny maneuvered Josh inside, and Maggie led the way to the dining table. "I'll sit here, closest to the kitchen. Rick will have the far end. Josh, you're over there next to Hope's chair. Danny, you sit here on this side."

"Where's Hope?" Josh queried. "Is she coming out?" His eyes were hopeful.

"She's still in her room." Maggie's own eyes dropped toward the floor. She struggled to keep a smile on her face. "She should be out soon," she said with more wishful thinking than conviction. "What would you like to drink? Lemonade? Coke? I think I have some Mountain Dew."

"Lemonade is fine for me," Danny replied.

"Same here," Josh said.

As Maggie returned to the kitchen, there was a light tapping on the door. Before anyone could move, it opened, and Rick stepped inside. "Hey, boys. How're you fellas doin'? Sorry I'm late. Joe Carr caught me at the General and kept going on and on about the rules around hunting the national forest. Despite how many times I told him that wasn't my jurisdiction, he wouldn't let up."

Maggie smiled. She gave him a light peck on the cheek. "No worries. You're here just in time. Lemonade for you too?"

"Sounds about perfect. I'm parched."

"Y'all sit down. I'll bring the drinks."

~

In mid-November, darkness came early in Indiana. At dinnertime, Hope found herself sitting in the dark, both in her room and in her heart. She could hear her mother moving around between the kitchen and the dining room, making preparations. Another dinner with Rick, and this time the boys were coming over. The smell of the food tugged at her will, but she doggedly resisted the urge to crawl out of the hole of her grief.

Josh and Danny. Her best friends. Hope missed them so much. Still, she had to block them out. She had to block everyone out. She even wanted to block her mom out, but she couldn't get away with that. If she could, she would, though—to protect her. To her grieving heart, everyone she loved was at risk. Everything that'd happened since September had wrapped around her soul—the people she loved had been put in constant danger. Because of her. Now, her dad was gone. Because she loved him.

A little sliver of light leaked in under her bedroom door. Quickly, she grabbed a shirt from her closet and stuffed it into the crack, blocking the light lest the shimmer be activated and the portal open. Despite her harsh words to Agahpey Hesed, she loved the elves, too. Yet, for their own safety, she couldn't let them come close.

As she bent to slide the fabric into the gap, she caught the aroma of the beef and noodles again, this time riding along with the smell of the fresh yeast rolls. "Mom," she groaned. "I know what you're trying to do, but I can't. I just can't."

Hope edged around her bed to her bedroom window. During the day, she drew the curtains closed. At night, she pulled them back so she could see the moon above the barren treetops. The indirect illumination of the moon didn't seem to be enough to activate the portal in her mirror, and it was the only hint of brightness she would allow. It soothed her melancholy like ointment on a burn.

The moon also brought some pleasant memories. Memories of walking at night with her dad. Holding his large, calloused hand. Joking. Laughing. Even crying a little. As she stood there staring at the lunar glow, another set of fresh tears streaked her cheeks.

Hope heard the doorbell and turned away from the window. She could hear voices—Josh's and Danny's. It was all she could do to resist flinging the door open and running out to join them. Especially Josh. Instead, she crawled back on her bed, pulling the covers up to her waist as she leaned on the headboard. The moonbeams fell across her lap as her friends' voices tugged on her heart. She leaned her head back, squeezing her eyes closed, and willed her friends' voices away.

She knew she couldn't stay locked up in this room, this house, forever. Life would force her out, sooner or later. Yet, her only plan was to refuse to see anyone for as long as she could get away with it. It was her intent to drive a wedge between herself and everyone she loved. It was the only way she could conceive of to keep them safe from the walking bad-luck charm—herself.

"Hope?"

Her eyes popped open, darting about. The voice was in the room with her, nearby. She looked at the door—still closed. Moving her gaze to the mirror—it was still a mirror. Had her isolation driven her a little crazy? *Am I finally losing it?*

The moonlight cloaked the room with its soft glow through the undraped window, casting everything with a slight white sheen. She closed her eyes again, listening to the low rumble of voices drifting her way from the dining room. Hope recognized Rick's voice as he arrived.

"Young one, what are you doing locking yourself away?"

Again, Hope's eyes flung themselves open. *That's not my imagination.* "Dad? Is that you?" Flinging the covers from her lap, she leaned toward her side lamp.

"Don't."

"Who are you? Where are you?"

"Look just to the right of the window."

Hope peered into the darkness beyond the incoming moonbeams. A misty form, amorphous, floated there, just a tad brighter than the air around it. It was tall, close to six feet. She swung her legs over, sitting on the side of her bed closest to the mist. "Can I please see you?"

"It's not possible. The lamplight would drive me away."

"Who are you?" She paused, thinking of Josh and the specter. "Are you a specter?"

"I'm no evil spirit. I've been looking in on you, though, these last two weeks. I see your pain. I asked the Mighty One for an opportunity to help you. You can't keep doing this to yourself."

Hope shivered despite herself. Not from the cold outside but from adrenaline. It poured into her muscles. The mist drifted slightly closer. She reached out, but her hand passed through.

"Why do you stay in this room and lock yourself away?" the spirit asked. "Your friends—your boyfriend—they are just in the other room. Yet, you stay in here all alone?"

"I had to cut them off." Hope's face stared at the floor. Her toes glowed in the moonlight. "I can't risk being around them, putting them in more danger. Everyone I love gets hurt. I got my dad killed."

"Nonsense." The entity's eyes were glowing with a golden

swirl. "He was killed by fallen elves—the result of one elf's greed. On the other hand, he had been lost in the darkness, but because you loved him, he found hope and joy and the brilliance that comes from true light. Your father was rescued because you poured out your love for him with selfless, reckless abandon. Keep doing that, Hope. Keep touching people the way you touched him."

"But what if they get hurt?"

"They will. It's life. Everyone gets hurt and everyone hurts others. If you love them, it won't matter. The hurts will dissipate as I will when my time with you is up."

Hope peered up. The entity was still there, a hazy form with golden eyes, hanging just outside the moonlight. "Do you have a name?"

"I do, but I won't give it to you. You have seen me in other forms and known me by another name." It paused to let that information sink in. "My time with you grows short. As for your father, you will see each other again. For you, it will seem like a long, long time." In Hope's mind, an image appeared. She was in another place with children running around her that she didn't know. She glanced at her hands. They were bony and thin, wrinkled. Then the image was gone. "For him, it will only be a blink of the eye."

"But I don't—"

"Hope!" The sound reverberated off her bedroom walls. Her prize basketball rolled off a nearby shelf. A stuffed pink bunny dropped from her headboard. "The pain you're feeling for him, you're inflicting it on your mother and your friends. You're not protecting them; you're hurting them. Now go out there and live your life."

Hope was quiet for a moment. She hadn't considered that. Was it true that all she was doing was transferring her pain to her mom, to Josh and Danny, also?

"Your father will always be with you. He awaits you, but you must live first. He said to tell you that he loves you, his sweet, little pumpkin."

The room grew still. The air changed. The soft mist near the window was no more. Hope knew the messenger was gone. The experience was real. The basketball still rolled around on the floor. The pink bunny rested next to her on the bed, its beady eyes staring up at her like little black and white accusations.

Muffled voices drifted from the hallway. The rich, savory scent of dinner on the table tickled her nose. She could almost taste those noodles. A chair scraped against the floor at the dining table.

Moving as fast as she could, she clicked on her bedside light, found her jeans and an Indiana University sweatshirt. After she slipped on some fuzzy house shoes, she ran a brush through her strawberry blond hair and edged her bedroom door open, moving quietly down the hall.

Hope rounded into the dining room as Danny was slathering a yeast roll with a large pat of butter. Josh dropped the ladle into the bowl of noodles. Everyone turned to look at her.

"Well, I couldn't let you turds eat all my beef and noodles," Hope quipped. She sat down at the spot left for her, scooped a glob of potatoes on her plate, then grabbed the bowl and ladle from Josh. "After all," she said to her friends, "I love beef and noodles more'n anything else in the whole world—even you bozos."

~

From her seat nearest the kitchen, Maggie smiled as she reached for Rick's hand under the table. *My Hope is back.*

Epilogue

Thanksgiving has arrived and Kay, as expected, plans to celebrate it alone. Well, not completely alone. Penny is there to share the occasion, the dog being the closest thing she has to family, having never had children of her own. Her parents never gave her any brothers or sisters before they died. They also had no siblings, leaving her no aunts or uncles. She bears no resentment in her heart. It simply is what it is. Kay is alone in the world.

The solitary life isn't for everyone, but now that she has her canine friend, Kay is good with it. It gives her time to think, to create, to write.

Writing is what she does when she isn't cutting wood or hunting for mushrooms in the forest. Reams of paper, some used and some unused, line opposing walls of her spare bedroom, the room she uses for her work. For income, she writes articles for magazines and newspapers. She also pens technical journals for businesses and does some proofreading and a little editing. For fun, she creates stories and builds whole new worlds. Once in a great while, Kay considers submitting the tales for publication, but that's a tough road, and who wants to read the words of a simple, humble, lonely woman from rural Indiana?

Being alone doesn't mean she doesn't enjoy great food, though. She often imagines herself in a large family sitting around a giant banquet table with a huge roasted turkey gracing the center. Delicious aromas mix and mingle as each plate is loaded with mashed potatoes, noodles, green beans, sweet potatoes, and turkey soaked in gravy. In her mind's eye, she sees a grandma and a grandpa on the left. To the right are children—the nieces and nephews she's never had. At the far end of the table sit her mom and her dad, now long gone.

Coming to herself, she finds that she's standing in the middle of her kitchen, having been lost in the daydream. In her hands, she holds the small roasting pan filled with the turkey breast she plans to share with Penny. On the table by the window rest her menu plan and supplies.

Evening light spills through the sheers, illuminating the assorted items—two potatoes to be boiled and mashed, a can of green beans and a can of whole kernel corn, both waiting to be heated with a little butter. She spies another can on the counter, this one filled with premade gravy. Finally, a fresh loaf of white bread, still sealed in its transparent wrapper, rests on top of her refrigerator. She usually eats wheat bread, but Thanksgiving calls for a little splurge.

The oven dings. Preheated. Carefully, she slides the roasting pan inside, feeling the heat through the checked, flannel sleeves of her shirt. Oven mitts protect her hands. Kay sets the timer, then pulls out some pans to boil the potatoes and heat the vegetables. Soon, the water is boiling, and the beans and corn have pats of butter as they rest on the burners, waiting for the right time to be heated.

Outside, the sun dips below the tree line. As dusk drifts across the landscape, Kay begins her nightly ritual of turning on lights. Starting in the kitchen, she flips the switch to the ceiling light and illuminates the under-counter lights she installed the previous year. At the backdoor, she clicks the outdoor lights to on.

In the living room, she clicks on the various bulbs—the replacement fixtures she purchased after the recent home invasion broke her decorative, antique lamps. Kay pauses to stare at the blank space on her wall—the space that used to be filled with her swords. The Civil War relics and the U.S. Cavalry swords are gone. The empty hooks remind her of where they used to hang. Only the broadsword remains, a lone remnant of her prized collection. She'd have lost that one too, if she hadn't shot that weird creature about to crawl through her mirror with it.

Kay slowly turns as she stands in the middle of the room until she faces the mirror on the opposite wall. Her own reflection stares back at her. Like so many other objects arrayed in this seldomly-used, formal living space, the mirror is special to her, handed down from her grandparents. Large, three feet by four feet, and rectangular, it takes up most of the wall above a rustic side table. For the last month, she's felt conflicted about that piece of painted glass. On one hand, she loves it and the memories it evokes, but on the other hand, those...those things used it as some sort of access port to her life. Part of Kay can never part with it, but another part wants it to go away.

Satisfied with the lighting in the sword room, Kay continues her nightly lamp-lighting ritual in the other rooms. The bathroom. Her bedroom. Her spare writing room. Wandering slowly, she clicks on switches as she goes. Penny follows faithfully at her heels.

Kay pauses again at the doorway to the writing room. Despite being a bedroom, it has no side tables, no bed. One lone bulb without a shade, screwed into a ceiling receptacle, illuminates the space. The room is filled with boxes of paper, a desk, and another family heirloom, an old dresser with another large mirror mounted on top. There are more reams of paper arranged on the surface of the brown wooden dresser—her most recent works, short stories.

"That's curious," she mumbles to Penny. "I don't remember leaving the lid off that box."

In that moment, an odd feeling rambles through Kay. It starts in her lower back, crawls up her spine, then raises the hairs on the back of her neck before ending in goosebumps on her forearms. With some trepidation, Kay inches across the room to the open box.

The lid sits top-down across the neighboring ream. A sealed envelope rests on top of the stack. Kay notes the label she scrawled on the side of the box—*Tales from Cutters Notch*. These are some of her short stories based on the local lore she's heard over the years. Picking up the envelope, she carefully slides her nail under the glued flap and tears it open. Inside, she finds one simple message:

Dear Ms. Sours,

I love your stories. You should most definitely publish them.
I apologize that some of my subjects stole from you and scared you so terribly.
I will see that it does not happen again.
Sincerely,
Queen Agahpey Hesed

The note falls from her fingers. It lands on the floor near her boot-covered feet. Raising her eyes, she stares at her reflection in the large mirror attached to the dresser. She considers it. *It's just glass.* Like a bad dream, she remembers those weird creatures crawling through the mirror in her living room carrying her swords. The fact is, she'd hoped it was only been a dream, a filament of fantasy filling in the gaps in the experience. Now, she knows it isn't that. It's all real.

A clatter echoes from the other room. Kay spins around, leaning back on the dresser. It sounds metallic. Penny trots out to investigate, ears perked, head cocked. From the other room, the dog whines.

Thinking quickly, Kay pictures the location of her shotgun. It's leaning on the wall in her bedroom, just across the hallway. Shivering, she tiptoes as quietly as possible across the room, leaning through the doorway, and peeking toward the source of the noise. All she can see is Penny's tail wagging. More whining. Her collar rattles like she's being petted. *Someone's in there. Someone or something?*

Kay darts across the hall, slipping into her bedroom. Moving fast, she retrieves the gun, checks the load, and marches toward the other room, barrel raised.

"You're not getting my broadsword," Kay screams as she barges into the living room, swinging the business end of the shotgun left, then right. "I'll blast you to hell first!"

No one is there. Penny is seated, staring at the wall mirror. Kay swears it ripples when she glances at it.

Her eyes drift downward from the reflective glass, spotting her missing swords resting on the wall table below the mirror. They are all there—the two U.S. Cavalry sabers and the two Civil War swords. Lowering the Remington, she rushes to inspect them. No damage. Clean. The blades still look sharp.

Kay Sours smiles. She stands there for several minutes, the joy returning as she lifts each antique weapon and looks it over. Carefully, she carries the blades, one at a time, across the room and hangs them back in their spots on the opposing wall. Finally, she stands grinning at her own reflection in the mirror. She doesn't know who this Queen Agahpey Hesed is, and she doesn't know how she found and returned her treasures, but Kay is grateful.

She's still grinning when she raises the butt of the shotgun and smashes the mirror. Whipping around, she marches to the bathroom where she shatters the mirror above her sink. Finally, Kay trots into the writing room and sends a blast of shotgun pellets into the mirror behind her box of *Tales from Cutters Notch*.

Kay Sours might be thankful, but she lives alone for a reason. She doesn't want anyone or anything intruding on her life—even some strange queen who returned her prized possessions. There's room for only one other in her personal space. That spot belongs to Penny.

Deciding to clean up the mess tomorrow, Kay walks back to her kitchen, reloads the shotgun, and places it against the wall before sitting at her table. With no more thought to the shattered glass in the other room, she sips her tea and ruffles Penny's fur with her free hand. She sighs as she picks up her copy of that morning's *Bloomington Herald*. Once again, everything in her life is as it should be, and Thanksgiving dinner will soon be ready.

Michael DeCamp, a native of Muncie, Indiana now lives in Indianapolis with his wife and best friend, Nancy. Together, they have two grown, very talented daughters.

He expresses his imagination through fiction (*the Cutters Notch books and stories*) but indulges his faith in his non-fiction works (*Loving Out Loud and related material*).

He enjoys traveling, reading, and podcasting (*Cutters Notch Podcast*). Visit to his website (www.authormichaeldecamp.com) to learn more about his books, read his blog, link to his podcasts, and enjoy a selection of his *Henry the Preacher* comics. Sign up for his newsletter while on site to receive periodic updates and news, plus a special, free, short story.

You can reach Michael through his website. He would enjoy hearing from you via his email (michael@authormichaeldecamp.com). Follow him on Facebook (@authormichaeldecamp), on Twitter (@MikeDeCamp1), or on Instagram (@mdecamp1985).